What the press say about
Port Moresby Mix

D1086721

Fascinating... highly readable.
ABC Radio National

Some very funny stories and some very quotable quotes.
The Cairns Post

Challinger writes well... probably the truth of the situation.
Sydney Morning Herald

Nicely-shaped old-fashioned stories, often with considerable satire and some comedy, sometimes with a deft punchline.
The Age, Melbourne

The rush for copies in PNG has depleted bookshop stocks.
Courier Mail, Brisbane

Challinger can't cover up the fact that he really is a good writer with a complexity of moral and social points to make.
Australian Book Review

A particular part of it is definitely obscene.
Post-Courier, Port Moresby

Port Moresby Mixed Doubles

Stories of Expatriates in Papua New Guinea

Michael Challinger

Pasa Press
Melbourne

First Published by Pasa Press 1992
Reprinted 1994
PO Box 5337 GPO Melbourne Victoria 3001, Australia

Copyright © Michael Challinger, 1992
Cover design by Bill Farr
Typset by Koodak, Melbourne

Made and printed in Australia by McPherson's Printing Group
Distributed in Australia by Advance Book Distributors Pty.Ltd.
Unit 18B, 64 Balmain Street, Richmond, Victoria 3121.
Distributed in Papua New Guinea by Gordon & Gotch (PNG) Pty.Ltd.
PO Box 107 Boroko, PNG.

National Library of Australia Cataloguing-in-Publication entry:
Challinger, Michael
Port Moresby Mixed Doubles: stories of expatriates in Papua New Guinea.
ISBN 0 646 11964 8.
1.Australians - Papua New Guinea - Fiction. I. Title.
A823.3

Contents

Glossary

boy-house .... Domestic servants' quarters.

boy-wire .... Steel reinforcing mesh, installed for security purposes.

cousin brother/sister .... First cousin

grilli .... Unsightly skin disease.

go finish(Pidgin) .... To depart permanently; used of expatriates leaving the country.

gumi (Pidgin) .... Rubber; condom.

hegeberi (Motu) .... Show-off.

Hiri Motu .... Simplified version of the Motu language.

Kairuku .... Coastal region west of Port Moresby; the people.

kina .... Unit of currency; worth around one US dollar

kokoruk (Pidgin) .... Rooster; virile man.

Koiari .... Tribal group inland of Port Moresby.

kunai grass .... Imperata Arundinacea; tough, long-bladed grass, growing to height of two metres

Laurabada (Motu) ..... South-east trade winds, the season from May to November.

long-long (Pidgin) ..... Feeble-minded, mad.

Motu .... The coastal people in the vicinity of Port Moresby; their language.

National .... Polite term for PNG citizen: replaces word 'native' which has colonial connotations

pamuk (Pidgin) .... harlot.

Pidgin .... Melanesian language based on simplified English, and containing elements of indigenous languages and German.

PMV .... Passenger Motor Vehicle, i.e. bus or minibus.

puri-puri .... Sorcery.

rascal .... Criminal; gang-member.

taubada (Motu) .... White man (literally: big man).

toea .... One hundredth part of a kina. (pronunciation: *toya*).

wantok (Pidgin) .... Clansman, family, kin (derivation and pronunciation: *one talk*).

Port Moresby Mixed Doubles

John Janssen's jowls were tinged with blue, and Alex disliked the smell of after-shave about him. Janssen was a good-looking man of about forty, but a bit on the heavy side. He had dark, unblinking eyes and an impressive manner. A good ten years older than Alex, he was doing well for himself. It made him just a little smug.

The two men first met on a special late night flight in the old Air Niugini 707. Both were taking up jobs in Port Moresby, and finding themselves in adjacent seats, they got chatting. John's wife Heather and their three boys, just babies then, were in the row behind. The little kids were fast asleep, and after the plane landed, Alex carried one of them through Customs and Immigration. The parents struggled with the other two, plus a lot of hand luggage. Even at midnight it was too hot to wear the light coats and cardigans they had unnecessarily brought with them from Melbourne.

John Janssen was on transfer within the bank. It was his chance to climb into the ranks of senior management. To begin with, he and his family were housed in a very nice place in the bank compound in suburban Boroko. When he was promoted to Assistant General Manager, the family moved into a house at the bottom of Tuaguba Hill. It was a tiny bit dated, but had beautiful timber floors and high ceilings, and you could see the harbour through the trees. It was almost as good as the General Manager's place.

Alex's situation was different. His employers put him up for a week in a guest-house, then told him to find his own accommodation. At first he stayed in a block of flats behind Waigani market. You'd never get an expat to live there these days. Then after a year, he changed jobs and joined the opposition for more

9

money. He decided he liked Moresby, and bought a rundown house, shack almost, on the crest of Chester Street. Bit by bit, he was fixing it up. He had part of the hillside bulldozed away and created a magnificent view out over the reef. Real estate prices were booming, and buying the place was the best thing he ever did. Home owners always say that.

The Janssens kept in contact with Alex, and used to ask him around for dinner. It became a regular thing, every month or so. Heather was an excellent cook and Alex got on very well with the boys, better in fact than their father did. When Alex had upgraded his own place he was able to reciprocate, though being a bachelor, he was no great shakes at the catering.

John Janssen was condescending about the house, with its unlined walls and rudimentary comforts, but Heather loved it. She encouraged Alex in all his plans and renovations. She restrained him from overdoing the improvements and thereby spoiling its rustic charm. For example, there was a passion-fruit vine which entered one kitchen window, and twirled itself around the security bars. At Heather's suggestion, Alex ran a cord across the width of the room, and trained the vine to exit through the side window. You could actually pick the fruit inside the house. The set-up lasted until the wet season, when the mosquitoes got so bad he had to sacrifice the vine to install insect screens.

In time, Alex came to know the Janssen family well. He was adored by the boys, the eldest of whom once announced that he wished Uncle Alex was his father. The comment, though embarrassing, was unsurprising. John was noticeably unaffectionate towards his children, and always spoke to them in a cold, forbidding tone of voice.

His manner of speech at the office was much the same, stern and formal, and the tendency became more exaggerated as he gained promotion. Only later did Alex learn that Janssen was Dutch-born and had gone to Australia as a boy of ten. Thereafter, Alex could occasionally detect the hint of an accent in Janssen's speech.

Perhaps Janssen's background was a factor in his relations with the Nationals. A bias is one thing, but Janssen's attitude verged on the objectionable. He always referred to them as 'coons' and was a bore with his endless stories, many obviously untrue, of how dumb they were. How a teller had done this or that, and a clerk had done something else, and had to be dismissed. It seemed to give him pleasure to sack them. Alex supposed it was the wielding of power that Janssen enjoyed.

The Janssens' own domestic servants were another case in point. They were fixtures with the house, and had worked over the years for a succession of Assistant General Managers. John was demanding and inconsiderate with them. Their kids were forbidden to use the pool and trampoline any more, and he only grudgingly gave the housegirl a lift in the car. It offended his dignity, apparently, to drop her off at the shops occasionally on his way to work.

To summon the housegirl, there was a buzzer in the kitchen wired up to the boy-house. John would press it at any time of the day or night to call her or her husband down to perform some menial chore which could easily have waited until the next day. Heather used to remonstrate with him about having them on call at all hours. "What if they're having sex when you ring?" she asked. But it made no difference to John, so she secretly cut the wire in a couple of unobtrusive spots and that was the end of the buzzer. Good on her.

Inevitably, John lacked a sense of humour. He took everything Alex said literally, and thereby missed the real meaning of much of his conversation. Alex often found himself exchanging glances with Heather. The two of them took pleasure at the many asides which went over John's head, and as time passed Alex came to the realisation that he liked Heather much more than he liked John.

Heather was intelligent and vivacious, and not bad looking either, though not really Alex's type. She was too old for him – not that he would think of anything with a married woman. He liked her as a friend. She had the liveliness and perceptiveness which John lacked, and he couldn't help reflecting how ill-matched she and Janssen were. Heather once showed him a photo from the days of their courtship. It was taken on a bridge or a pier, with a beach scene in the background. Janssen was standing, dressed in a blazer – presumably the height of fashion in those days – feet astride, arms akimbo. He looked full of himself even then. Clinging to one arm was Heather, in a frowsy cotton frock and with her hair blowing in her eyes. The angle was unflattering. She looked a bit of a scrag.

"John had a lot of female admirers in those days," she said. "There was plenty of competition for him. I was pretty proud of myself when I managed to land him." She raised her eyebrows. "That's hardly the way I feel about it now, though. I was a fool. I married too young."

Since John was never home until the dot of 6.15, Alex used to arrive for dinner before five. While the housegirl fed and supervised the children, he and Heather would sit and chat. She would give vent to her dissatisfaction with a husband who was humourless, vain and preoccupied with his job. She had no one else to grumble to, and Alex didn't mind listening. He enjoyed her company. Her confidences were full of insight and often funny.

With John's arrival at 6.15, the atmosphere would immediately turn solemn. Alex would then willingly allow the boys to claim his attention until they were taken off to bed just as dinner was served. The three adults would eat, and then chat or play Scrabble. Both Alex and Heather made efforts not to thrash John, whose play was woeful. Once only, Alex played John at draughts. He won twenty-odd games in a row despite every stratagem to let John win at least once for the sake of politeness. Somehow, the slow-witted Janssen always managed to blunder. It became embarrassing.

One day towards the end of the year, Alex was at work as usual at his office in Boroko. It was mid-morning when the girl at reception rang through and announced that there was a Mrs Janssen to see him. It was an unexpected distraction. She had never called at Alex's office before, not once in four years. He was delighted to see her.

His immediate guess was that she needed some insurance, that she'd forgotten to renew her cover and then smashed her car up, for instance. In fact her purpose was quite different, and characteristically, she came straight to the point.

"I've come to ask you a favour," she said.

"Whatever you want," he answered immediately. In an emergency he could always oblige a friend with a back-dated policy.

"You don't know what I want yet."

"Well, ask away."

"Can I use your house?" she asked. "Tomorrow."

He agreed right away. "Of course you can."

"Don't you even want to know why?"

He hadn't given it a thought. "Go ahead, tell me why," he said. She obviously wanted to tell him.

"I need somewhere private where I can meet someone. A friend, you know." She paused again, and flushed ever so slightly. "This is the hardest thing I've ever done."

"What is?"

"Asking you."

Then it dawned on him. He realised what she was talking about. It was utterly unexpected. He couldn't think what to say, but his silence was from surprise, not disapproval.

"It's weird, you know. John and I have been married for eight years, and I've never looked at another man. Never even thought about it, until now. It must be something about this place." She meant Port Moresby.

"I think you're right."

"You don't think any less of me, do you?"

"Hell, no," he said, but with a momentary hesitation. "Not less – no, no far from it. Just surprised." In fact, he kind of approved.

"I'm surprised at myself. I'm not in love or anything like that," she said. "I don't honestly know why I'm doing it. I really like Carl, he's from the Seychelles. He's a lovely man, but it's nothing serious. Just something to do, I suppose. Nothing may come of it. I mean, we might not even do anything."

Alex made no comment.

The next morning, he felt a sort of anticipation himself, a vicarious excitement. He made sure he left the house neat and tidy, and hid the spare key under a cement brick in the agreed place. The sheets had been changed the day before, and though he'd slept on them that night, no-one would ever know. They looked pristine.

As it happened, Alex was quite busy the whole morning. Only at lunch-time did he remember Heather and wonder, you know, how things were going. He half expected a telephone call in the afternoon, but Heather didn't ring.

It was with an almost indecent curiosity that he returned home in the afternoon. He didn't know what he expected to find, but somehow he thought there would be some evidence. Evidence they'd been there. He went into the bedroom and looked at the bed. Was it indelicate to make an inspection? Bad manners? Prurience? After all, it was his bed. The sheets though, were as smooth and neatly tucked-in as he'd left them. It was as if no-one had been there. There was no trace. They had covered their tracks well.

Heather phoned him the next morning, chirpy and humorous.

"How did you go?" he asked, not having thought of a better choice of words.

"We couldn't find the key."

"What? How did you get in?"

"We didn't. We sat in the car for twenty minutes and then we went home."

He was disappointed. He felt he'd let her down. He wanted her to try again the next day, but Tuesday at ten was her only possible rendezvous; it was the youngest boy's morning for play-school. So, in elaborate detail Alex explained once more where to find the key. There could be no misunderstanding the next time.

The following Tuesday, Alex left the key for them again. He prepared himself for another anti-climax, and deliberately avoided giving Heather a thought all day. Again, there was no phone call in the afternoon.

But when he arrived home, he noticed at once. The spoon left in the sugar-bowl, the folded tea-towel, the Bougainvillea in a vase. He had forgotten he even owned a vase. He had never used it, never had cut flowers in the house before. It was unprecedented. A woman's touch.

She phoned the next day to thank him.

"We only had a cup of tea and talked. We lay down on the bed, but that was all. You know, nothing happened."

"Good oh," he answered, and wondered what else he should say.

"Don't you believe me?"

"It's not that at all, Heather. It's entirely up to you. Good luck to you."

"Aren't you curious?"

"I am curious, yes. But I don't think you should tell me too much. After all, I know John, too. He's my friend as well. It's simpler if I don't know more than I have to."

"But I want you to meet Carl. I want to introduce you. Then you'll know what I see in him."

"For goodness' sake, Heather! That's the last thing I want."

And she understood why. She knew Alex was right, but it was difficult for her. She wanted to talk about Carl. She had to tell someone. And though she did her best to curb her enthusiasm, week by week she let fall more details about him. How she had met him, where he lived, what work he did, what he looked like. Every Wednesday, little by little, Heather told him more. It was their secret together.

In a way, Alex felt himself almost as guilty as this fellow Carl. Yet it gave him a strange satisfaction, the adventure of it. At the Janssens' for dinner, he would make risque comments to Heather in John's presence. Nothing incriminating, but remarks about Bougainvilleas, brands of biscuits, little domestic details which only Heather knew. Childish, really. It never struck him that John would draw any conclusions. The man was too unimaginative for that.

But news was already getting around. Alex was alarmed when he heard the gossip at the club. Galloway spread the word. Some bloke from the Aero-club was knocking off Johnny Janssen's missus. Half his luck. You couldn't blame her. Nobody would call the Dutchman exciting. And the bloke was a coon into the bargain – what a laugh! Alex studiously took no interest.

Then he heard from Heather. She phoned him at work.

15

"I thought I'd better let you know," she told him. "John has heard I've been seeing another man." She was completely calm about it.

It was more than Alex was. A thought flashed through his mind. Not about the Janssens' marriage, their children, divorce, the break-up of a happy home. None of that. Just about himself.

"He doesn't know you used to go to my place, does he?"

"No. I'll never tell him that."

"He might find out."

"He won't. He thinks we go to Carl's place. We had the whole thing out last night. He made a dreadful fuss at first. You know what he's like. He threatened to throw me out, divorce me, all the usual things."

"Good God! Does he mean it?"

"No, it was just talk. I shut him up in the end. I told him it was fine by me, that I'd take the kids and go and live with Carl. You remember, Carl's from the Seychelles. He's a bit dark-skinned, like a coffee-coloured Frenchman. John's such a bigot. He just couldn't cope with that part."

Alex could imagine. "So what's going to happen?" he asked.

"We've worked it all out. I think he's been suspecting something for a while now, so after the initial storm he took it fairly well. I told him it was just an interlude. We'll be back in Melbourne in a year's time, back to normality. Port Moresby just won't be real any more. I mean, it's so abnormal here. It's not as if anything that happens here really matters. I wouldn't dream of doing this in Australia."

"What do you mean 'doing'?" he asked, with concern. "Surely it's all over now?"

"Why should it be? I didn't make any promises to him. I hold all the trump cards. My taking off with Carl — he could never stomach that. Not that I'd ever do it, even if Carl did leave his wife. No, John will just have to put up with things a bit longer. You know, the Port Moresby mixed doubles. I'm not the first to do it."

"For God's sake be careful," he warned her. "Don't push him too far."

16

Alex was worried at his own involvement, but Heather was heedless to the risk. She felt completely in control.

"Don't worry," she reassured him. "I know you're concerned because we go to your place. But we'll be absolutely careful. I promise you, John will never find out."

A week passed, and Alex was in his office, when the girl at reception told him he had a visitor. It was the visit he'd feared. There was a Mr Janssen to see him.

"Can I tell him to come in?" asked the girl. "He wants to see you right away."

Alex blamed himself more than Heather. It was his own fault entirely: he had been mad to let himself get involved, to become an accomplice. It seemed so sordid now. John had been bound to find out: the husband always does. And now there was no knowing what the man might do. It might even come to blows. He decided to keep the office door open, for safety's sake. He could think of no other precaution. He took a deep breath and told her to show Janssen in.

The Dutchman entered and closed the door firmly behind him. He didn't shake hands and he didn't sit down. The two men faced each other across the desk.

"I've got something to discuss with you," said Janssen in his stern, portentous manner. Alex remained standing. He'd be too vulnerable, sitting down.

"I suppose you know Heather's been playing up on me?"

Alex didn't reply. He wondered which was best – incredulity, shock, sympathy? Half-heartedly he tried all three, and was unconvincing.

"Don't pretend. You know very well. Everyone does. Some French bastard."

Alex made no further attempt at dissimulation. He just looked serious. He was worried about what was to come.

"Anyway, I'll handle that. I've come to you to ask something. About your house."

Alex's mouth went dry. He tried to swallow.

"I'll tell you something first Alex, man to man. The fact is, if that's the way Heather wants it, it's all right by me. Two can play at that game. Port Moresby mixed doubles they call it."

17

Alex wondered at first if he'd heard right. But he had, and his uncertainty changed to astonishment, then relief.

"Look, Alex, I know Heather's your friend too, but well, she started it, and in actual fact there's somebody I'd like to meet. You know, privately. And well, I wonder if I could use your house? I've always liked your little place. It's what I call discreet."

Alex hoped the relief didn't show on his face. He hoped only the amazement showed. It was extraordinary. He had never imagined John could have such initiative. What was it about this country that made them all like this? The heat, the boredom, the isolation, what?

"Don't think ill of me," said John defensively. "Heather started it, and if that's what she wants ..."

"Not at all," said Alex. "It's just that you've taken me by surprise. When do you want to use the house?"

"Tomorrow morning," answered the Dutchman.

Alex had to think. "What's today?" he asked.

"Today's Monday."

"To tell you the truth," said Alex, "it's not really convenient tomorrow. But the day after would be all right. What about Wednesday?"

Every Six Months

Ivan heard the news about John Porter at the club. That's where you hear all the news, even about the things that never happened.

What happened to Porter was real enough, though. Some rascals got into his house, goodness knows how, because it's got security like a fortress – chain-mesh fences, razor wire, bars on the windows, deadlocks, the works. They must have used a car jack to to prise the bars open.

Porter heard some noises in the middle of the night, and got up to investigate. He never did find out how many there were. All he knew was that he grabbed the last of them, just as the bastard was squeezing out the window to the patio. Porter grabbed him by the scruff of his neck and started pulling him back inside. He's a big bloke, Porter, and he would have succeeded if the rascal hadn't been armed. John didn't even see the knife. He just felt a pricking to his chest and realised he was bleeding. Not even a sharp pain or anything. The next thing he knew, he was waking up in Intensive Care.

Ivan heard all the details from Porter himself. He went out to the hospital with a few of the blokes from the club. They took him a bottle of brandy for a present. The man was lucky to be alive. The rascal had used a fishing knife on him and actually stabbed him in the heart. He was clinically dead in the ambulance, but they got him to the hospital in time and managed to revive him.

They had to cut him right open to do the heart surgery, and he had an enormous scar from one side of his chest to the other. No kidding, all cross-stitched, the way they show railway lines on maps. Porter's about as big as a gorilla, so it was really a sight.

John himself was pretty cheerful. They were going to send him down to Brisbane in a couple of days, so at least he had that to look forward to. He was resigned about the whole thing, fatalistic almost. He'd lived in Port Moresby long enough to know you have to expect anything. The only hard part is accepting how random the risks are. You can take every precaution under the sun and still not be safe, or you can just be lucky. John said he always reckoned on something nasty happening every six months or so.

Now that he thought about it, Ivan agreed with the estimate: every six months was about right. For example, the Christmas before last, Ivan's own place was broken into. He slept through it all. Luckily, he'd had a skin-full the night before and didn't hear a thing. In the morning he noticed the missing louvres and the hole in the boy-wire. (That stuff's no good at all – you need bars nowadays.) Half his personal possessions were gone, and he wasn't exactly happy about that. But he found a carving knife on the chair near the window, and counted himself lucky he hadn't woken up and disturbed them.

Then, in about June, driving through Hanuabada one night, Ivan copped a beer bottle through the windscreen. And six months after that, his car – it's a little Suzuki jeep – got stolen. The police recovered it within a few days without much damage, but they wouldn't give it back. They claimed they needed it as evidence and impounded it in the yard at the back of Boroko Police Station.

About a week later a mate told Ivan he'd seen the Suzuki cruising around town with some off-duty cops aboard. Sure enough, when he went to check on it, the car had more damage than when it was first recovered. Ivan had to tackle the Chief Superintendent and make a big scene to get it back. Maybe that story's true after all, how a bloke got his car impounded and they raffled it for the Police Club Christmas party.

Anyway, about six months ago there was another incident. It gave Ivan a real fright at the time. He's a pretty light sleeper when he's sober, and there are noises all night long in Moresby. You know, dogs barking, cars revving, the boys down the hill at the labour camp beating 44 gallon drums, cocks crowing, mystery footsteps, you name it. In fact, when he went south on leave, Ivan had the opposite problem: it was too quiet to sleep, but that's beside the point.

This particular night was hot and oppressive, the sort when you're up and down every hour, turning the ceiling fan on and off because it's too cold with it on and too hot with it off. Ivan couldn't get to sleep with the shadows moving on the trees outside, and all the creaking noises he kept hearing. So he lay there, wide awake, straining his ears and thinking that he'd heard voices on the front porch. A few minutes passed and there was nothing. He relaxed a bit, thinking he was just imagining things. Then he heard whispering again, and the noise of glass on metal. There was no mistake this time, and Ivan's heart started to beat double time.

It's easy to be wise after the event. What he should have done was to go through the connecting door into the bathroom. From there, he could have looked directly out to the porch without being seen. Instead, he barged straight out the bedroom door, not even quietly. He would have been history if the rascals had already got inside. Luckily, they were still outside, and too busy to notice. They had torn the flywire and removed a glass louvre below eye level. They still didn't see him. A hand was reaching through the window towards the deadlock.

At the sight of that, the adrenalin really started pumping. Ivan lived on his own, and he wasn't to know how many of them there were. Even worse, he wasn't entirely sure whether the door was locked or not. He'd had the door open that night, and he wracked his brains as to whether he'd turned the key before he hung it back in the dresser. It becomes second nature. You do it automatically, and that's why you can never be sure whether you've done it or not. You never have a specific recollection. Ninety-nine times out of a hundred you do it, but was this the hundredth time or only the ninety-ninth?

The hand reached further towards the lock. Ivan shuffled a bit and the hand stopped dead. They'd heard him. He gave a shout, something pathetic like: "What's that! What are you doing there?" He heard whispers and a mad scramble on the wooden steps. They started making off.

"Peter, the gun! Get the gun!" shouted Ivan. Of course, there was no gun and there was no Peter, but Ivan felt braver with his own shouting and when he was sure the rascals were at least out of sight, he checked the door. It had been locked all the time.

Then he started thinking about those bastards. They would have smashed his head in if they'd had half the chance. And for all he knew, they were still outside on the road, waiting to try again. He switched half the lights on and made a lot of noise. It's usually a waste of time, but he phoned the police, too.

"Phone us tomorrow and tell us what they took," they said.

"They didn't take anything. They didn't get in."

"Well, what do you want us to do?"

"I think they're still outside. They might come back. Can you come around and check?"

"Sorry, all the vehicles are busy."

"But what if they come back?"

"If they come back, you can phone us tomorrow and tell us what they took."

Next day when Ivan told them up the club about the break-in, everybody was full of helpful suggestions. They told him what a dill he was, how he should have crept up and grabbed the hand and bitten a finger off. It's really easy, they assured him, provided you bite just on the joint. According to the experts, it's like biting through a thin Hungarian salami. "You've got your own teeth," they told him, "It would have been no trouble. Even if you'd only got the top joint, it would have been the bit with the fingerprint. The cops could have used it for identification."

Then they started with their own scare stories, and all the latest rumours. How rascals busted in to Henderson's place and he ran one through with the wartime bayonet he keeps on the wall for decoration. How the bloke made it into the street, before he collapsed and died from loss of blood. The cops removed the body before anyone saw it, but Neville Martin saw the blood along the road, puddles of it.

"How come Hendo hasn't been charged?" asked Ivan.

"Charged with what? The cops don't care. It happens all the time. They're pleased to be rid of another rascal."

"How come they didn't mention it in the newspaper? Or have an inquest or something."

"Don't be stupid. They hush it all up. They told Hendo not to tell anyone – that's why everybody knows about it."

In the old days the rascals were a laugh. They used to do the houses over almost weekly, and leave cheeky notes: "More beer next time, thanks," and things like that. They used to eat the stuff out of the fridge and you didn't mind over-much because it showed they were hungry. And most importantly, they used to run away when they were disturbed. It's different now. They'll turn on you if you disturb them, and they're always armed these days. Guns even, half the time. You need a gun yourself, and you shouldn't hesitate to use it either. Fuck the rascals. They'd use the guns on us. Strike first, don't muck around. At any rate, that's the way everybody talks at the club.

Shortly after Porter went south, a few of the blokes stayed on at the club one night to finish a game of snooker. It was getting latish, so they decided to go up to the Travelodge to eat. Greg and Terry went together in one car, and Darrell drove himself. Ivan had the Suzuki. It's a handy little thing, high off the ground and much nicer than a car in the evening. Canvas roof, no doors, you just jump straight in, and enjoy a cool evening breeze instead of the stuffy smell of Japanese plastic.

Ever since the cops had driven it, the ignition had been a bit dodgy, so the others waited to make sure it started. Then they led the way down Douglas Street, with Ivan bringing up the rear. The town area was dark and deserted at that time of night.

The Travelodge Hotel is perched right on the crest of the hill, on your right where Douglas Street meets Hunter Street at a T-intersection. There are two levels of carparking, and most of the blokes use the lower level, which you enter from Douglas Street. You can always be sure of a vacant space there.

Ivan followed the other two cars, and this time for some reason they both went past the ramp to the lower level, and turned right into Hunter street. They must have decided to park on the top level. Ivan didn't give it a thought. He acted from habit.

He turned sharp right up the ramp to the lower car park, almost a hairpin bend from that direction, and a steepish climb too. As soon as he straightened out, he saw why the others had gone on to Hunter Street. Swarming across the entry ramp was a mob of drunken Nationals. There were a dozen or more of them, swaggering, aggressive, and brandishing half-full stubbies of beer to show how tough they were.

The worst thing you can do in a situation like that is to drive fast. It only antagonises them. But Ivan had been accelerating to get up the slope, and he was taken by surprise too. There was no time to pull up and try reversing. He was in the middle of them before he knew it; he had no choice but to keep going.

They scattered before him, shouting belligerently and pounding the bonnet with their fists. Some lunged forward as others jumped clear. A bottle flew in Ivan's direction and shattered on the asphalt; the aim was bad. Ivan felt the fear welling up in his chest, but by now he had almost reached the entrance to the car park itself. They weren't likely to follow him in there.

Just as the Suzuki was entering the basement, the last of the drunks caught hold of its side and tried to clamber into it. Ivan turned the car sharp left into the carpark, and the drunk's dangling form was swung wide in the shape of a letter C.

The enclosed carpark was hot and sticky, and eerily lit with fluorescent lights. There was no sign of life. The few parked cars were down at the far end. The place was a gloomy, low-roofed cavern, supported by concrete columns like the trunks of trees. It was suddenly quiet after the hubbub outside; there was no sound but the squeaking of the tyres on the smooth cement floor.

The drunk was struggling to lower his head enough to get fully into the passenger's seat. With him in that exposed position, the car drew near the first concrete column. The seconds seemed to slow down for Ivan. There was time enough to think everything out. With deliberation, he calculated his closing distance to the column on the left. Take it close enough and he could knock the fellow off. Indeed, fast enough and close enough and he could maim him, kill him even. And why not? Strike first, that was what everybody said. He could do exactly that.

Yet what did he have against the poor bastard? The clamour outside was left behind. There were just the two of them now, and Ivan felt no wish to injure a fellow man. On the contrary, for all the tough talk, he didn't want to hurt him at all. The bloke was only drunk, after all, and showing off. Just like Ivan himself sometimes. Live and let live, he thought. And drove carefully wide of the column, reaching for the fellow by the shoulder to help swing him safely into the passenger's seat. "Be careful," he said. "Careful, or you'll hurt yourself."

For the moment, the fellow seemed taken aback. Perhaps he sensed Ivan's feelings. Brotherly feelings: that all Ivan wanted of him was to sit tight and settle down. For the fellow did sit still. He sat, muttering drunkenly, as Ivan drove to the far end of the basement, close to the entry door into the hotel.

Then, when the car had come to a stop, the drink in the fellow reasserted itself, or some primeval instinct, or God knows what. In the cramped confines of the Suzuki, the fellow swung a punch at Ivan's head. He must have been right-handed, for the swing with his left hand was so clumsy that Ivan easily ducked out of range. He grabbed the keys and jumped down from the jeep.

Even then, Ivan felt no malice. Just annoyance. The bloody fool, making trouble – he would get himself hurt. "Don't be stupid," he snapped at him, and started walking to the heavy door which led to the hotel lobby. He didn't run, he didn't even feel like running. He felt calm enough to turn his back on this drunken fool. What was there to fight over?

The door opened and two uniformed security men emerged, big blokes with wooden batons. One raised his hand in warning, and at the same moment Ivan felt a blow to his back. It sent him reeling to the concrete, and the guards rushed to help him. He picked himself up. He wasn't hurt, but he was angry now. Why had the fellow done it? He'd given the bloke a chance and been attacked from behind. And a kick too! Now it was Ivan who bristled with aggression. His assailant was making off and he moved to give chase, but the security men held him back.

"Grab that man," Ivan shouted to them. "Don't let him get away."

Perhaps it was having an audience that made the difference. We can all act the hero if there's somebody watching; and anyway it was three against one now. Yet surely, it was the fellow's violence that had made the difference? Till then, Ivan had wished him no harm at all: the fellow was only drunk and stupid. What of it? But now he wanted to knock the bastard down.

"Don't worry, taubada," said the security men as they dusted Ivan down for long enough to let the drunk disappear altogether. They had no intention of pursuit. Perhaps they knew of the mob outside. Or perhaps their concern for him was genuine.

Just then the door opened again, and Terry and Greg hurried into view.

"Didn't you see them?" Greg asked. "That's why we came the top way. Are you blind or something?"

"I never saw them till too late," Ivan answered.

"Don't you ever use your bloody eyes? You were asking for trouble."

Then Greg realised Ivan was a bit shaken and that there was no sense in rebuking him. "Anyway," he said, "It doesn't matter. No harm done."

"Yeah," added Terry, who had lost three teeth to a rascal with a bushknife the year before, and was wholly unimpressed. "Let's go and eat."

Their chatter helped restore Ivan's sense of proportion, and as they ushered him into the carpeted and airconditioned lobby, Ivan was already becoming philosophical. After all, it was no big deal. As they said, he was all right. And according to schedule, he should be all right now for another six months.

Dorcas And Her Auntie

He had only met Dorcas once before. It had been early in the dry season just before the south-easterlies really started to blow.

It happened in the inevitable way. It was early afternoon and work at Pinnock, Lamb & Company seemed even more dreary than usual. Colin had no appointments, just mounds of paperwork. The others were taking a long lunch, and anyway Mr Lamb was out of town for a few days.

Colin gazed out the window and down two floors to the road. A group of National girls sauntered down from the Bankers' College. They moved beautifully, not swaggering, but loose-limbed and carefree with their arms swinging in wide arcs through the air. He studied the one on the left. Even at this distance he could make out the outline of her panties under her dress. His mind became fixed on that certain subject from which it was always so difficult to dislodge it.

Why try? He took his car-keys from the desk drawer and left his office, closing the door behind him. Luckily, his expatriate secretary was broad-minded. She frowned only half in disapproval as he announced he was going out on an 'audit'. It was a euphemism she had coined herself. She liked to quiz him after these forays and be shocked by his escapades.

He walked down the stairs. The glass louvres were fully open and admitted a slight breeze with a hint of sea-salt. It mingled with the smell of coffee from the stairwell kitchen and the slightly sour, scented smell of the tropics which was always present.

The office airconditioning was just a bit too cold for that time of year, so it was pleasant at first to climb into the driver's seat and be enveloped by the heat. Colin started the car and drove out from the carpark at the rear of the building.

It was no use prowling around the town area. The girls there were mostly employed, busy with work to do and bosses to watch them. And you might run into anybody in town; clients, colleagues, their wives. Colin was interested in girls with nothing to do and plenty of time to do it in.

So he took the usual route, along Ela Beach Road, up Three-Mile Hill (sometimes a chance, but too difficult to stop), and down Angau Drive. That was where you might run into Diana or Ruby. Colin's friend Mullen claimed he had met a cute little Madang girl there, only last week.

Colin did two full circuits without luck and turned into Taurama Road. The wide grass verge was still greenish, not yet brown and shrivelled from the dry wind. It was dotted with litter, but looked not so much unkempt as decorative. His speed was on the slowish side, and a couple of cars banked up behind him. Let them overtake if they wanted.

Just past the hospital there were a couple of raintrees and beneath one was a National girl, alone, leaning against the trunk. Colin's car stopped almost of its own accord, and the cars behind braked and then went past. The girl came over to him straight away.

She was in a pale blue cotton frock which buttoned up the front. It was a detail not usually lost on him, but at that moment he was too busy making eye contact. The girl was very young with short, but not overcurly hair, and a finely featured face. Her eyes were bright and direct and her smile dazzling. She was quite lovely.

She rested her arm along the open window of the passenger door, and Colin noticed a few sparse hairs gleam in the sun against her dark, even skin. His pulse quickened, as they say.

"Hello." Colin spoke first. "What's your name?"

"Dorcas."

"Want to come for a ride?"

"Okay." And with a glance behind as if someone might be watching, she quickly opened the door and jumped in.

"What were you doing there?" he asked as they drove off.

"Nuth-thing," she shrugged in a singsong voice.

She looked so young and innocent that Colin almost had second thoughts. He wondered whether she entirely understood what sometimes came from accepting lifts from strangers.

"How old are you Dorcas?"

"I'm sixteen."

Colin hesitated momentarily. That was very young. Colin's conscience debated with his hormones, but the debate did not last long.

"Dorcas is a nice name. Where does it come from?"

"It comes from the Bible."

"Really?"

"Dorcas was the one who wiped Jesus with a cloth. That's all I know about it."

Colin glanced at her with a smile and remarked, "You could wipe me with a cloth, anytime."

She laughed with a look both cheeky and innocent. Colin wondered again whether she knew what was in his mind. Perhaps after all, she did have the same thing in hers.

By this time they had reached the crest of Gavamani Road where the sea came into view, dazzling and blue across the entire horizon. Below them was open country, dotted with gardens and mango trees. Even the squatter settlements looked pretty, nestling between the hills. The road curved down the hill to the market, then turned right, back towards town. Dorcas sat low in the seat as they passed the market, but there were few people on the road, and none looking their way.

The turn-off to Colin's place was not far ahead. "Do you want to come to my house for a drink?" he asked.

"Okay," she said.

"Dorcas, you speak English very well."

"Yes, my mummy wanted me to keep schooling. But me, I'm tired of schooling, so I finished."

"What school?"

"I was schooling in Samarai, but my mummy wanted me to school in Moresby, so she sent me the ticket. Her boss paid. He told her to make me keep schooling."

"Where does your mother work?" Colin asked.

"She's a housegirl. She works for one European man."
Dorcas became quite chatty. "My mummy is from Samarai and
my daddy is from Sepik." It explained her good looks. "Only my
mummy and my auntie are in Moresby. They wanted me to keep
schooling. I told them yes, but now I don't feel like it any more."

"So what do you want to do?"

"I just like to go for a spin."

"And to meet people?"

"Oh yes, of course."

"Like me?"

"That's okay."

The edge of her frock rested slightly on the handbrake
between them. Such are the advantages of small cars, even in a
hot climate. He reached down and tucked the hem clear of the
brake, and in doing so, he contrived to rest his left hand on her
thigh. She showed neither resistance, nor assent.

They turned off the main road, and drove down the street
towards his flat. To make the turn, Colin had to lift his left hand
back to the steering-wheel, but he exaggerated the motion of the
turn and leaned towards her. His shoulder made brief contact.
The road straightened out and this time he placed his hand on
hers and lifted it to rest it on his own thigh. He glanced at her.
She bit her lower lip gently and grinned mischievously, displaying those lovely white teeth. Her hand remained.

"Dorcas, I think you know some things they don't teach in
school," he remarked.

"Oh yes," she answered, missing his meaning, "but they still
want me to keep schooling. My mummy was cross when I told
her I don't want. And her boss too, the one that paid for the
ticket."

"Yes. He's wasted his money".

"Maybe he's going to make my mummy pay him back, now.
I don't know." She paused. "Do you know that man? He's very
kind, Mr Lamb."

Colin gave a start and Dorcas noticed. Samarai was small
enough for all the expats to know each other, and Dorcas had
assumed the same was true in Moresby.

"You know him? Mr Keith Lamb. He's got an office in town. He's gone away till Thursday. He's a nice man. He paid for the ticket." She looked at him.

"There are lots of expats in Moresby," said Colin. "I don't know him."

But his brain was working fast. What if Keith Lamb got to know? He pays for the housegirl's daughter to come to Port Moresby for her education, and the junior accountant picks her up and screws her! It would be his job, his reputation, everything. It didn't bear thinking about.

"I think you're a nice man too." She smiled and this time she moved her hand on his thigh. Half patting, half stroking. The pressure was gentle but the effect was profound. So much for job, reputation, conscience. He turned into his street and then hard left up the steep drive to the flat.

He led the way up to the verandah and unlocked first the security door, then the front door. She walked in ahead of him and looked around her. He locked the deadlock behind them and they faced each other.

Then, and only then did he notice the buttons on the front of her dress. There was just an instant to consider the possibilities, for without any hesitation, she reached her arms around him. She pressed herself against him and they kissed. All conscience dissolved.

"Do you want a drink?"

"I don't mind."

"Or shall we go upstairs?"

"Okay," said Dorcas.

They went upstairs together and the buttons came undone without difficulty.

Later, they lay together and Colin studied her. He noticed she had a scar along the inside of her right arm.

"What is this?" he asked her.

"A burn."

"How did you get it?"

"I got burnt."

Her simplicity touched him; half her charm for him was her innocence. His anxiety had left him, just as his desire had. It was

31

too late now to worry. Indeed, he became bold in his curiosity, enjoying the irony.

"Tell me about Mr Lamb."

"Oh he's a very kind man. I told you already."

"Yes, you did."

"So why do you ask me again? You don't know him."

"I do."

"Oh." His previous denial seemed of little account. "So you know everything about him already."

"Not exactly."

"He's coming back on Thursday. I'll tell him I met you."

"No, don't do that," said Colin in alarm.

She laughed. "I won't tell him anything else."

"Better not mention me at all."

"Okay", she said in agreement, "And I won't mention to Mummy either."

When she had put her panties back on, she went through his wardrobe. The doors were already open. She found a Hawaiian shirt.

"Can you give it to me?"

"It's a man's shirt."

"I like it." She tried it on and it fitted loosely, but well. It suited her. It was in vivid green, a pattern of leaves with a dash of orange and yellow flowers. It was nothing special. He had bought it in Steamships supermarket.

"I can give you some money, and you can buy a better one yourself. Buy two." He wanted to give her something, something more than the shirt.

"No, I like this. Why can't you give it to me?"

He smiled at her insistence. "Of course you can have it."

"Thank you," she said. "My mummy says to say thank you to the Europeans, when they give you something. That's what Mr Lamb told me, too."

And she got dressed. Just the frock, that's all there was to put on. She looked with surprise as Colin buttoned the front for her. It had been no surprise earlier, when he had unbuttoned it.

She drew away and picked up the shirt again. She put it on over her frock, and smoothed it against herself. She admired herself in the mirror.

"Won't you be too hot wearing it?" Colin asked her. "Why not carry it with you?"

"No, I like it. I want to show my auntie."

They went downstairs. Colin felt a slight anxiety returning. He wanted her to stay and yet he wanted her gone for safety's sake. He made a resolution: this once would have to be enough. To try it some other time was asking for trouble, much as she attracted him.

"Don't forget. Don't tell Mr Lamb," he told her again as he drove her back.

"No, I won't," she said emphatically. "I promise." She had a sense of prudence. More than Colin, actually.

They said little else in the car. She must have understood that he would not see her again. When they neared Taurama Road she told him to stop. He patted her thigh in farewell and she got out and closed the car door behind her. She walked off without looking back.

Colin pulled out onto the road and drove past her, making no sign of recognition. He was heading back to the office by Taurama Road and the highway. When he was well past her he looked in the rear vision mirror and picked her out in the distance, in the bright green shirt. Suddenly he remembered it was the shirt he had worn to drive Keith Lamb to the airport on Saturday morning.

But nothing ever came of it. Dorcas was as good as her word. A couple of times Colin thought of pretexts to call round to Keith Lamb's house, in the hope of seeing her. Queries about work, say. But Lamb was a very private man and rarely had his staff visit. The thought of encountering Mrs. Lamb was also a deterrent. Indeed, Colin had only ever been to the house three times in eighteen months, and he'd been invited inside only the once.

In the following months, Colin occasionally caught a glimpse of a girl in the street, and momentarily fancied it was Dorcas. He would feel a brief excitement, but it was never her. Perhaps she was attending school after all. Perhaps she had been sent back to Samarai.

After a false start, the wet season finally arrived. It was just before Christmas. The parched and fire-blackened hills became suddenly green. The moist air was heavy with the smell of damp and decay, and of prolific growth.

It was Sunday and the town area was deserted. In the breaks between the clouds the sun was intense. Colin had been finishing some work before he left on Christmas leave. He had parked at the front of the building to get the shade of the mango tree opposite.

About three o'clock he called it quits. He walked downstairs and crossed the road to his car. As he unlocked it, two girls came around the corner into view, ambling towards him. There was no footpath on that side and they walked on the road.

Colin fumbled with the keys to give them a chance to get closer. He opened the driver's door and wound the window down. They were slow walkers, so he played for time by leaning across to open the front passenger window. He glanced again and saw unmistakably that one of the girls was Dorcas. His heart leapt.

She was wearing a skirt and blouse, a white one with short sleeves. Modest, yet beguiling. It showed off her figure well.

The woman with Dorcas was older, in her mid-twenties or so. She lacked the grace of Dorcas and her fine features, and she was not as dark. The two exchanged remarks as they approached. It was obvious they were discussing him.

The woman with Dorcas was too young to be her mother, but discretion was still called for. Colin intended to wait and see if they spoke first, but he could not help himself. "Hello there," he called while they were still some distance away.

"Hello," Dorcas replied, but without any hint of whether he should acknowledge an acquaintanceship with her. He thought he'd better not, and he addressed himself to them both.

"Would you like a lift?"

They hesitated and exchanged glances. Colin waited. The encounter was pure chance. He hadn't sought Dorcas out, but now having met her again, he could not bear to let her simply walk away. In his anxiety he added a banal remark. "It's almost Christmas."

It was unnecessary. Dorcas answered as if he had spoken to her alone. "Can my auntie come too?"

"Of course," he answered jubilantly. He unlocked the rear passenger door for the auntie, while Dorcas went around the back of the car and got in beside him.

He headed straight for home. The two made no enquiry as to their destination. Colin turned it over in his mind. They had interpreted him at first as offering a lift to Dorcas alone, and the auntie had raised no objection. She surely realised that Dorcas knew him from before.

Partly to confirm his supposition and partly because he could scarcely restrain himself from touching her, Colin reached across and brushed an imaginary fleck from her bare right forearm. The momentary contact with her soft, smooth, bare arm sent a charge through him. Did she feel it too? He couldn't tell.

Colin looked in the mirror at the auntie. She had seen his manoeuvre but obviously thought nothing of it.

Instead she asked, "You got aircon?"

"Yes," he answered, and they all wound their windows up. After a while they felt the cool draught from under the dashboard.

The auntie began to talk. "I got married to one European. That was five years back. He was a German. It was here in Moresby, and after we get married he wants to go back to his place. So he take me to Germany."

"You went to Germany?" asked Colin, surprised.

"I live there one year."

"Did you like it?"

"It was okay."

"Wasn't it cold for you?"

"Too cold. That's why I have to come back."

It was difficult to look at her while driving. "Where did you live in Germany?"

"I don't know."

He thought she had misunderstood the question and asked, "I mean, what was the name of the place?"

35

"I forget," she answered.

It was hard to know what to make of Auntie. Colin looked at her again in the mirror. She caught his glance full in the eye but her manner was ambiguous. Was it disapproving? Hostile? Had she really lived in Germany?

By this time they were almost home and Colin's eyes were all for Dorcas. As soon as they reached the flat, Dorcas sprang out and led the way up the steps. He tried to brush against her as he went to unlock the doors, but Dorcas backed away.

As he found the keys, the auntie caught his eye again. "You work for Mr Lamb?" she asked, and he wondered anew how much she knew of himself and Dorcas.

As soon as the front door was open, Dorcas went in. She noticed the new video at once.

"Oh, you've got a video now! Have you got any cartoons?"

No, he told them, but he'd got tapes of the Commonwealth Games.

"Doesn't matter," said Auntie "That's okay. You got boxing?"

Colin turned the video on, and the two women stood leaning against the backs of the lounge chairs. It was athletics.

This time Colin stood beside Dorcas and taking hold of her wrist, said, "Come upstairs. I want to tell you something." He tried to appear calm and matter of fact. Dorcas turned casually and preceded him up the stairs. Auntie seemed unconcerned. She watched the long-jump. She said she would help herself to Coke.

Colin caught up with Dorcas at the top of the stairs. As they entered the bedroom she turned and embraced him. She put a hand to each side of his face and kissed him violently, using her tongue. "Quickly," she said and pulled him to the bed.

Later, they came downstairs again, Dorcas first. She kept a studied distance ahead of him. It was the discus throw now, and Auntie was at the fridge, replenishing her glass of Coke. She was amiable enough, and she seemed at ease. She told Colin he had a nice place and that she liked javelin throw best.

Dorcas joined her aunt in the kitchen and the two of them spoke to each other in whispers. Colin thought he noticed their manner change. Though they lowered their voices, he could hear them distinctly, but it was in their own language and he couldn't understand anything of it. Their tone was serious, tentative; not a disagreement, but a difference of opinion. They looked towards him and Auntie's expression, especially, was almost solemn. He wondered if it was trouble.

Suddenly, Colin felt worried. He wished he hadn't brought the women home. He had decided after the first time not to dally with Dorcas again. He should have kept his resolution. Yet the auntie knew Dorcas had been there before. She knew why they had been upstairs together for thirty minutes. She knew who he worked for, his name. Why make a fuss now, after the event? What was the problem?

Dorcas came towards him, and said with formality: "My auntie has a question."

Inwardly, Colin braced himself. "What is it?" he asked.

"Can she have a fuck too?"

An Important Consular Duty

Consider for a moment the links of history, language and culture between Spain and Papua New Guinea. It takes only a moment, for there are none. Trade between the two countries is unheard of, and as for Spaniards living in PNG – there could only be half a dozen of them, say twenty at the very most. It's therefore remarkable that the Spanish government is represented in Port Moresby by an honorary consul; and even more remarkable that the position should be filled by Neville Martin.

The explanation on both counts is historical. Years before Independence, some Spanish chap had run an import agency which was later taken over by Martin and Gardiner, Neville's family firm. In return for a minor political favour, the Spaniard had wangled himself the appointment, and when he left the country the job passed to old man Gardiner. After the old man died three years ago, Neville somehow just took over – inherited it, you could say.

Neville had few qualifications for the position, though it was true he looked the part. He was a big man with an impressive manner, only just fifty, and still good-looking. His greying temples gave him the appearance of a distinguished statesman. In some ways he was intelligent, but his was an intellect undermined by the tropics; undisciplined, lazy, shallow. He was far from ignorant, but he was a show-off and a bit too fond of playing the buffoon.

Besides his looks, his other attributes for the job were these. He had lived his whole life in PNG, apart from a few years in Australian boarding schools. He was financially well-off, having inherited a long-established family business and sufficient shrewdness to employ good staff to keep it profitable. He had plenty of contacts and was a born gossip. Perhaps, indeed he was not such an unlikely choice for a consul, provided he didn't actually have to do anything.

In the event of action being required, Neville's limitations were considerable. Even by Port Moresby standards, he was lazy and incompetent. His only talent in practical matters was to carry thrift to extremes. His meanness was legendary, and extended even to ungenerous treatment of Max Lovett, who had worked for the firm since Neville's father's time. Though nominally the second in charge, Max was really the one who ran the place.

Max was short and fair-haired, energetic and efficient. He had a slightly off-hand manner with fools such as Neville, but a valuable knack of getting on with the Nationals. They respected him for the way he got things done, and they liked him for his good nature. After all his years with the firm, he was used to Neville, but still found the man exasperating. He knew the firm's business backwards, and Neville would have been lost without him, a fact not always fully borne in mind by the latter. Max stayed on with the firm more from sentiment than anything else. He knew he was underpaid, and by way of recompense felt justified in taking occasional liberties with the book-keeping.

While Max actually did the work, Neville occupied his time by lunching the big clients and making rash promises for Max to keep. Apart from that, Neville merely interfered, altering orders for example, or changing staff rosters for no good reason. In either event, one of the shop-boys would tell Max, who would immediately countermand him. That would be the end of the matter. Neville took no interest in seeing his orders carried out. He was preoccupied with the idea of being busy, not with actually getting a job done.

In Neville's three years as Honorary Consul, a few Spanish tourists had passed through and collected their mail from him. Like most tourists who turn up to see their consul, they hoped for a free meal, and asked questions to which the answers could be found in any guidebook. As soon as he saw they were on the make, Neville would give them a cool reception. Sometimes he had his revenge by selling them film that had lain in a crate on Moresby wharf for a whole wet season. "They won't be back here," he used to comment. "Let them complain to Kodak."

Neville was both jealous of his status and insecure about it. He felt aggrieved that he lacked the trappings to which he considered his office entitled him. At the very least, the other consuls had flags or plaques or brass plates. All Neville sported was a miniature Spanish flag on a stick, which he had acquired one leave from a toy-shop in Brisbane. He displayed it, faded and limp, on the desk in his office. He dared not draw attention to himself with the powers-that-be in Madrid, lest having become aware of his existence, they made enquiries as to his suitability. It goes without saying that he could speak no word of Spanish.

But Neville's accreditation to the position was definitely official. He enjoyed the only perk which went with it: duty-free liquor on the Spanish national day. Neville would stock up with cut-price spirits at home, and throw an annual shindig for his clients and intimates. Don Quixote's Birthday Party, he called it, pronouncing it Quick-Zote of course. He would get full, propose toasts and hold forth on the subject of things Spanish.

"Intelligent race, invented marmalade you know. And what about those wine-skins like a football bladder with a whistle on the end. You just open your gob and squirt the stuff in. Terrific!"

Then, when he was sufficiently merry, he'd lower his voice confidentially to make mention of Spanish Fly. "Wouldn't mind getting hold of some of that stuff. Lorna could do with a dose, I can tell you." That part was a joke. His comments were roughly the same every year.

One afternoon a telegram arrived out of the blue from the Spanish Embassy in Canberra. Neville was thrilled. For a whole day he carried it around to flourish in front of his acquaintances as evidence of his importance in international affairs. The cable was written in Spanish, but with the aid of a Spanish-English dictionary and some common sense, Max was able to make a rough translation. It requested the Consul to take charge urgently of the affairs of one Caserras.

By asking around, Max learned on the grapevine that the said Caserras was a Spanish scientist who had been doing research in the Highlands. Apparently, he had fallen down a cliff while collecting specimens of insects and was only found by villagers two days later. By then the unfortunate fellow was dead.

Neville's excitement was intense. He blabbed for hours to his cronies, confiding to them that he was presently occupied in important consular duties. He made telephone calls to the Post-Courier and the radio, promising to keep them informed of 'developments'. Max, who couldn't avoid overhearing the calls, merely shook his head. He wondered what developments there could possibly be, short of resurrection.

Neville was anxious to report back to Canberra with all the details. Naturally, it was Max who was ordered to contact the officials at Kainantu to make the necessary enquiries. Where was the body now? Would there be an inquest? Who had to certify death? What was to happen to the remains? Max knew nothing of such things. He spent the morning on the telephone, identifying himself on Neville's strict instructions, as the Secretary to the Spanish Consul. He had to phone the District Office – pretty hopeless; the police – worse; the hospital; a Dr Wayman at the local mission and so on.

Further instructions arrived from the Spanish Embassy in Australia and were to this effect: Ramon Jose Caserras, aged 34, entomologist of Bilbao, Spain, had died unmarried and without issue. The deceased's next of kin desired that the body be returned to Spain for burial. The Honorary Consul was to make immediate arrangements and report back. All expenses would be met in due course.

At first Neville was disappointed. He had been looking forward to a funeral in Port Moresby with himself as star mourner. He rather fancied himself as a public speaker and had been thinking up some apt phrases for a graveyard eulogy. He had even got out his tie and long-sleeved shirt in anticipation of the occasion, lamenting how times had changed: a hundred years ago, people in his position had fancy uniforms to wear with gold braid and epaulettes. He had seen pictures of them in a book.

Once Neville realised he had been cheated of the chance to make a funeral oration, he turned a little suspicious of the whole business of sending the body to Europe. His meanness began to assert itself over his vanity.

"I reckon they're having me on," he said. "I mean who's going to end up paying? Meeting all expenses indeed! I can see it a mile off – I'll bust my gut with all their dirty work and I won't get so much as a thank you from the Costa Brava."

A more immediate problem arose. The body could not be released by the coroner in the Highlands until it had been identified by the Spanish Consul. "They're bloody joking," complained Neville. "I don't want to see some gruesome sight and have nightmares for the rest of my life. Anyway, how would I know this bloke from Adam?"

Neville tried to coerce Max into making the trip, but without success. Max was already wasting more time than he could spare, and on his own initiative drew a company cheque for the freight on a body-bag, and notified the officials at Kainantu. He correctly foresaw that their eagerness to be rid of the body would overcome strict adherence to formalities. Sure enough, a day or so later, news arrived that the mortal remains had turned up in the coolroom at Port Moresby General Hospital. As a bonus, the body came accompanied by a certificate from someone at the Sub-District Office who really had been acquainted with the deceased. The Consul was therefore spared the sight of the corpse after all.

Further arrangements were now required, and in spite of himself, Max was drawn into helping with them. Neville needed him to make contact with the undertakers. The year before, Neville had been on the RSL Committee which had arranged a funeral for an ex-serviceman. It had been a big send-off: a colour party and bugler at the graveside, and so on. Unfortunately, funds were insufficient to meet all the expenses, and the under-taker was still harassing Neville and the rest of the committee for the outstanding balance.

So Max was sent out anonymously to make arrangements for a casket. At the funeral home, he was politely received by a businesslike gentleman who expressed his condolences, and promptly gave him a message to take back to Neville. "Tell Mr Martin that when his last bill is paid in full, plus interest, he can send you down again. And after the trouble we had last time, it's strictly cash up front from now on."

Max reported back, but Neville was unperturbed. He announced his intention to cut out the middleman. By this he meant that he would bypass the undertaker entirely. One of his mates had told him of a National chap who was a registered coffin-maker. He was said to live somewhere in Hohola, and all that was required was for Max to locate the fellow and engage him to custom-build a coffin for them.

"Why can't you send one of the drivers?" he protested.

"This is a consular matter, Max. It's too important to leave to the boys. It needs an expat."

"Well, do it yourself."

"I'm delegating you."

Inevitably, Max was made to embark on the search. He systematically scoured every street in Hohola between the barracks and the rifle range, attracting crowds wherever he stopped to make enquiry. At length he found the place. It was a reasonable looking fibro house on stilts, with a wrecked van on blocks out the back. There was a kind of workbench set up under the house, but the coffin-maker appeared to have no work in progress.

Max's arrival was greeted by a horde of children who ran up the steps into the house and could be heard shouting at somebody to wake up. After a minute or two, the master-craftsman himself emerged. Yes, he was a registered coffin maker. He had a certificate to that effect, but the kids had been playing with it. He would look it out and show Max next time. His name was Sailor Baruka and he was happy to accept a private commission at short notice. He was a nice old bloke with a good-natured face and thinning hair which stuck out in tufts like the ears of a toy koala.

The price was agreed at 150 kina plus materials on condition that Max would help get the timber. Sailor had none on hand just then, and his vehicle was out of action. However, he was most anxious to get the materials and start work. Max was pleasantly surprised at Sailor's keenness, and rather than return to town to get one of the firm's vans, he decided to take the old fellow there and then in the company car. So they piled into the car amid much discussion and running back and forth by Sailor's

44

relations. Various family members ran and got in, and were ordered out and made to change places. A few lengths of rope were produced.

With difficulty, Max was able to limit the passengers to Sailor Baruka himself, a younger man who was the so-called apprentice, and a young boy. Max was assured that the timber available in town was of decidedly inferior quality. Whilst the living might find it satisfactory, the dead deserved something better. Sailor explained that the best coffin timber could only be obtained at Erima sawmill, where it so happened that a wantok of his was employed. Max, anxious to be done with the fiddling around, agreed to do as he was told and take them to Erima.

En route, Sailor insisted on a short detour. He gave Max directions, and they ended up outside the Electricity Commission offices, because the power to Sailor's house had unfortunately been disconnected. An advance on the contract price was then requested and carefully recorded on the back of a cigarette packet.

The apprentice was sent inside with 36 kina and after a while returned for another ten kina to pay the reconnection fee. There was a further wait during which Sailor gave a protracted explanation of how he had come to be called Sailor, which Max was not quite able to follow.

In due course they reached the sawmill, where the wantok assisted in assembling the necessary timber. Another 72 kina was paid out and the timber arranged on the roof of the car. The rope proved to be a single length about thirty metres long, and Sailor would not hear of its being cut.

So the rope was woven in and out the open windows, wrapped round the timber, and finally secured by special knots which Sailor declared had been taught him by his grandfather. Since all the car's doors had been tied shut, the four of them had to climb in through the windows.

No sooner were they on their way, than it was noticed that grandfather's knots were unravelling, and the planks of timber were beginning to swivel open like a giant pair of scissors. Some unsightly scratches appeared on the roof of the company car, and in all, they had to stop three times to secure the cargo before they made it back to Sailor's place. There, Max was asked for another ten kina advance for smokes, and assured the job would be ready by the following afternoon. Sailor promised to work through the night.

In Max's absence, the hospital had been pestering Neville to remove the body. He was therefore relieved that construction of the coffin was underway, although outraged at the price of 350 kina plus materials. Having spent hours arranging for the coffin, Max needed to put in extra time at work to make up for the lost morning. He therefore considered his slight adjustment to the price to be fair in the circumstances.

Next day, Max returned to Sailor Baruka's to find that work had not progressed as speedily as hoped. The power had still not been restored and so Sailor had been unable to actually start on the job. However, some further measuring had been carried out and Sailor's new calculations disclosed that they were short a couple of planks.

Max left with the helpers to get another 22 kina-worth of timber, with only a short detour to take some female relations to buy betel-nut. The ladies were rather short of cash, so Max outlaid another four kina. This time, Sailor remained at home to carry out further measuring.

On Max's return, Sailor announced that his original calculations had been correct, and the extra timber would therefore not be required for the coffin. However, it would be just right for some shelves he planned to build in his house. Sailor promised to make proper allowance at the end of the job, and the cigarette packet was duly produced and the records updated.

Max's car became well known around Hohola. He called at Sailor's place at least once a day, usually more, for seven days running. By reason of the discrepancy in the price for the job, it was essential that Max continue to deal in person with Sailor Baruka. He had come to agree with Neville: consular duties like this were too important to entrust to any of the National staff.

Finally, the coffin was ready. This even included the airtight metal lining for which Sailor had paid a sub-contractor 40 kina and charged Max 80. The coffin was placed on the top of Max's car and taken off to the hospital. In all, Max had paid out 368 kina, although this did not tally with Sailor's recollection, the cigarette packet having been lost.

Max did not quibble; he had kept Neville informed of the various escalations in price, always adding his own surcharge. He had also come to like Sailor and he didn't care what it would cost the embassy. It had given him pleasure to see Neville's agitation both at the price rises, and the delay. The hospital and the embassy had been hounding him remorselessly.

Arrangements were made for the cargo to be sealed into the coffin the next day. The waybill and paperwork were prepared, and Air Niugini was set to collect the Spaniard for the Manila flight. Customs and the Health Department were on notice to do their stuff. Max was looking forward to washing his hands of it all at last.

When he returned from making arrangements at the airport, Max could see immediately from Neville's expression, that he had something up his sleeve. Neville was trying to be ingratiating, always a sure sign.

"Max, you've done a splendid job. You must be the only bloke in Moresby who knows how to get a first-class coffin constructed. And as a gesture of appreciation," with a flourish he produced a wad of notes, "here's a bit of a bonus for you."

Max was certainly taken by surprise. The generosity was unprecedented: there was bound to be a catch. At first Max refrained from touching the money, which Neville now placed temptingly on the desk in front of him. It looked to be more than a hundred kina, and Max couldn't resist counting.

"What's the catch, Neville?"

"No catch. Just appreciation for a job over and beyond the call of duty."

"From the sight of this," Max nodded towards the money, "I can only assume that you intend swindling the Spanish Embassy."

"Not at all. Don't be so suspicious, Max. Take the money, it's all yours. Handsomely deserved for a job well done." He paused. "And in anticipation of future services."

"What future services?"

"Well, as a matter of fact Max, I'm in need of another coffin. Pretty urgently, too."

"What? Another one?"

"Exactly so. Same size, same finish, same tin lining."

Max was bewildered. "Don't tell me another Spaniard's kicked the bucket?"

"Not at all. There's still only the spider-man, but it's like this," explained Neville. "It turns out a Japanese tourist just dropped dead of a heart attack, and it's action stations at the Jap Embassy. I got a call from Mr Osamu, who'd heard I was an authority in the coffin business. Indeed, I let him know that I'd got an export special – the kind with the metal lining – actually in stock. And he was so anxious to get his hands on one, that I kindly offered to oblige him with ours."

"For a price, no doubt," commented Max.

"Not a bad price, either," Neville gloated. "Twelve hundred bucks – those Japs will pay anything. Bloody lucky with the timing, too. Another two hours and the spider-man would have been all sealed in."

"So now the Spaniard's going to rot for another two weeks! You disgust me, Neville."

"Look at it this way, Max. These coffins turn out to be more valuable than we thought. They actually cost – what, about 600 kina? What say we bump up the price to the Spaniards by another three hundred? That still sounds fair, and we earn ourselves a bit of commission."

"And what about your so-called commission from the Japs? How did you work out my cut?"

"Let's not argue," pleaded the Honorary Consul. "Tell you what, I'll give you another hundred as your share from the Japs, and we go halves on the new coffin. How's that?"

Max looked thoughtful while he did a further calculation in his head, and then he nodded. Neville was delighted he agreed with so little haggling.

Tropical Dinner Party

Christine had made it compulsory for them to be uncomfortable. They could have been eating in the dining-room like normal people at a table and chairs. At least by the open louvres they would have caught a bit of the evening breeze. Instead, they were made to sit Melanesian-style on the floor of the crowded lounge, dining off a huge tabletop – in fact an old door – on which a bed-sheet did service as a tablecloth.

The seating arrangement was Christine's brainwave. The idea was to give the dinner party a tropical atmosphere. The armchairs had been pushed against the walls to make room and the cushions arranged for the guests to perch on while they ate. The Sepik carvings and the new wall hangings from Pacific Arts looked nice enough, but they all got a shocking cramp in their legs, and the heat was stifling in spite of the ceiling fan going full blast.

Christine was fortyish, intelligent and politically radical. She was the type one expects to find teaching Women's Studies in some inferior tertiary college. However, she'd had troubles with her work permit and the best she could do in Port Moresby was an office job at the Harbours Board for local wages. She was not bothered unduly by the low salary. It intensified her feelings of solidarity with the exploited Nationals. What rankled was to be classified by Immigration as a dependent of Malcolm.

He, ten years her junior, was an engineer. They had arrived in Papua New Guinea together eighteen months before, but they were not married. Christine was at pains to let it be known that they never would be. Her oft-repeated assertion provoked no reaction from Malcolm. He treated it as he did most of her pronouncements, with good-natured indifference. He was the easy-going type. Somehow he had meandered into Christine's orbit, and lacked the will or energy to break free.

Neither of the other couples had enjoyed Christine's catering before, and they were surprised to find that at home she was a vegetarian. In the capacity of guest, she had been known to partake of roast beef, lamb casserole and assorted barbecue meats without demur. Tonight she served vegetarian tacos with little bowls of shredded this and that. None of the others had known what to expect when she first announced the menu, and all were disappointed. Christine accepted their polite praise without embarrassment. "Low in cholesterol, plenty of fibre," she informed them. "Better than all that processed shit from Steamships." It tasted all right but nobody felt full.

The guests were four in number. Frank and Kate were newcomers, and felt outranked by Christine's year and a half in the country and her pushy manner. They were dull and inoffensive. Kate, especially was rather proper and naive. She was too polite to express offence at her hostess's language, but was actually quite shocked, not just at hearing so many "fucks", but at hearing them from a woman.

The last couple were Tony and Weka. Weka was a National, quiet and pleasant, but not very sophisticated. Tony had lived in the Solomons for some years and had been in Port Moresby longer than Christine and Malcolm. He was the only one who stood any chance of successfully contradicting Christine. With bad grace she had to acknowledge Tony's authority in matters Melanesian. But she did so unwillingly, like the cleverest girl in the class who resentfully yields seniority to a middle-ranker from the year above.

To ensure she remained in total control of the evening, Christine steered the conversation away from anything specifically about PNG. Her topics ranged from natural childbirth, neocolonialism and traditional medicine to the capitalist system and male power conspiracies.

"Look at the medical profession," she lectured them, "totally dominated by men, while it's the women, the nurses, who provide the real patient care. It's a fact you know, you can't deny it. The women have got no power at all. The doctors just treat them like shit, especially the surgeons. The only women who challenge male hegemony are the midwives, and because they're a threat they're persecuted.

"Yes, persecuted in the full sense of the word. Just a few hundred years ago they were hunted down as witches and burned at the stake. Millions of them, just because of male insecurity. Something like nine million – murdered out of hand during the course of the Middle Ages. Just imagine, nine million! And people talk about Hitler and the Jews!"

Malcolm had heard Christine on this subject several times before, and he noticed that the number of victims was rising steadily. With difficulty, he stretched across the table to top up everyone's glass with warm white wine. Christine paused to draw breath and looked to the other women for support. Neither responded.

Kate was too polite to enquire of Christine's source for her figures. As for Weka, she had said nothing all evening except "please" and "thank you", having been given strict instructions by Tony to say and drink as little as possible. A dinner party to her was as formidable as sitting an examination, and she wasn't game to venture the slightest comment. She had nice table manners, but not the vaguest idea of what Christine was talking about. Indeed, the conversation was over Tony's head, too.

Their hostess digressed to the adverse terms of trade for developing countries.

"And did you know that in 1969 a hundred tons of jute would buy two and a half tractors? But ten years later, a single tractor cost the equivalent of a hundred and fifty tons. That's the point President Nyerere is trying to make. You know, of Tanzania."

Except for Malcolm, they all nodded in dazed agreement. It peeved him that of the six of them, only Christine was enjoying herself.

"The West completely manipulates the system. I mean it's just international capitalism all over. It's a fucking rip-off. No wonder the Third World can't meet its debts! They ought to default and just bring the whole rotten system down."

"What's jute, anyway?" asked someone.

"Isn't it that stuff they make sacks out of," suggested Tony, glad of a chance to say something. "And rope".

"Well jute's just an illustration. It's the same with all commodities. It's the system that I'm condemning. With the odds loaded against them like that, I mean, what can they do?"

"Build a polyethylene plant," suggested Malcolm coldly.

Christine turned on him. "And how are they going to do that?" She resented any reply to a rhetorical question.

"Well there's not much of a market in burlap sacks these days. They should have invested in a factory to make that artificial rope, the stuff that cuts your hands."

"Oh yes," she challenged him sarcastically. "And how could they possibly do that, in their position?"

"I don't know how they could do it, but the Taiwanese and the South Koreans manage to. Why can't the Africans?"

"I'll tell you why not," she snapped, raising her voice. "Because they take their advice from arseholes like you."

In the moment of silence which followed, Christine noticed she was rather overdoing it in present company. The others, it seemed, were unused to rigorous debate. So she added: "Only joking", and gave a little smile.

There was a respite while she busied herself in the kitchen. Kate felt she ought to help, but she was wedged in one corner and couldn't get out. Malcolm and the guests exchanged desultory remarks among themselves but, even from the next room preparing dessert, Christine's forceful presence was sufficient to inhibit conversation.

Chocolate mousse was served (processed shit from Steamships), and Malcolm was ordered to turn over the record of Chopin's Greatest Hits. The halting initiatives of the four guests began to bear fruit in the form of polite small-talk. Frank and Kate had volunteered that the day before had been their fourth wedding anniversary. They were tentatively launched on the subject of how they had first met, when Christine returned to the table and resumed immediate control.

"My wedding anniversary is something I'll never forget. Getting married – the greatest mistake I ever made. Sixteen years wasted. To think what I could have done with my life."

Malcolm interrupted her. "Spare us all that," he said with irritation. He was finally losing patience with her.

"Well, I don't want other women to make the same mistake as I did, no offence to you, Frank."

By now Malcolm was sufficiently roused to let fly a few barbs of his own.

"Why don't you just leave out the marriage part and tell us about the real highlight, the divorce! How you paid the poor bastard back tenfold and skinned him alive."

"Really Malcolm, you know nothing about it. You don't know what I went through. I didn't even meet you until a year later."

"You told me all about it yourself, you tell everyone. What about the property settlement and the house?"

"Malcolm, you never even knew the man. He was just a pig. And he got worse as the divorce went through. I mean, I didn't care about the money at all. He could have burned the bloody house down for all I cared, but out of principle I dug my toes in. I mean, fuck him, it was my house too. I wasn't going to let myself be walked all over just because he's a man."

"So you met Malcolm a year later?" enquired Frank, in a brave attempt to deflect the verbal barrage.

"Oh yes," answered Christine with scarcely a pause. "That was a laugh as well. I used to meet him in the lift when I was working in North Sydney. He always used to look so lost. He's younger than me, you know. He must have played on my maternal feelings or something."

Malcolm slumped back against the wall and pursed his lips as Christine continued. There was no stopping her.

"I could see Malcolm wanted to ask me out and I realised I shouldn't take it out on all men, so I made it easy for him and asked him out, myself. A reception for a poet friend of mine. She'd just published her second volume of poems. I've got it over there, I'll show you later.

"And what I remember most was that Malcolm drank Campari and soda. I suppose it was trendy in those days, but I thought to myself: 'This poor mutt is trying to impress me'.

Imagine! Campari indeed. Nobody's even heard of the stuff nowadays."

Malcolm was making a face and shaking his head. "Christine, I drank it because they offered it to me. That was the sort of do it was."

"You could have drunk beer. You were trying to impress me, admit it."

"God help us," said Malcolm. "Do you want to hear how it really happened?" he asked, turning to the others.

He was displaying unusual determination, and for a moment Christine thought he would actually insist on giving his own version.

"Let's hear from the others, Malcolm," she interjected, suddenly a champion of free speech. "What about giving someone else the floor for a change. Kate and Frank were just telling us how they first met. If you don't mind."

And for once Kate and Frank were keen to speak. Indeed, they were busting to tell their story; this was a topic, perhaps the only topic, on which they had a tale to tell. Kate looked doe-eyed at Frank, and left it to him to narrate the story of their first encounter. The mood of the gathering mellowed remarkably.

"It was on my trip to Europe," recounted Frank. "I was in London and the travel agent booked me to go to a symphony concert. I'd never been to one before – you know, some of that music's a bit heavy for me.

"I got lost on the Underground and reached the hall just as they were shutting the doors to keep the latecomers out. They don't let you in once the performance has started, you know – it's a good idea, really. But I pleaded with them, and I was absolutely just in time. They let me in. I was the very last one.

"I had no time to find my proper place because the conductor had already come in. So I just looked for the first empty seat I could see and I plonked myself down."

"Yes", added Kate, "It was row K."

"K for Kate," said Frank.

"And it was next to me," said Kate, taking up the thread. "Frank was really panting and I whispered something to him, and I could tell from his accent that he was an Australian, too.

So at interval, we just got talking. And we hit it off from the very first moment."

The two of them told the story as a well-rehearsed duet. There was something sickly about it. No doubt it was all true, but the sentiment was horribly overdone.

"It was such a coincidence you know," continued Kate, "because I was in London, doing Europe with a girlfriend. She had bronchitis and didn't want to come to the concert. I almost didn't go myself – it's not much fun really on your own. Then I thought it was silly to waste the tickets. But if it wasn't for her being ill, there wouldn't have been an empty seat beside me, and Frank and I would never have met."

"And if I had been on time I would have found my correct seat and we would never have met either," concluded Frank. They were exchanging glances all the time now. "We always feel that it was somehow planned that way, you know, that fate intended us to find each other."

"Whenever I hear the Merry Widow waltz, I feel my eyes start tingling," said Kate.

There were conventional words of acknowledgment.

"Mmm."

"Well I never."

Christine did not join in. She had been decisively silenced. How, she wondered, could they still talk like this after four years of marriage?

There was a pause, and it was Kate who turned to Weka and asked her how she and Tony had met. "Was it anything like Frank and I?" she enquired, confident that nothing could have been quite so romantic.

Weka looked blank, and glanced at Tony to speak for them.

"There's nothing to tell, really," he shrugged.

"Oh, but there must be," exclaimed Kate in disappointment. "Do tell us."

Tony hesitated and looked to Christine as if hoping she would recover the power of speech and take command once more. But the others pressed him.

"Well," said Tony, "It was like this. When I first arrived in Moresby, they gave me a scungy little flat in Badili with no furniture. I had to hunt all over the place and get stuff second-hand.

"A bloke advertised a fridge in the paper, and I went to have a look at it. Weka was there too. She lived with the bloke. He was selling the fridge because he was going finish, and he wanted ninety kina for it. But it wasn't worth that much, so I offered him seventy-five.

"We haggled a bit and in the end he said that if I gave him eighty for it, he'd throw Weka in as well. She looked all right to me, so we loaded the fridge in the ute and Weka got her clothes and that, and we've been together ever since."

There was a brief, stunned silence and all eyes turned to Weka. She took it as her cue to say something. In her own way she was as delighted with the tale as Kate and Frank had been with theirs. Now was her moment: the occasion for her first complete sentence of the evening.

"Yes," she agreed, "and the fridge is still working good. We keep it downstairs and Tony put his fish in it after he been fishing."

Two Tea-Boys

I wasn't keen on having two middle-aged tea-boys: the thought of even one was bad enough. So I resolved to get rid of them both at the first opportunity.

The question of tea-boys arose with the amalgamation of our firm with our rival, Harold Harvey and Company. Harold had retired from active work and got himself a government sinecure, leaving his partner, Richard to run the business. My bosses in Sydney negotiated the merger pretty well over my head. They had long complained that the PNG operation wasn't profitable enough. It peeved me at the time, but in the long run it worked out well for all of us. Naturally, we took the opportunity to put up our prices straight away.

Harold's was the bigger firm and its office was far better, so we moved all our records over to join them on the second floor of the Cocoa Board Building. The combined business was to be run jointly by Richard and myself. Harold was rather an old fogey, and the terms of the merger ensured that he didn't interfere too much. It was specifically agreed that only Richard and I had the power to hire and fire. I intended to use it.

When I mentioned as much to Harold, just before merger day, he seemed a bit dismayed. He knew I had the tea-boys in mind.

"Herman and Raka have worked for me a long time," he said. "I wouldn't like to see them just sacked out of hand."

"How long?" I asked.

"About seven years for Herman and a bit more for Raka. That's a long time in PNG."

I had to agree.

The weekend of the move was a bit chaotic, of course. One of our clients lent us a flat-top truck and a couple of his boys.

We got no help from the Harvey brigade. Richard was in and out of the office to keep a eye on us, but he kept well clear of doing any work. In fact, the only time he showed any active interest, was when he noticed what the boys were doing to his vinyl floors when they dragged the filing cabinets in.

By the Monday, I was established in my new office, looking out over the dazzling blue expanse of Fairfax Harbour. It was a better view than the retaining wall in Cuthbertson Street. My own staff of three had come across with me, and I made a point of keeping them busy while I tried to get organised and settled in. I kept my office door closed while I sorted out a few trouble-some items which had come to light. I had planned to lose all my problem files during the move, but inevitably, it was only the important stuff that went astray.

Meanwhile, Richard was busy in his own office, creating a very misleading impression of diligence and efficiency. He professed to be too busy to introduce me to all the office staff he employed, and I made a point of strolling around to meet all the girls. I didn't bother with the tea-boys. I knew I'd encounter them in due course.

Raka was the first. Around mid-morning there was a gentle knock on my door. Between the bottom of the door and the floor, there was a gap of about six inches. A hunk had been sawn off all the interior doors to improve the circulation from the airconditioning. Framed within this gap, a pair of shoes appeared, rubber soled with plastic uppers, and about size twelve. From their position, I could tell the wearer was standing to attention.

"Enter," I called out.

After a pause there was another knock, equally timid.

"Come in."

No further knock, but no movement either.

"Yes," I said loudly, and after just a slight hesitation, the door opened.

The fellow came in. He was of medium height but strongly built. He was very dark-skinned and had short, almost shaven hair like steel wool. He had a low forehead and coarse, atavistic features. There was a menacing look about him; the sort of bloke whose only pleasure is to smash someone's face in. His age was impossible to guess, but according to Harold when I asked him later, was around thirty. Not middle-aged at all.

He came to attention in front of my desk.

"Excuse me, Mr Peter. Would you like some tea or coffee?"

He had a deep voice and spoke respectfully. That part was appealing.

"Are you Raka or Herman?" I asked him.

"I'm Raka, Mr Peter."

I studied his expression more carefully and realised that first impressions had done him an injustice. He was earnest, solemn, uncertain. There was a look of concentration about him as if it were a great effort for him to pay so much attention.

I exchanged a few pleasantries and ordered white coffee with one sugar. Raka nodded – almost bowed, and left the room, noiselessly closing the door behind him with the utmost care. Again, I saw the shoes motionless outside the door for a few moments before they disappeared from sight. Raka was not a fast mover.

About fifteen minutes passed before he returned, serious and apologetic, to enquire whether it was tea or coffee I had ordered, and how many sugars. He had remembered that I wanted milk. This time he brought paper and pencil, and took notes. I was beginning to like him.

When the drink and a biscuit finally turned up, I asked him if it always took so long to make a cup of coffee.

"I make the teas for all of them," he answered.

"Listen, Raka," I told him. "Next time, bring mine first. The others can wait. And I tell you what, bring me two biscuits too."

He looked worried. "Mr Richard told me to give one biscuit only."

"One biscuit for the others," I said, "but two for me."

Raka grinned briefly.

"Do you always have biscuits?" I asked.

"First time today," he answered.

It was late that afternoon that I met Herman, who was a different type entirely. He was taller, with real fuzzy-wuzzy hair and the clear skin and good features of the people from Marshall

Lagoon. He was not a tea-boy at all but a clerk, with a lot of responsibility at that. He certainly knew what he was talking about when it came to Bills of Lading, and was bright, alert and obviously very capable. Where Raka engaged your sympathy, Herman invited your respect.

Harold Harvey's firm acted as agent for clients in the Highlands, and it turned out that Herman virtually conducted the agency business on his own. He had a separate company chequebook for outlays, and the cheque-butts were reconciled before he drew his next float. The butts were meticulously written up in his neat, mission-school handwriting, and always balanced to the toea. Subject only to Richard's supervision, Herman ran his own one-man department, even preparing his own invoices. In recognition, he was well paid, and had the use of a company car overnight, and often at weekends.

Raka's duties were less exalted, but they kept him busy. He would collect the mail at the post office, write up the mail book, empty rubbish bins, make the tea and act as messenger within the town area. He had a typed list of his duties, to which he referred far more frequently than I would have expected, after his eight or nine years in the job. However, I learned that the list had only been compiled by Richard just before merger day. In carrying out his duties, Raka had about reached the limit of his capacities, but it is only fair to record that in performing them, he was conscientious and, dare one say it, efficient.

Both Herman and Raka were likeable and useful, and thoughts of dispensing with them were soon forgotten. Whereas Richard maintained a certain formality in his relations with them, I got to know them well, and allowed myself to take an interest in their personal affairs. Before long I became something of a benefactor and protector to them, especially Raka.

The kitchen was Raka's domain, and indeed, the gathering place for the National staff generally. The door was always open, as the room had no window and was unbearably stuffy otherwise. Richard never went near the place, but I frequently ventured in, both in order to hear the office gossip, and more often, in impatience at the delays at morning-tea time.

There was an occasion when I was surprised to find the kitchen door locked from within. I rattled the handle a few times, but there was no sound. I waited a full minute, and all kinds of ideas flashed through my mind. I really began to wonder what was going on. There was somebody inside all right, and I felt sure it was Raka.

"Open up, Raka," I shouted. "What are you doing in there?"

I knocked furiously until I heard the bolt slide. Slowly, the door opened and Raka stood back, smiling sheepishly. The teacups were arranged in neat ranks on the bench.

"Sorry, Mr Peter. Tea is ready soon."

"What's the idea? Why did you lock the door?"

"I was saying the prayers."

"What prayers?"

"I was saying the prayers to Lord Jesus, you know, thank Him for the coffee, thank Him for the tea, and also for the biscuits and..."

"Never mind the prayers," I interrupted, "get on with the teas. We don't pay you to say your prayers."

"Sorry, Mr Peter," he answered, but he knew I was only kidding.

This was my first intimation that Raka was subject to bouts of religious devotion. As well as prayers, he went in for Bible-reading, moving his lips and emitting a deep rumble like an electric motor. He was a Seventh Day Adventist, and I used to rubbish him for that too, though I never meant it unkindly. His interest in religion was decidedly intermittent, and was a useful barometer to his general state of mind. It helped keep him off the drink: Harold had told me that Raka had been a terrible drunkard in his early days.

Knowing he was an SDA, I used to ask him sometimes to work overtime on a Saturday.

"Oh no," he would say, "cannot come tomorrow because it's the day of rest. I can come on Sunday okay."

"You've got it wrong, Raka," I would tell him, "Sunday's the day of rest. You've got to come on Saturday. No excuses."

It became a standing joke and indeed, quite unnecessarily, Raka would come into the office some Sundays to sweep the place out. He had his own key, and often I wouldn't have known, had I not come in myself for some reason and found him there. He would never mention it or ask to be paid overtime. Joking aside, I used to tell him not to come in, that it wasn't expected of him.

"I got to finish my cleaning, Mr Peter. No time on Friday."

I made sure we paid him a bit extra when I knew he'd been in over the weekend. He was certainly conscientious, though I suspected he came to the office sometimes to get away from his wife, or perhaps to purloin some sugar and tea. The latter was something I was happy to overlook: unlike Herman's use of the car, Raka's job provided no fringe-benefits.

Of course, Raka did benefit from the car too, for he often got a lift home from Herman after work. At other times I used to give him a lift myself, part of the way. I would let him out at the Karius Road turn-off and he walked the two or three kilometres further on to Kila Kila Horsecamp, where he lived. On these occasions, he would often invite me to come to his house and meet his family. Though I was curious and I wanted to please him, I felt reluctant. Horsecamp teemed with people, and it was no beauty spot. Even the main road past the market had an unsavoury reputation.

The place took its name from the old quarantine station. Originally, the area had been properly laid out for low-cost housing, but the facilities had not kept pace with the influx from the provinces. Squatters had moved in, and a proliferation of shacks spread untidily up the hill. The part of Kila Kila in which Raka lived was an enclave of people from the Gulf, a group which few would claim to be the most appealing of the country's many tribal groups.

One day, Raka was especially insistent on my visiting; unknown to me, he had an ulterior motive. So we drove past the High School and I followed his directions along a series of unnamed streets. The last of them was crossed at right angles by a deep trench, which I negotiated in first gear. Perhaps the trench was a deliberate speed trap, for the road was thronged with people. Many sat in groups in the middle of the road, making no effort to move aside for the car's approach. At least the road was sealed, and there were communal water taps, a street light or two, and evidence that the dustman sometimes called.

The standard of housing deteriorated as we went further up the street. In the rear-vision mirror, I saw all eyes following us as we drove up the hill to where the road came to a dead-end. Here, the houses were constructed from scrap timber and old packing cases. Most were roofed in crumpled, secondhand iron, and some even in plastic. One house was a lean-to added to an old truck body. The sight of it reminded me of nursery-book illustrations of the Old Woman Who Lived in a Shoe. The rest of the rhyme probably also applied: the having so many children she didn't know what to do.

Raka's house was beyond the dead-end. Where the road finished, a track led steeply up the hill, weaving between the shacks of his neighbours. I made sure the car was locked securely and followed Raka up the dusty track. It was dry season and the hills behind were brown and bare, with black patches where grass fires had burned what little grass remained. The place smelt of dog shit, and we had to be careful where we stepped. Raka jumped a dry ditch and I followed suit. We scrambled up the last incline to the open space in front of his hut.

By this time, about twenty children were following us, squealing and yelling insolently. Raka hissed at them and shooed them away. Some girls, who proved to be his daughters, ran up; skinny, dark-skinned, petulant. He scowled at them and loosed a burst in his own language, lips curled, spitting the words at them. I had never seen his manner like this before. They answered him back with equal violence.

"What's wrong?" I asked.

"Nothing wrong, Mr. Peter. Only, Madia not here. I tell them go to get her but they don't know where. Gone to the market maybe."

The crowd of children began to encroach. They were all grubby, not exactly in rags, but in clothes too big for them. They were dusty and unkempt. I tried to avoid looking at the faces of some of the little ones. Between nose and mouth, they sported a shining mass of solidifying snot. Another had a green tusk of snot dangling. She noticed me look askance, sniffed, and the

63

stuff disappeared upwards into its home nostril. Their personal grooming left much to be desired. Poor little buggers.

A few adults sidled over and they were friendly, but restrained. From time to time they tried to subdue the rabble of children. Raka raised his fist as if to hit one of them. The child cowered, and momentarily the crowd receded.

"Children very cheeky. No good," he frowned in disgust.

I waited to be introduced to Raka's children, but no such formality took place. I had to ask him to identify his own from the neighbourhood urchins.

Raka's house was worse than I had expected. The walls were a patchwork of old planks and off-cuts. They were nailed at irregular angles, creating chinks which in turn were patched with parts of old crates. The house was set on a bare patch of earth which had been swept clean of every leaf and blade of grass. Scabby dogs sniffed the jagged, empty bully-beef cans which had been tossed to them. They ventured tentatively in my direction until kicked away by the adults, and pursued by the children who pelted them with stones.

On this first occasion I failed to meet Raka's wife, and to tell the truth, I wasn't terribly keen to make another home visit to do so. However, Raka was insistent. He assured me that Madia was anxious to make my acquaintance, and so I accompanied him home again, the very next day.

She was indeed there to greet us as we drove up. The contrast with Raka was extreme. Raka, in the environment of work was grave, respectful and gentle to the point of saintliness. His wife on the other hand, struck me from the very outset as dirty, lazy, slovenly, and cunning. She spoke fluent English, not correctly, but with facility and great speed.

The reason for Raka's eagerness for me to meet his wife was immediately made clear. He knew I needed a new domestic for a day or two a week, and the moment I met her, Madia volunteered for the post.

"Raka say I can come and work for you. I work as domestic plenty of times, know how to do washing clothes, iron shirts, washing dishes I can do it everything. I got references before but Raka lost it already. I used to work for plenty of expats, Raka can tell you. First day, I come tomorrow, how much you going to pay me?"

All this she said at high speed, without pausing for breath, or reply. I was rather taken aback by her; her manner was objectionably forward and familiar. As she gabbled, various children squirmed for attention and pushed their way as close as possible. Those out of favour were shoved away, and Madia shouted both at them and, for no reason that I could see, at Raka too. He pursed his lips in irritation and embarrassment. I only engaged his wife out of sympathy for him. Goodness knows, his family needed the money.

Madia turned up on time the next day. Contrary to my explicit instructions, she was accompanied by several children. By the end of the day, the washing had been done, it's true, but the children had created as much mess as had been cleaned up, principally by digging handfuls of dirt from the garden and scattering it all over the verandahs. Madia was still there when I got home. She had waited to be paid for the day's work. When I pointed to the mess on the verandahs, she answered offhandedly, "No time now. Do it next time." And of course, they had sampled something from every open packet in the fridge and cupboards. Madia only worked for me another day before I had to sack her, something which she never held against me in the slightest.

However, the experience gave me some insight into Raka's home life. And Madia was only part of the problem, for Raka had four children, aged up to twelve or so. They were all girls, three of whom closely resembled their mother in appearance and temperament.

The fourth one was a special case. This was little Gladys, three years old, who could not walk and sat up only with difficulty. She held her spastic hands strangely and her head would flop about as the older children carted her around. A Red Cross van sometimes came to take her to a day centre. She was a cheerful little soul, and always the centre of attention. The wantoks couldn't pronounce her name, and called her Cassette. The entire family, Madia included, treated the little girl with the

65

utmost love and kindness, infinitely more than they ever showed towards Raka.

As for Herman, whom I knew slightly less well, his home environment was very different. His children were girls as well, but sensibly, he had only the two. He was buying a Housing Commission house out on the edge of town at Gerehu, but it was properly constructed, on a bitumen road, and with power and water. His wife was neat and pleasant, but very shy. The two girls of eight and ten were lovely kids, always clean and well-behaved when I saw them. Herman and his wife clearly managed the household money well, for the family was well-dressed, and they had a kitchen table and chairs, a washing machine, brand new fridge and so on. Unlike many in the office, Herman always had just enough money to last him through to the next payday.

Herman and Raka were very good friends, but quite a contrast. Herman seemed to do well for himself without too much trouble, while Raka battled hard for what little he had. The one had a quiet, reliable wife; the other a sharp-tongued slattern. Herman showed a brotherly concern for his friend, and would quietly bring it to my attention when Raka was having domestic problems.

"Raka got a problem with Madia," he would tell me.

And before long, I could tell for myself, simply from the presence or absence of the Bible from the kitchen. Only when Raka's family life was serene did he read the Holy Scriptures. When times were bad at home, it was nowhere in evidence; in adversity it apparently provided no solace. For that, he reverted to the bottle, and increasingly, came to work a bit the worse for wear. This worried me. I ceased to ridicule his religious interests, and I helped him stay out of Richard's way.

Around September, Raka took a lot of time off work. Malaria, he said, but I thought there was more to it.

"Mosquito always bite me in the night," he told me, "because they burn my mosquito net."

"Who did?"

"Madia's people. They burn it with a match and make a big hole in it."

I shook my head in sympathy.

"So I sew it up with cottons but next day they burn it again. Then it's got too many hole so I throw it away."

"Did they do it on purpose?" I asked.

"Yes."

"Why?"

"I don't know. Maybe they're cross or something."

That's all he would say. I bought him a new mosquito net.

It was from Herman that I learned the details of the discord. Madia wanted Raka to pay for her younger sister, Lucy, to come from the village. The plan was for her to live with them, at Raka's expense of course, and attend Kila Kila High School. For a time Raka succeeded in resisting this scheme, but Madia continued to apply pressure. Horsecamp was full of her wantoks and they all took her side. Raka's only comment was: "Madia is not happy. She is a strong woman."

A little later, Raka was away from work again. He returned in time for payday and explained his absence. He had had no clothes to wear. To get her own way, Madia had been making things difficult for him and had cut up his clothes with scissors. He confessed too, that he had been doing his own washing for weeks. Herman lent him some clothes, and he resumed work.

Next, he turned up to work with his head entirely shaved: they had poured paint in his hair while he was sleeping, so he had cut it all off. His life was becoming impossible. I don't know how he was eating, for all their cooking pots and enamel plates were ruined by Madia, who drove nails through them with a borrowed hammer.

Finally, Raka relented and borrowed seventy kina from me to pay for Lucy's fare. It seemed a bad idea, but the lesser of two evils. In the event, the people back in her home village had already saved enough to pay Lucy's fare, so Raka's payment, instead of being returned to him, was used to send not just Lucy, but her younger sister Karo, too. This made a total of eight mouths for Raka to feed.

I met Lucy the week she arrived; she came to visit Raka at work. Physically, she was a well-developed sixteen. She had a large mouth and a nice smile, but close up her skin was rough and pock-marked. And she reminded me of Madia sufficiently to leave me unimpressed. She told me she was a "Christian girl," and her naivety did seem genuine. She had never been out of the village before.

The arrival of Lucy and Karo placated Madia for a time. Raka became noticeably less strained, though now he bore the extra burden of Lucy's school fees and school uniforms, besides feeding and housing both her and the younger sister. It was a relief to see that Raka was back to reading his Bible in the kitchen. He produced it from its place of hibernation behind the cups and saucers.

Raka now seemed to get through his fortnight's wages in a week. Madia noticed that there was less money to go round and so did I, for it became more frequent for him to turn up unannounced at my place to ask to borrow money or food. When he told me they had nothing to eat at home, he meant it literally – not anything. I have been to his house when there has been not even a spoonful of salt, much less a handful of rice or a solitary biscuit. Only little Cassette was assured of never going short, for the wantoks would feed her even if they refused to share with the others.

Now Raka was treated with ingratitude. Madia blamed him for failing to provide for their increased numbers, as if he were to blame for the two new arrivals. Herman used to speak to me of Raka with sympathy, but just a trace of condescension.

"Poor old Raka, he's never got much chance with all those women. Why he's got so many? I reckon things are getting worse for him."

Raka was absent again and again. We all tried to shield him from Richard, but his attendance was so erratic, that it was becoming hopeless. Richard was not interested in Raka's domestic difficulties. He claimed I was undermining staff discipline and converting the office into a sheltered workshop. I pointed out that Raka had been an employee of the Harold Harvey side of the business.

"Not for much longer," he said ominously.

Then came a climax of sorts. Raka took things into his own hands. I wasn't surprised. I had worried about violence all along.

"I chase all those women away," he told me proudly one day. "Four pastors come from the church and they cool me down. They were saying all sort of things from the Bible. Madia was scared of me. I was holding her, you know, with some dangerous thing."

"A dangerous thing?"

"Yes."

"Like what?" I asked.

"Like a knife."

It seemed he'd threatened Madia with a knife. The pastors and the Kila Kila Peace Officers had called the police.

"The Peace Officers tell them, 'This man holding a dangerous thing. He must be dangerous'."

But it was all sorted out. The police did nothing besides turn up. Madia and Lucy and her sister went to stay at a pastor's house for a few days, and soon after, Lucy left at short notice for Kundiawa in the Highlands, where there was another wantok. I don't know why she didn't go back to the village; the fare would have been about the same. Karo, the younger sister, remained in Moresby but moved into another household. So that was that. I hoped.

Raka was glad to be rid of Lucy, but things did not settle down. When Madia returned from the pastor's house, she was unrepentant. She began to shame him. She told people that he couldn't provide for them and no doubt there were other grievances too. At any rate, relations between Raka and Madia did not improve. Raka knew his job was in jeopardy. He made sure he made it to work every day, but this led to Madia's appearing outside the office to make trouble. Raka would go out to her and the two would stand arguing under the trees on the traffic island. Then Raka would return to work, brooding and self-absorbed. I warned Madia to stay away, but there was really nothing else we could do to help.

The marital storm waxed and waned. It bothered all of us. Herman looked distinctly worried. It was he who kept me supplied with some of the details. At one stage, Madia squandered a week's housekeeping to engage a puri-puri man from Vabukori to make Raka sicken and die. At least the fear of

69

magic gave Raka something else to worry about. For a week or so he believed his life was in danger unless he slept in a different house every night. Among others, he spent a couple of nights at Herman's and finally, one night at my place. Then he must have run out of houses, or the puri-puri got weaker. He moved back home without fatal consequences.

Then, without warning, Lucy turned up again at Horsecamp. The wantok in Kundiawa had bought her a ticket and simply sent her back. By her earlier departure, she had forfeited her place at Kila Kila High School, so Madia decided she should enrol instead at Gordons High, three suburbs away. New uniforms would be needed and daily PMV fares. First, Raka talked about divorce, about going away somewhere. Cassette was the only one he would take with him. Next he decided he would get rid of all the women. His desperation was pathetic.

Then, one Sunday morning I awoke with a start and the feeling that I was being watched. It was bright and sunny and I got up and went into the kitchen. Glancing out of the window, I saw Madia sitting out in the yard by the dustbin. I don't know how she had got over the security fence.

I opened the door and called to her, but she hung back. She had never been so reticent before. I had to go outside to speak to her.

"What are you doing here, Madia?"

"Peter, I been waiting since six o'clock."

"Why didn't you knock?"

"No, I just wait."

"What's happened?"

"Peter, it's Raka. He got a trouble. You got to help him."

"What trouble?"

"Big one. They put him in jail. At Boroko now."

"What's happened? What's he done?"

"Something bad."

"What?"

"You go to Boroko and see Raka. He tell you himself. Something about Lucy."

I had never seen her so serious. I must have looked worried myself, because mercifully she added, "Lucy, she's all right. At home now."

She would tell me nothing else, and when I promised to go to Raka, she agreed to leave. I went and got the keys and opened the gate for her.

"How did you manage to get in, anyway?" I asked her.

"I can do it," was the reply.

I hunted around the house and succeeded in scraping up forty kina. It was about nine o'clock by then, and the roads were empty except for the church-goers. I was at Boroko Police Station in ten minutes.

The place was packed. They were two deep on the public side of the counter, with only one policeman attending to them. About a dozen other police skulked behind the partitions to avoid helping. I suppose it was their busiest morning of the week, after all the arrests on the Saturday night. Like me, the crowds were there to locate their friends or family, and get them out.

Being white, I was served quicker than most. Yes, Raka Nalau was in the cells. Yes, I could go and see him, and I was led through a door and out to the watch-house. The counter there was placed in full view of a cage-like cell which was crammed to capacity. The prisoners crowded at the bars, reaching their arms out like monkeys in the zoo. The place stank. I scanned the faces, but there was no sign of Raka.

My arrival was greeted by a chorus of pleas.

"Hey, taubada. You help me, please."

"Masta, you know me!"

"Galass, galass." This last, a reference to my wearing glasses; but still no sign of Raka.

A couple of police sat on the watch-house desk. One held a clipboard with the list of names. They nodded immediately when I asked for Raka.

"We got that one," they said.

"Raka Nalau," they called out loudly. "One taubada come to see you."

The crowd of inmates parted and Raka made his way slowly between them, from the back of the cell. He reached the bars and avoided looking directly at me. "Hello, Mr Peter," he said in his deep voice, quietly and with dignity. To my surprise, he didn't seem particularly relieved to see me. He just looked very thoughtful.

"You okay Raka?" I asked him.

"I'm okay."

I turned back to the police and asked what he'd done.

"Indecent assault," they answered. "Did it to his sister."

"Wife's sister," I corrected them.

I asked if I could bail him out. They consulted the price list glued to the back of the clipboard. There was Assault, Common at 10 kina, Assault In Company at 20 kina, and Assault, Serious at 25 kina, which seemed a bargain at the price. But there was no Assault, Indecent on the list. Bail refused.

"But that's crazy," I told them.

"Sorry, taubada," they said.

I consulted the list myself and saw that accused rapists could get out for a mere 50 kina and burglars for the same. I pointed this out to them.

"Sorry, taubada, he never rape that girl. So can't give him bail."

I called for a sergeant and after a while, succeeded in persuading him that whatever assault Raka had committed, it was serious and therefore warranted bail at 25 kina. I filled in the forms, paid the money and waited ages for a receipt. Then they brought Raka out to sign his name and we finally got out. He cheered up slightly on the way to my place, but all he would say was, "I only try to get rid of those bloody women."

It turned out that the deed was done on the Friday night and that Raka had been arrested on the Saturday morning. He hadn't been able to contact me that day and had waited until Madia turned up to tell her to fetch me.

According to Raka, what had happened was this. On Friday, he had stayed on at the office, cleaning-up, until the rest of us had gone home for the weekend. Lucy was waiting by arrangement, and he let her into the office with the promise of getting her a job. Instead, he asked her for sex, but she refused. The next morning he let her free, instructing her not to tell anyone. That was all there was to it.

"So you kept her there all night?"

"Yes."

"Didn't she want to go home?"

"Yes."

"Wasn't she upset you were keeping her there?"

"I don't know."

"Well didn't she cry or something?"

"Oh yes, she was crying and screaming."

"For how long?"

"Long time."

"Raka, I think this is pretty serious."

"Yes Mr Peter," he said philosophically. "I make a big trouble. Maybe I go to jail now. Anyway, no more Lucy at my place." He seemed happy at that.

As if as an afterthought, he then produced a record of the interview that the police had conducted with him. Raka had signed at the bottom of every page with his studiously formed handwriting.

"They tell me I got to say the truth, that's better for me, so I tell them everything."

I had never seen a police record of interview before, much less one like this. The grammar and spelling were remarkable throughout, but the contents seemed innocuous enough to begin with. I sat at my kitchen table with Raka, and read it aloud. First of all was a caution under the Constitution, that the defendant had the right to remain silent. Then the interviewing police identified themselves and asked Raka to state his name and address, which he did. They asked his age, but he didn't know it. He gave his occupation as Office Work, Harold Harvey and Company.

The incidentals continued down to Question 24. where Raka was asked what had taken place on the 26th of November at 10pm. Thereafter, the document made alarming reading.

"I went in there and asked her to sleep with me and I told her if you don't let me sex with you I will kill you ..."

I was horrified. "Raka, did you really say that to her?" I asked.

"Oh yes," he answered ingenuously, "but I was just tricking. I only say it so I can sex her."

His answer continued: "... and also I told her to take the pants off. She then lay down sleep sideways and she wouldn't give me space for chance to have sexual intercourse with her. She scream and shouted and sit up and also was crying.

"I told her that I got the job and will take you to the company car and give you job, but that's not true because I want to have sex with her. I didn't sex with you, you don't have to go and tell your sister about this. If you let your sister know about this and she's upset about it I will kill you."

I looked at Raka. My expression elicited another bashful admission from him: "I was only tricking again, Mr. Peter."

His account concluded: "I told her keep this secret. It's only for you and me. Sorry I forgot the first thing I did was I went and grabbed her. She was shouting and crying and I let her go. That was the first attempt. That's all."

There were lots more questions:

Q.25   Is it true you trying to have sexual intercourse with her?

A.   Yes.

Q.26   She was by herself or with someone? You by yourself or with someone?

A.   By herself and I was by myself.

Q.27   What had happen then?

A.   I asked her to lay down.

Q.28   Did she laid down?

A.   Yes.

Q.29   Who took the dress and pants off?

A.   Myself, but she didn't took her dress off.

Q.30   Who took your short and pants off?

A.   Myself.

Q.31   Did she scream and shout and cry?

A.   Yes.

Q.32   Did both of you had sexual intercourse?

A.   No. Only I try to.

Q.33   When you try to have sexual intercourse was
        your penis fully erected?

A.   Yes.

Q.34   At this time was your penis in full swing?
        (How did they think of these questions!)
        Answer: Yes

More details followed, but I felt I had read quite enough. Raka
seemed to have enjoyed the reading, or perhaps my reaction; he
was almost cheerful now. Nevertheless, he was concerned that
Madia might turn up, and asked me to take him to Herman's
place. So I gave him some money and drove him to Gerehu to
stay with Herman. Herman was at home and not surprised to see
us. He seemed to be fully informed. The bush telegraph works
well in Moresby.

On my way back home I called in at Richard's; I felt I should
break the news to him. He too was unsurprised. "I can believe
anything of Raka," he said.

On the Monday morning, Herman informed us that Raka was
going to see Madia and sort things out with her. He might not be
in to work that day.

"Or ever," commented Richard.

My view was different. Raka had given eight or nine years of
faithful service, and now he was at great risk. More than ever, he
needed our assistance, and it would be no help to him to be
dismissed from work, and without means of support. If he went
to jail, his family would suffer soon enough. I must say too, that
I really did accept that his motive had been to get rid of Lucy. It
was the way his mind worked. And quite frankly, I couldn't see
the experience doing Lucy too much permanent harm.

Richard was unforgiving. I argued with him at length, and as
a last resort insisted that Harold Harvey be consulted. As I had
hoped, Harold took my side, or rather Raka's. He argued that it
was up to the court to decide whether Raka went to jail, and that
we shouldn't punish him first. After all, his crime had nothing to
do with work.

"Except that he committed it in this office," said Richard grimly.

"But not on a client," I pointed out, and the whole question was left in abeyance.

Raka, rather subdued, was at work that afternoon. He recounted the morning's events at Kila Kila. Mostly, Madia's relations had taken an even-handed view of things. Popular opinion was that she had pushed Raka too far. During the course of discussions, one of her wantoks partly demolished Raka's house, and stripped all the iron off the roof. On the other hand, some others had punched Madia and an auntie. On balance, Raka was quite pleased with the way everything was turning out, apart from the prospect of three years in jail.

The court hearing was unexpectedly prompt and took place only about a week later. I engaged the cheapest lawyer I could, and Harold and I went to give character evidence for Raka. Really, the facts supported a more serious charge, attempted rape for example. But Raka was lucky; the police were content to accept a guilty plea on the indecent assault. They seemed to want to go home early.

It carried a lot of weight that two expats were sitting in court, ready to say nice things about Raka. And the Magistrate was influenced too, by our readiness to continue to employ him. He imposed one hundred kina surety for Raka to be of good behaviour for the next twelve months. Harold and I were amazed the court was so lenient. I paid the surety with a company cheque: we would charge it to Raka's loan account.

"I'm very happy to stay out of jail," declared Raka.

The three of us returned to the office, relieved and cheerful. The outcome was certainly better than I had ever expected. But the mood in the office was tense and gloomy; some other drama was being enacted there of which Harold and I were as yet unaware. Richard called us in, and announced the news. It was Herman's turn to be brought to account, and Raka's misdeed was quickly eclipsed.

Herman's affluence had always been a little puzzling. Several times Richard had audited his records and chequebook, but they were always in order, and his figures always balanced.

The possibility of his wangling the duty stamps was eliminated; everything there tallied as well. But like a tax inspector, Richard had found it impossible to reconcile Herman's income with his acquisitions of consumer goods. Herman's discomfort of recent weeks had been not only out of sympathy for Raka, but also from the knowledge that he himself, was under investigation.

This time, Richard had obtained all the original cheques from the bank. Certainly, the butts and the debits balanced, but some unusual discrepancies now came to light. Cheques to the Chief Collector of Customs proved to have been drawn in favour of the Kone Tigers Football Club. Cheques to the Registrar-General were made out to Herman's wantoks and endorsed 'Please pay cash.' He had been charging the clients for spurious outlays, and pocketing the proceeds. The clients in the bush had been none the wiser, and nor had we. Herman had made a full confession.

"How long has it been going on?" asked Harold.

"Years."

"And how much does it all come to?"

"At least three thousand, from what I can see. I've only got the cheques for the last two years. He was certainly good at budgeting – he didn't get greedy. Just twenty or thirty a week, except at Christmas time. That was for presents, he told me."

"What are we going to do?" asked Harold.

"We can't ignore it," I said. "We'll have to sack him. But do we tell the police? That's the question."

"Sack him?" exclaimed Richard. "We can't do without him. It'll take months to train someone to replace him, and I can't spare the time. We're not talking about Raka now, you know. Herman's not just the bloody tea-boy."

"But we can't trust him!"

"*We* can trust him. It isn't the firm's money he's been embezzling. It's the clients'. They're the ones who can't trust him."

It was perfectly true. From the point of view of the firm, Herman could still, in a manner of speaking, be considered trustworthy. Perhaps there was a flaw in the logic somewhere, but this line of reasoning appealed to me, and Harold didn't seem disposed to argue. After all, for something like this, Herman would surely go to prison. It wasn't as if he'd only tried to rape someone. This was serious; it involved money. In any event, and this was the main argument, none of us wished to lose Herman's services.

We discussed it back and forth for an hour or more. If Herman wasn't going to go to jail, and wasn't going to lose his job, it seemed at the very least that he should repay what he had stolen. But since it wasn't our money, we could scarcely dock his pay and take it ourselves; and needless to say, we weren't going to draw the clients' attention to it by volunteering a refund. Repayment would take years, anyway.

As was often the case when Harold joined in, the discussion grew more and more drawn-out and inconclusive. We had almost strayed from the point entirely, when there was a knock on the door and Raka brought in our teas and biscuits.

Howden

Reluctantly, Howden had come to the conclusion that he was married to a whinger.

Charmaine had always been a bit neurotic, a worrier. Over their eight years of marriage she had gradually got worse. When they first decided to transfer from Townsville, she was all in favour. She said a complete change would do them good.

But not long after they arrived in Port Moresby, she turned sour on the place, decided she wanted to go back to Australia, for goodness' sake. She started grumbling about everything: the climate, the food, the prices, the security, the Nationals. Most of all she grumbled about Howden. According to her, he drank too much. Her big whinge was that he never spent any time at home, that he was always up the club.

That was all bullshit. Of course he went to the club; it was part of his job. You had to meet people, have a few drinks, make contacts, keep your ear to the ground. The firm picked up half its business at the club. You'd never know anyone else's tenders unless you mixed with the other blokes. Anyway, how could he spend more time at home when Charmaine was always such a pain in the neck?

As for drinking – sure he drank, but so did everybody. It was a hot climate and you needed to get fluids through your system. And it was only beer, after all. He hardly ever drank anything else. The bottles of spirits laying around at home were just for special occasions.

And he did enjoy a drink at the club too, but what of it? "Aren't I entitled to a bit of relaxation?" he asked her. "I'm the one that bloody works all day."

Howden himself was content with his life. He would never have gained such a senior position if he'd stayed in Townsville.

Instead of Deputy Sales Manager in a provincial town, he was Assistant National Manager of a whole country. They had a company house, a company car, business class fares for their annual leave, quite a few perks. He could wangle a trip out of town whenever he felt like a change of scene, or time off from Charmaine. The company even paid for his club membership.

So he made it quite clear to Charmaine in a tearful scene that he intended staying on in Port Moresby for quite some time yet. That was the only way to handle her when she threw one of her tantrums; just lay down the law.

Anyway, she had her own life – an easy life too. Talk about not counting your blessings! The houseboy, Henao did all the work at home. Charmaine hardly had to lift a finger if she didn't want to. She did the shopping, but that's recreation to women. Otherwise, she could swim every day at the Aviat pool, have her lady friends in for cards or Tupperware parties. She could please herself entirely; Howden never complained once.

For a while Charmaine would be all right, and then for no reason at all something would stir her up. Like a fortnight ago, when she carried on something stupid. He got home from the club about nine, not very much later than usual. He wasn't pissed or anything, but she just got it into her head to make a scene. She provoked him that much he did turn a bit ugly.

She'd kept his dinner hot in the oven and it had got burnt. Big bloody deal. He'd told her a hundred times not to bother with cooking for him. Not that her cooking was bad: he just never had much of an appetite.

"Just leave a salad out and I can take it or leave it," he used to tell her. But no, she had to be the martyr and cook something fancy, hours before the club closed.

"But I want to cook for you," she said.

"Well, I never asked you. Please your bloody self."

So then it was on for young and old.

"You're my husband. I need you with me."

"What for?"

"I need your company. You're never here."

"Company?" he said. "You've got the dogs."

Then she just started raving. "I can't stand it any more. You're destroying us both." All that kind of rubbish. He did say a few unkind things to her. After all, you can only take so much from a neurotic woman, and quite frankly he was sick of all the tears.

Next morning relations were a bit grim, but that was nothing unusual. By the afternoon though, he was all set to humour her when he got home, tell her what a lovely dinner it was and so on. However, the minute he walked in the door he saw she had one of her real sour faces on. What was the use of even trying?

He went to the fridge for a beer, but it was completely empty – apart from food, that is. Not a beer to be seen. Howden wasn't too happy about that. It was Henao's job to make sure there were always a dozen or so cold in the fridge, but it was in the back of Howden's mind that Charmaine had been up to her clever tricks. He kept his cool and went into the laundry where there had been a couple of cartons. But there were none there either.

He still kept his temper, but he couldn't help sounding a bit surly. All he asked was what had happened to the beer.

"It's outside," she told him, all sort of drawn and tearful.

The security lights were already on, and when he looked out onto the patio, the whole barbecue area was illuminated and covered with broken glass. It smelt like a brewery.

Well, Howden went right off. "You stupid bitch. What's the fucking idea?"

But she couldn't answer, what with the sobbing and carry-on. Really, she just went plain hysterical.

"What about the dogs? They'll cut their fucking paws to shreds."

Even in a situation like that he could think straight, think of consequences. Not like bloody Charmaine, thinking of nothing but her own bloody whingeing.

He did yell a few choice comments at her, but he managed to control himself. Anyone else might have hit her, but Howden would never hit a woman, no matter what. You had to give him that. He wasn't perfect, but he knew right from wrong. He'd never played up on her and never hit her, not once.

He shouted for Henao to clean the glass up right away, and Henao whispered to him that the missus wouldn't let him do it earlier. You'd think she'd have had some self-respect and kept the houseboy out of it.

Once he calmed down, Howden left Charmaine alone. He read a magazine and had a couple of gin and tonics. You can't reason with a woman in that state. All she said was that she would sleep on the couch.

"Please yourself. I couldn't give a stuff what you do," he answered.

Actually, it suited him fine. They had slept in single beds for years, but he probably wouldn't have got any sleep with her in the same room. All that sniffling the whole night long.

The next two weeks were pretty quiet. When the club closed he'd head for the Davara Hotel and make sure he didn't get home till late. It was best to keep out of her way. It's no fun living with a loony. He wondered if she needed professional help. Anything he said was bound to be wrong.

On the Friday, Howden was due to take the early morning flight to Rabaul and be back the next day. He was looking forward to a day out of town, even though Charmaine had actually started to snap out of it by then. He'd even managed to sneak a few beers back into the fridge – cans this time, just in case.

It was only a routine inspection of the Rabaul office. Howden or the National Manager went every three months or so, and this time it was Howden's turn. Charmaine knew that, so it was no use her acting pathetic and pleading with him not to go. You would think she'd be happy to have a break from him. No doubt she couldn't bear to think of him having a good time with Monty.

Monty ran the Rabaul branch, and a very good operator he was too. The office was always in great shape. Usually, they could get through all the work by lunchtime, and then concentrate on putting a few drinks away. And could Monty drink! He was a wild man all right.

Charmaine knew Monty's reputation – didn't everyone? – and that was her excuse. It was her usual line; the drink was killing him, destroying her love for him, destroying their marriage. "Monty is an alcoholic, and so are you, Geoff," she said. It was all stuff he'd heard plenty of times before.

Then she made a really stupid remark, how one of these days Howden would be so terribly sorry.

He flared up at that, being threatened.

"What do you mean by that?" he said. "So it's back to Mum and Dad in Mackay, is it? That'd be the day, you've got it that easy here! I wouldn't be so terribly sorry anyway, just terribly bloody relieved."

Charmaine's parents were rather a sensitive issue, and later he wondered whether he'd gone too far and said a few things he didn't really mean. So he tried to placate her a bit, and told her he'd be back by the Saturday morning. Indeed, he promised her he would. He needed her to drive him to the airport.

Well, the trip was great. Monty had everything organised and the work was all out of the way in time for a late lunch. They started at 1.30, finished up at 5.30 and went straight on to Monty's club. Howden visited Rabaul often enough to know a few of the blokes there. They're a pretty friendly crowd anyway.

It was hard to remember all the details, but by the time dinner came around, they had already had more than a skin-full. They had dinner in the Queen Emma room. Fresh vegetables and local beef, better than you ever get in Moresby. They had plenty more to drink too, two bottles of red and two of white between them. Or was that lunch? What does it matter?

Somehow, they got themselves back to Howden's room at the hotel for a few nightcaps. Even by their usual standard it had been a big night out, and it was starting to tell on their systems. It was about two in the morning, and Howden wondered how he was going to manage to make the morning flight.

Monty suggested an alternative; stay at his place on the Saturday night, and catch the Sunday flight back to Moresby. They could take it easy on the Saturday; have a nice quiet day, recovering. Monty's a thoughtful bloke.

It seemed a good idea, but Howden wondered whether Charmaine would be entirely happy about it. She might need a bit of talking round and he thought he'd better give her a ring and break the news to her. The sooner the better, he thought, and Monty agreed. Between the two of them, they managed to get a line out and dial the right number.

The phone took a long time to answer, but finally Howden heard his wife's voice. When he announced that he wouldn't be back till Sunday, Charmaine gave a kind of wail.

"No Geoff, no. You agreed to just one day. You promised you'd be back tomorrow and that things would be different." The wailing continued. "It was a promise."

It was true he had given his word, and for the moment he couldn't think of anything to say. Monty grabbed the phone and babbled drunkenly into it.

"Hello Charmaine, you remember me, Monty..." but the sound of sobbing from the other end did not abate.

Howden felt suddenly very much the worse for wear. A wave of seediness came over him all at once. He felt the urge to pass wind, and half raised himself from the chair. Yes, he felt better for it, but as he eased himself down into the seat again, he realised with mild surprise that he had shat himself.

Now he felt positively ill, terribly hot, and he wanted to vomit. He opened the door of the room and stumbled out onto the landing and down the stairs to the hotel courtyard. He staggered to the swimming pool and threw himself into the shallow end. The water was warm but it revived him and he waded around fully-clothed. He tried to wash himself.

Before long, the manager came out in shorts and thongs and ordered him out. He couldn't remember anything that happened after that. In the morning he woke up on the floor of his room, still in his wet clothes. That was as much as he knew. Monty had gone, and he, himself felt far from well. What he did remember was that he had a flight to catch. He changed his clothes, threw all his belongings into his suitcase and got a lift to the airport.

The early flight had already left, but there was a Bandeirante which would get him back to Moresby with a few stops on the way. He was lucky to get a seat at all. They sat him in the last row, just in front of the passengers' luggage which was secured under a net at the rear of the cabin.

The smell was terrible and it was only halfway back that Howden reconstructed the events of the night before and realised that it was his rolled-up trousers, stuffed into his suitcase, which were the source of the stench. Worse luck, there were three stops on the way. It was the late afternoon before he finally reached Moresby.

Of course, Charmaine wasn't there to meet him. Typical, just when he needed her. If she'd looked at a timetable, she would have known he'd be on this flight. Once he'd missed the early one, it was the only other possibility. After all, she knew he'd be home that day. He'd promised her.

It wasn't worth phoning her to come out to the airport for him, even if he'd been able to find a telephone that worked. So Howden waited around, keeping a studied distance from the wretched suitcase until he managed to grab a taxi and get home.

Henao had the weekends off, so only the dogs met him as he let himself in the security gate. They were pleased to see him, but the house was strangely quiet. Howden guessed Charmaine was sulking somewhere, waiting for him to apologise or grovel or whatever, but why should he? True, he was a bit late, but it was still Saturday. He'd kept his promise.

Howden walked up the hall to the bedroom and saw Charmaine laying at an angle on her bed. Then he noticed the Chloroquine jar. For a moment he thought – hoped – it was one of her silly acts. He went to shake her shoulder and saw the trace of cold vomit on the coverlet. And he knew at once she was dead.

It was like a physical blow, the rush of grief and incomprehension. Why had she done it? It made no sense. Tears welled up in his eyes and he needed a drink badly.

Staring vacantly, he made his way to the lounge and opened the buffet cupboard. It was a stiff brandy he needed before anything. His hand groped for the bottle among the glasses and table mats, but found nothing. He wiped his eyes clear with the heels of his hands, and bent down to look into the buffet. There were no bottles there at all, not one.

In the kitchen he found them, upturned in the sink where Charmaine had emptied them. Her note to him was nearby.

The Native Regulations

Kevin and Hilary were holding a barbecue, just a couple of blokes from work and the people next door. It was a cloudless day in the dry season, and not too hot. The cooking fire was just right and the chops were sputtering. Everything was going fine.

The men stood around the fire with their drinks, chatting about tax rates and their new contract terms. The children, all toddlers, were ignoring each other nicely while their mothers looked on. Hilary was in her element, displaying her Tupperware and hoping to talk the other women into ordering some, she being the local agent.

The dogs could be heard barking furiously down at the front gate, and after a while Hilary told Kevin to go and check what the fuss was about. He strolled down the steep drive to the chain mesh gates. There were half a dozen Nationals gathered at the fenceline with the dogs snarling ferociously. Kevin was mildly curious. After a few beers, and the last hour discussing his tax-free termination payment, Kevin was in the best of moods. He felt equal to any situation.

As he reached the gates the dogs put on a real performance, poking their snouts through the gap and baring their fangs. The Nationals backed away. Kevin's face assumed the expression he reserved for dealing with Papua New Guineans he didn't know; tough, yet approachable. "What's the problem?" he asked. He couldn't pick their province, but maybe Morobe. He didn't recognise any of them.

"We looking for Mr Kevin Sanders."

Kevin was surprised that they knew him by name and, without thinking, identified himself right away.

"You Mr Kevin Sanders?" asked the spokesman.

"Well, what's it all about?" he said, struggling to keep the three dogs quiet.

"We come about a big trouble."

Kevin had no idea what they meant, but he didn't like the sound of it. These Nationals seemed too purposeful for his liking; they seemed to be up to something.

"What trouble?"

"Trouble belong you, masta," interjected one of the others.

The first fellow resumed: "My cousin brother say you spoil his wife."

"What?" exclaimed Kevin in genuine surprise. And as the fellow repeated himself, part of Kevin's mind began sifting through half-forgotten misdeeds in an effort to make some connection with this group on the other side of the wire.

"What are you talking about?"

"You go to Kermadec Street and Mr Darlington's house, and you spoil my cousin brother's wife."

Then Kevin understood. His vague unease congealed into unpleasant comprehension. It was something that had happened months before. It was true he had been to Tony Darlington's place in Kermadec Street. Darlington was a colleague from work who was at that very moment enjoying his hospitality, probably helping himself to potato salad from Hilary's special Tupperware bowl. These Nationals were wantoks of Darlington's domestics. They were there to make demand on behalf of the housegirl's husband.

Involuntarily, Kevin glanced up to the house lest Darlington was wandering down to see what was detaining him. Or even worse, Hilary. But there was no-one in sight. They were all still at the barbecue, thank goodness. Kevin turned back to the delegation, still not knowing how to handle the situation.

The spoiling amounted to this. Kevin had called in one day to see Darlington, but he wasn't there. The housegirl was a cheeky little thing with a pretty face, and nipples that showed like buttons through her frock. A certain look in her eye was giving him the come-on. So he decided to wait for Darlo to arrive – and before he knew it, Bob's your uncle.

The first time was on the camp-bed in the spare room, with the housegirl's dress pulled up around her tits and Kevin having trouble slipping his pants over his shoes and socks; a real lightning job. The other times Kevin knew Darlington would be out for some time and it was all a bit more leisurely. They tried out the cane furniture, not to mention Darlo's double bed. Kevin only succumbed a couple of times. Well, five to be precise. It would have been six, except for the occasion when Darlington arrived home unexpectedly.

The Nationals shuffled their feet in the gravel. They were waiting for some sort of answer from him, but Kevin was at a loss what to do. He was cursing himself for his stupidity. Why had he done it? He must have been mad. If Hilary ever heard of it, there would be hell to pay. He wished it had never happened, but he didn't deny the accusation. His only thought was to be rid of these people before any of the guests came down to the gate.

"So what do you want?" he asked.

"Two thousand kina," said the chief negotiator without hesitation.

Kevin was stunned. "What!"

"Okay masta, one thousand."

"You must be joking, mate."

But the leader was playing it tough. "Not joking, masta. You spoil that lady," he said. "You pay two thousand kina or we court you."

Before Kevin even grasped the meaning of the threat, the fellow produced a light blue baton of paper and poked it through the chain mesh wire. Kevin took it and unrolled it.

The printed form was headed "District Court" and had his name filled in as defendant in ballpoint pen. It was a court summons. He looked back at the faces, now pressed eagerly to the wire. They showed genuine delight at the effect of the document on him. Kevin loosened his grip on the curled paper and it sprang back into a tube.

The leader gestured to the others to stand back from the fence. He was alert to the risk of Kevin's poking it back to them and refusing to accept service. Apparently the fellow knew of that trick, but Kevin hadn't given it a thought..

The group milled around uncertainly. Kevin was immobile with shock. Each side waited for the other to make the next move. Kevin wished the dogs would start barking again, but they had headed back up to the barbecue for scraps. It was the spokesman of the Nationals who took the initiative; he had concluded correctly that Kevin was not about to produce a wad of banknotes.

"Okay," he announced, "we going now, Mr Sanders," and with unexpected promptitude, the whole group about-turned and headed down the street.

By now Hilary and a few of the guests were at the top of the drive, calling to Kevin and starting to make their way down. He stuffed the summons in his hip pocket and pulled his shirt down over it. "It's all right Hilary," he shouted, "I'm coming back now. Don't come down". And he started thinking fast of an explanation to give them.

Everyone noticed his change of mood, and wanted to know what had kept him so long. "I feel sorry for them," he explained. "Their father's just died and they wanted some help from the Arnotts." This was the family who had previously lived in the house, and had left two years before. "I told them I couldn't help them."

"That's the oldest one in the book," commented Darlington. "You should have told them to piss off. Just forget it."

But Kevin did not cheer up.

On the following Monday he took the Summons to Simon Gaffney, the lawyer. He didn't dare go to any of the big firms. He was on edge that someone would find out, especially Hilary. For all her do-gooding attitudes, she would have just about killed him if she'd known he'd been with a black girl.

Gaffney handled criminal cases and accident claims, especially the dubious ones. His clients were the less respectable whites and some of the black politicians. He didn't do commercial work, but for blackmails, rapes, all that sort of thing, he was well regarded, if a tiny bit crazy.

Gaffney was in his forties. He had a pleasant but permanently screwed-up face as if he were always looking into the sun. It gave him a shrewd, but slightly humorous look. Originally it had been a deliberate expression, put on for effect, but now it had become a habit. People were used to it.

The lawyer had just eaten a packet of Twisties for morning tea, and Kevin noticed the empty bag still on his desk. The bookcase along the wall was impressively filled with thick lawbooks, some even bound in leather. There were piles of papers on the desk, on the chairs, on the floor. The office was untidy in a reassuring way. It was located directly beneath a dentist's surgery. The drill could be heard intermittently.

"This is a summons for adultery," Gaffney told him. "It claims that you committed adultery with this Pala woman, contrary to the provisions of the Native Regulations. The husband wants you punished and he wants compensation. Probably not in that order."

"What do you mean punished?"

"Well, adultery carries a penalty. A fine or possibly jail. Up to three months, I think from memory."

"But how can it? It's not a crime is it?"

"My word it is," answered Gaffney.

"But I've never heard of such a thing. It's outrageous."

"Couldn't agree more," nodded the lawyer cheerfully.

He fumbled with a thick, battered volume, its black spine detached along one side and flapping like an unclosed door. There was already a bookmark in the appropriate place, and he read the relevant parts aloud. Kevin felt beads of sweat gathering on his forehead and his shirt was sticking to him in spite of the air-conditioning. The drill started upstairs, and Kevin would willingly have swapped places with whoever was in the dentist's chair.

"It's a strange state of affairs really," explained Gaffney. "You'd think they would have repealed these regulations after Independence. I mean, we don't dare even use the word 'native' these days, yet they haven't even changed the name of them. They date from the twenties, I think – real colonial stuff. They're regulations to keep the natives under control.

"Another funny thing. Only the husband can lay a complaint. A wife can't charge her husband for his adultery. How's that for equality!"

Gaffney was warming to his topic, but Kevin had been following his own train of thought.

"Well, if it's a crime, doesn't that mean the woman's equally guilty?" Then he added cagily, "That is, assuming anything happened." He was keeping all his options open still, for Gaffney had so far spared him the embarrassment of a direct question.

"My word she is," agreed Gaffney eagerly. "But you can forget about a counter-claim. The obstacles are insuperable." The last thing Kevin had in mind was a counterclaim, but Gaffney did not pause. His exposition was word-perfect, and Kevin suspected this was far from the first time the lawyer had expounded the subject to a client. Small comfort.

The first problem was that Kevin himself could not counter-claim since he had been a participant, assuming that something had taken place, Gaffney added with delicacy. So the counter-claimant could only be Kevin's wife who, being a woman had no standing. Furthermore, the Native Regulations applied only to natives, and so Hilary as a European was disqualified on that score too.

"But if it only applies to natives, then why does it apply to me? I'm not a native, thank you," argued Kevin, taking offence at the imputation.

"Just so," said Gaffney with the pleased tone of a school-teacher to an unusually bright pupil. "It's really amazing, isn't it? One law for the Nationals, one law for the Europeans. Just like South Africa."

Kevin couldn't shut him up now.

"I think it was the missionaries who made sure it wasn't repealed. Just narrow-mindedness really, though I must say they take it seriously in some provinces. Northern Province for instance, it's just about worse than murder there. That's the Church of England for you!"

But Kevin again was a step ahead of the lawyer. "But if the Native Regulations don't apply to me, haven't I got a defence?"

"A complete defence," responded the lawyer. "You are absolutely correct." He paused for effect. "But there is a further factor which is this. Although you are right in law, unfortunately the magistrates don't know it. Well, perhaps they do know it, but they don't like it. They look at things a bit differently. They reckon it's unfair that if they screw each other's wives they can go to jail, but if you screw their wives, you get away Scot-free. I mean, if you did".

"I did," Kevin admitted sadly.

"That's the way these magistrates approach it, I'm afraid. They don't share our view that the Native Regulations do not apply to foreigners. It doesn't help to tell them that they're wrong. It's palm-tree justice all right in this jurisdiction. They'll happily make an order against an expat, no doubt at all."

Kevin was horrified. The news offended his lofty notions about the law. "But if they're wrong, surely you can appeal?"

"By all means! Marvellous! A test case. That would be excellent. Let the magistrate make an order, and then appeal to the National Court. It might even go to the Supreme Court and make it into the press and the PNG Law Reports. I'd be delighted to conduct an appeal for you."

Kevin was more horrified. He had no wish to reform the law or create a legal precedent. He wanted the business hushed up and disposed of as quickly as possible. At all costs his wife must not find out. Nor must the press or the law reports. Nobody must find out. Gaffney must keep it all as quiet as possible, and Kevin was prepared to pay whatever was required.

"I understand the situation perfectly," smiled Gaffney.

On the appointed day they met at Gaffney's office and walked together past Burns Philp's freezer to the court-house. Gaffney told Kevin not to look so conscience-stricken, and to leave everything to him. Kevin had been losing sleep and had phoned the lawyer umpteen times for reassurance that he wouldn't be sentenced to jail. He still felt very nervous. He had never been to a court before.

They made their way up the wooden steps of the court-house and through the chewers of betel-nut and the hordes of children obstructing movement along the wide verandah. Kevin was left to wait in an alcove while Gaffney tried to pull a few strings in the registry where the staff knew him well.

"I've tried to organise it so we'll be first on," said Gaffney, returning.

In the meantime, Kevin had noticed that he and Gaffney were the only white faces in the vicinity. It restored a little of his confidence. He stopped worrying about jail and publicity and began grumbling about the expense. He had already paid the lawyer four hundred kina in advance.

"This is costing me heaps, when you add it all up," he complained. "I mean, I always gave her a few kina every time."

Gaffney turned on him, and it was impossible to know whether he was testy, or was only joking. "Well, do you want me to mention that?" he asked. "Shall I ask them to give you a discount on the fine?" Kevin said nothing.

Mercifully, the case was to be heard in Courtroom Number 3, beyond the registry and away from the crowds and confusion of the main courtroom. Number 3 looked out through the trees towards Ela beach. So many louvres were missing from the windows, that the view was excellent. The adultress and her wronged husband already occupied two seats in the back corner. A couple of other people were there too, perhaps the ones who had served the summons.

They did not have long to wait. The magistrate, Mr Velikiri, in trade-store shirt and Indian sandals entered and everybody stood. The lawyer bowed to the magistrate, the magistrate nodded back and they all resumed their seats. Mr Velikiri sat at a wooden table in front of the PNG flag. With difficulty, a clerk read out the names of the parties. Kevin's was the first case called.

At the mention of his name, the cuckold stepped forward with dignity, followed by the woman, Pala. Kevin noticed that by design or chance, the housegirl was wearing the same dress as when he had first met her, the one he had rolled to the level of her armpits. She sashayed to a chair at the front, glancing cheekily at Kevin and clearly revelling in being the centre of attention. What a farce!

Briefly, Kevin was made to stand while the charge was read. Then Gaffney took over. The husband said little because the lawyer announced that the plea was one of guilty, and so the necessary facts were all admitted.

Gaffney was really very good: above all he was dignified. Kevin felt much better once the man began to speak. His words even laid to rest Kevin's irrational fear that somehow Hilary would get to hear of the case, and burst in on the scene. That had been his very worst fear, much worse than the ignominy and the money, and even the risk of jail.

Now Kevin listened to his lawyer and realised that what he was saying was exactly right; it was exactly how it had all happened. Gaffney put it so well. It had been an inadvertent and unintended lapse. Indeed, several such lapses. Five momentary lapses in all. But the defendant had had no intention of damaging the lady's marriage. The thought hadn't entered his head. He was now very conscious of the great injury he had done to the lady's husband and to their marriage. He regretted it deeply. Mr. Velikiri looked sage and seemed to examine his fingernails.

In order to make amends, continued Gaffney, to partially redress the injury to the complainant's marriage, his client wished to offer a sum in compensation. This was in addition to the penalty which he knew must be imposed. The figure which his client had instructed him to offer, he said, was fifty kina. Then Gaffney sat down.

The husband jumped up in protest at the mention of fifty kina. No doubt he had a four-figure sum in mind, but Magistrate Velikiri silenced him with a gesture. Kevin was impressed with him, too

"This is a serious matter," declared Mr. Velikiri, "and I therefore impose the fine of twenty kina. Also, I order the compensation."

He turned to the complainant whose wife, for all the world appeared to be winking in Kevin's direction. "The defendant sex your wife five times. So I order the compensation of fifty kina. That's ten kina each time, and that's enough for you."

The husband tried to remonstrate, but Gaffney rose and asked for a month to pay. It was granted. He gathered up his papers and an impressive but irrelevant lawbook which he had carried for display purposes only. He nodded to Kevin and the two of them left the court and made their way to the alcove near the registry.

"That's it," remarked the lawyer. "You got off rather cheaply. There's usually some increase over the first offer."

They exchanged a few words about the payment of the fine and so on, Kevin expressing his gratitude and relief. He was keen to get away, but Gaffney insisted they wait for the housegirl and her mate to leave first. It would be bad form if they ran into each other on the way out.

"She was a regular coquette all right," commented Gaffney in a tone which sounded almost understanding.

The lawyer walked to the steps and looked down the courthouse drive to see if the litigants had somehow got past them, but there was no sign of them. Then he had an idea, and leaving Kevin where he was for the moment, he walked back to Courtroom 3 and pushed open the door. Bowing, he entered.

Mr Velikiri was still presiding and was hearing the second case of the morning. The same aggrieved husband sat in the front while Pala the housegirl was now in the witness box. She was pouting in the magistrate's direction while the defendant, a National man this time, was interrogating her.

"Did he pay bride-price for you, or what?"

Gaffney understood at once what was happening. Unlike Kevin, this defendant was pleading not guilty to committing adultery. He was conducting his own defence. He was disputing that the housegirl and her consort were actually married. Gaffney hadn't thought of that.

The Bushwalkers

In spite of his name, Dr Schreier was a third generation Australian. He was not a big man, but tough and wiry and very fit for his age. Patrick was amazed when he mentioned one day that he was 73. He looked at least ten years younger.

It seemed natural to call him Dr Schreier, though he was not a doctor of medicine, but of mathematics. He was the Deputy Chief Government Statistician and still worked full-time. Though respected in his job, and liked well enough, he was not close to any of his colleagues. His manner was detached and aloof and he kept people at a distance. Even with Patrick he was often reserved, and the young man learned not to trespass on his privacy. When it suited him, the doctor would simply ignore a comment or question, pretending he had not heard it. Yet when he felt so inclined, Schreier would confide his past, unasked. To Patrick, at any rate.

The doctor's passion was bushwalking and that was what had brought the two together. They had first met one day on a track in an abandoned rubber plantation. Each had been alone, and they had teamed up. Thereafter, Schreier would telephone Patrick during the course of the week and arrange for a walk each weekend. Strangely, it was Schreier who cultivated Patrick and not the other way around. Patrick concluded the doctor saw in him something of the independence and solitariness which the doctor himself possessed.

In time, Patrick learned something of the doctor's background: that he had a wife in Adelaide, but he had not lived with her for many years, though they remained on good terms at long distance. They had no children, and it crossed Patrick's mind that perhaps the doctor looked on him as something of a surrogate son.

They almost always went walking alone, just the two of them. There was a bushwalking club and occasionally they joined in, but the club was full of Pommies and simpering women, and their noisy day-walks resembled school excursions. The two of them much preferred their own company.

Their walks took them in every direction; out past Brown River one weekend, up the range the next, down the coast towards Hula the one after that. After a while it became understood between them that Dr Schreier would decide their route. He had an amazing knowledge of the district and was never at a loss for somewhere new to go.

Patrick was in his late twenties and much bigger and stronger than the doctor. He preferred to walk just a fraction faster than Schreier's regular pace. But for endurance the doctor could certainly match him. In the punishing heat of mid-afternoon the doctor just kept plodding along at the same steady rate, even after three or four hours of tough country.

The two found they had other things in common. Both had travelled a lot and they shared an interest in music and books, very much a minority interest in Port Moresby. Most of the time they walked in silence, Patrick leading the way and gradually drawing ahead.

Every now and then he would wait for Schreier to catch up and they would walk together, chatting for a while. Schreier disliked banal chatter; he would not talk just for the sake of politeness. When he spoke, his comments were always significant, though Patrick was sometimes disconcerted by his abrupt changes of subject.

"Have you ever been to Leningrad?"

"Yes, I have."

"Do you know those drinking places near the Griboyedov canal? Where the sailors go, I forget the names now."

"I was only there for three days."

"Pity. Fascinating place."

And then it would turn out that Schreier had worked in the cipher section at the Australian Embassy in Moscow during the fifties. He could speak Russian as well as German, and could recite slabs of Pushkin in the original and then in English.

"Strange name, Griboyedov. It means mushroom-eater you know."

He said these things without boasting or showing off, but just because they were interesting and he was with congenial company. It was fascinating to listen; the doctor often seemed to be reviewing his life aloud. He had led an amazingly varied and adventurous life. Patrick envied him his experiences. Port Moresby seemed mundane by comparison.

Gradually, the walks which the doctor chose for them became more demanding. Patrick enjoyed the challenge and to begin with he did not mind.

Once, they explored some caves beyond Musgrave River. The doctor deliberately took a rugged track well away from a nearby village so that none of the locals would know they were there. He had brought a torch for each of them and they slid down a muddy crevasse into a maze of tunnels and galleries.

The torches were only small and their batteries stale. If only the doctor had told him, Patrick could have taken his spotlight and a really good fluorescent torch. As it was, they didn't even have warm clothes.

That was the doctor's style. He was an ascetic, and he enjoyed making do. He created difficulties for them just for the sake of it. One wouldn't have thought him short of money, but he always wore cheap trade-store boots and carried an ancient, and heavy, army surplus knapsack. Even his water-bottle was just an empty plastic detergent bottle. Not even a cordial bottle, mind you: he said a drop of detergent in their water would do them no harm.

The caves were said to go for miles and the two of them kept up quite a feverish pace, for they felt cold whenever they stopped to rest. Patrick assumed the doctor knew the way. Before long they were bruised from wriggling through narrow gaps in the rock, and wet from blundering into unseen pools of water. Patrick began to worry about finding their way out again, but the doctor was determined to press on to reach a certain gallery with some special stalactite formations. To conserve the batteries they took to sharing one torch between them, Patrick stumbling behind the doctor and knocking his head against rock ledges.

At length, the doctor abandoned the search for the stalactites and agreed to turn back. They tried to retrace their steps, but every fork and turning looked unfamiliar. Every now and then Schreier claimed to recognise some rock feature, but Patrick had come to the conclusion that they were hopelessly lost. The dark and the echoes, and the darting shadows from the movement of the torch got on his nerves. He was angry with the doctor for getting them lost, and with himself for his anxiety. Dr. Schreier's unconcern made Patrick feel himself a sissy.

They argued over which passage to follow and whether they were going in circles. The doctor remained unperturbed at every false turn, while Patrick struggled to conceal his growing fears. Finally, they caught a glimpse of light ahead, and succeeded in squeezing through a fissure under a cliff. They regained the surface about half a kilometre from where they had entered. The doctor thought nothing of it, and merely commented that it was useful to know of another entrance.

Another time, the doctor got them lost for hours in kunai grass. Patrick preferred this to being entombed, but he could not summon up the same fortitude and fatalism as the doctor, who seemed genuinely indifferent to hardship or adversity. Indeed, it was clear that he relished these ordeals. The doctor had the sense of adventure of a man of twenty.

Imperceptibly, their excursions crossed the borderline of good sense. One Sunday they tried to climb the back face of Hombrum's Bluff. As usual, the doctor had kept their destination to himself, and they tackled the climb without any proper equipment. Just a rope and a different pair of boots would have made a lot of difference. They were lucky to come through unscathed. The doctor had persisted in following Patrick too closely, subjecting himself to showers of rocks which the young man could not avoid dislodging. A fall would have been disastrous.

They were no longer being daring or adventurous; they were being reckless. The doctor deliberately arranged it so that no-one ever knew of the direction they took. They could expect no help in the event of a mishap. Schreier seemed to court disaster more closely with every week.

Patrick finally discovered the reason on their trip to Variarata. That Sunday he was not free until mid-afternoon, and disinclined to go out walking at all. But Schreier phoned and insisted on their driving up the range for a short walk. They would just go to the National Park for an hour's stroll, he said. It was unusual for Schreier to suggest so tame an outing, or indeed, for him to tell Patrick their destination at all.

It was late in the afternoon when they reached the park entrance, and the ranger had given up for the day. The doctor was delighted to get in without paying. As they arrived, the weather grew suddenly worse. Thick cloud descended and a strong wind blew up. The last of the picnickers headed for their cars.

Patrick and the doctor started out on a track for a circuit which brought them back to the car by way of the tree-house. This was a Koiari hut of the kind the local people originally inhabited. Made entirely of native materials, it perched about twenty metres up in the fork of a tree.

By the time they reached the tree-house, the wind was blowing a gale. The upper branches of the trees thrashed the air and the whole structure creaked and groaned. Inevitably, the doctor insisted on climbing it.

A ladder led to a landing about halfway up, and a second, even steeper ladder then led to the hut itself. The steps of both were sticks bound in place by vines, but many of them were missing and the entire construction was in poor repair. Yet it was completely authentic; there was not a nail in the whole thing.

Dr Schreier went first and made his way up, sprightly and nonchalant. Patrick followed and went as high as the landing. The movement of the tree was unnerving and the noise of the branches whipping in the wind, even more so.

As Patrick reached the landing, the doctor headed up the second ladder and got to the hut itself. It was the size of a children's playhouse, with a thatched roof and walls and floor of woven cane. Patrick had no wish to join him there. He was not fond of heights at the best of times.

"I don't think it's very safe, doctor," he called above the wind.

"That's where you're wrong, my boy," shouted back Schreier. "The Koiari lived in these things for centuries. A wind like this is nothing. These people knew their environment, don't forget."

And to show the strength of the hut he stood in its doorway wrenching it from side to side with the wind, like a child on a swing. There was a loud crack and part of the wall gave way propelling Schreier forward off the platform.

An entire panel of the wall toppled end over end to the ground and smashed to smithereens. The doctor had been caught beneath the armpits by a floor joist and a protruding horizontal spar on which the hut itself rested. He dangled momentarily, then nimbly scrambled to his feet.

"You okay Patrick?" he called. "This thing needs some maintenance."

Back on the ground, he allowed no discussion of the incident. "It was nothing. Those things are perfectly safe. I've been up them scores of times."

But the message was not lost on Patrick. Unbelievable though it seemed, it was now unmistakable: Dr. Schreier was trying to kill himself. He was determined to end his days with his energy undiminished. His life had been adventurous, eventful, vigorous, and he wished to end it in the same way. He had deliberately chosen Patrick as his companion. In Patrick, the doctor saw himself and his youth. The young man was to be his successor and at the same time, witness to his death.

Patrick was certain he was right, yet the idea was too bizarre to be possible. He felt he should do something, but what? He merely avoided the doctor for the next two weeks, until one day Schreier phoned him at work and invited him for dinner. He had never done so before.

The doctor lived in an old administration house, overgrown and falling apart. For some reason the front door had been nailed shut, and to reach the side door, one had to step over a low locked gate on the verandah: it had been in that condition for five years.

Inside, there were unexpectedly few books. Instead, every shelf overflowed with specimens of natural history: sea-shells,

102

samples of grasses, fragments of unglazed local pottery, parts of animal skeletons, roots, driftwood, strange misshapen seed pods. The stove and furniture were standard admin. issue of twenty years ago and the lights were bare bulbs. A dusty transistor radio was the only evidence of modernity. Piles of frayed, yellowed typescript lay about with letters and months-old Australian newspapers.

The house produced a strange impression. It was weird, Spartan, like an explorer's hut in some remote outpost. Everything seemed makeshift and impermanent. Metal patrol boxes occupied two corners of the main room. The doctor seemed to have lived out of them for half a decade. Or, Patrick wondered, had he packed his possessions in them only recently, in readiness for the closing phase of his life?

Schreier fussed incompetently in the kitchen. He had fed himself from cans for years and now for his guest, he heated Peck's Braised Steak and Onions in a blackened pot, not even a saucepan with a handle. The rice was already getting cold in claggy lumps on the enamel plates. There was just enough cutlery for the two of them.

"Do you know Amman?" asked the doctor.

"Who?"

"The city," said the doctor with impatience.

"In the Middle East?"

"Jordan."

"No."

"Shame. Marvellous place. Make sure you go."

Patrick perceived in such comments, both the content and the tone of voice, confirmation of his conclusions about the doctor. Indeed, Patrick now noticed in Schreier's conversation constant hints of his intentions. He paused significantly for instance, after pointing out that his age, 73, was a prime number. Then he digressed to other subjects: Tolstoy's enthusiasm for bicycles; Beethoven's only opera; the discovery of laughing-gas; the coming weekend.

On this last subject, he announced he had something special planned. "It's a marvellous walk, just splendid," he said. "And

I'm depending on you," he added so pointedly that Patrick was powerless to refuse.

So they started early, driving in Patrick's car up the range and well beyond Sirinumu Dam. They left the road and followed a jeep-track running along the top of a ridge and parked in an open spot where the track petered out.

A walking path led directly down into the valley beneath. It was a steep descent for half an hour or so, crossing numerous small watercourses which ran down to the river below.

The river was not wide, less than ten metres, but it was deep and fast flowing over rocks and through miniature chasms. They crossed by an ancient wire bridge which swayed as they inched sideways over it, stepping across the gaps where the planking was rotten or missing.

The bridge had been put in years before for Hamaru village, but was now disused. The village had been relocated some miles south, adjoining the road, and the old site was now abandoned. The bridge was gradually falling apart.

The doctor was right: it was a lovely walk, but strenuous. The old village site had reverted to kunai grass and a few struggling banana plants. Not a stick remained standing of any of the houses. The surroundings were entirely deserted.

The track was overgrown, but led gradually uphill round the folds of the hill until a steep climb led them to a gap on the very crest of the next ridge. There was a superb view in both directions of jagged blue peaks and rock outcrops. There was nothing but the silence of nature, a magnificent solitude.

"If I believed in heaven," declared the doctor, "This is what I would expect to find."

Their route back led down the other side of the ridge to a creek which they crossed without difficulty. They then followed the creek for several miles, descending all the time. The track was undulating, but easy walking now. The afternoon wore on and at length they heard again the sound of the river they had first crossed. They were some kilometres downstream from the wire bridge, but to reach the jeep-track and the car, they had only to cross the river and climb the steep hill on the other side.

But the river here was compressed by high rock banks and ran fiercely between huge boulders. The two of them jumped from rock to rock on their side of the river, the doctor in the lead. He appeared to be looking for something. Then he stopped atop a huge spherical boulder. Directly opposite was a similar rock, and between the two was a gushing maelstrom of water about seven or eight metres wide.

"This is it," announced the doctor, and when he saw that Patrick did not quite understand, he added: "This is where we cross."

Patrick was taken aback. "But it's impossible, Doctor. We can't cross here!"

"Oh yes, this is the place. It isn't hard, although the river is a bit higher than usual."

Patrick argued, but the doctor would have none of it. He said there was a ledge on the side of the rock they were standing on, and another on the boulder opposite. All that was needed was to jump from the one to the other. It was a pity both ledges were submerged. When the river was low, you could see quite clearly where to jump.

Holding the younger man's hand, the doctor gingerly lowered himself to mid-thigh into the water. Patrick had thought this purely exploratory, that the doctor was trying first to locate the foothold he spoke of. But Schreier's intentions were otherwise: he hardly hesitated. Without warning, he slipped his hand from Patrick's, and with a shout over the noise of the water – "Here we go," he launched himself from the boulder.

It was not a clean jump. Nor was it a leap through the air, but across the rushing flow of water. The jump was more of a stumble into midstream, and a brief clawing motion towards the far boulder. The doctor stood no chance.

To Patrick, everything seemed to take place in slow motion, even his shouted remark, which was strangely drawn out and distorted. The doctor's canvas knapsack flapped in the flow and in one clumsy movement Schreier himself was turned upside down. There was a glimpse of the soles of his boots as he disappeared from sight. The noise of the gushing water continued uninterrupted. Patrick could scarcely believe what had happened.

He looked downstream, hoping to see the doctor surface, but there was no sign. He scanned the spot where Schreier had disappeared. The seconds passed and his eyes swept further and further downstream for a trace of his friend. In short steps he edged further down the rock and back again. He turned around, somehow hoping the doctor might reappear beside him, where he had stood only a few moments before.

Patrick's fear grew. His little twisting dance of desperation on the rock made no difference. The surface of the water bubbled and boiled and Patrick was alone.

Reality now dawned on him, the dreadful realisation of what had happened. His lips trembled and spittle gathered in his mouth before his tears began to flow. He knew he was alone and it was safe to cry. The pressure built at the back of his throat and produced a sound like steam escaping. Then the steam took full voice and Patrick's wail swelled in volume over the noise of the river. It was the wordless, dribbling wail of a little child, and it was his only comfort.

How long he cried, Patrick had no idea. Seconds or minutes, he knew not. But all of a sudden he was seized by a physical agitation. He sprang back from the rock and struggled headlong into the bush downstream of the big boulders. It was his body rather than his mind which demanded that he do something, that demanded the expenditure of energy in activity, however futile. He blundered along the bank and among the rocks. He slipped and clambered among them, plunging waist deep into the water, scratching and grazing his legs and hands on the sharp edges.

In a frenzy of desperation, Patrick worked his way down the river bank. His tears over, he still panted aloud with panic and pointless exertion, half moaning in a drawn-out singsong chant.

At the tangled bank itself, leaves and fallen branches collected behind rocks out of the direct flow of the current. In such a backwater Patrick caught sight of the doctor's plastic water-bottle, bobbing cheerfully from side to side in its effort to return to the main flow.

With a stick, Patrick could easily have flipped it towards himself and reached it. But the sight of the plastic bottle, its pathos, moved him and he felt only the compulsion to retrieve at once this vestige of the doctor. He lunged at it with outstretched hand and missed his footing on the slippery rocks. He did not try to recover himself. His impulse to grab the bobbing bottle was too strong, and as he succeeded in grasping it, he felt himself swept bodily away.

The powerful current dragged him below the surface and he saw only a dim green light and dark objects. The force of the water hurled him against the massive shapes, and he deflected them with kicks and with his shoulders. At last he broke the surface, and scrambling between two rocks, realised that he was now on the opposite side of the river.

On this side, it felt spongy and yielding underfoot. His fear now was to be thrown against the doctor's body, and he dragged himself feverishly clear of the water. He had recovered the doctor's water-bottle; that was enough.

A fine red line across his right thigh widened and a curtain of blood descended his wet leg. He had other gashes too, and the sight of them was a relief. The doctor was lost and it seemed indecent for him to be unscathed. Now he too, had suffered physical hurt.

Without conscious thought, he clambered through the bush heading upstream. He kept away from the river bank, for fear of the sight of the doctor's corpse, snagged on a rotten log, or curled in the scum in the still pools among the innermost rocks. His wounds and bruises began to hurt.

He was more composed now, though he felt drained of feeling as well as strength. He still moaned slightly as he moved through the undergrowth, moving parallel with the river. He aimed to reach the track leading up the hill to the car. Then he would drive to the dam site and raise the alarm.

Suddenly, below him and close to the river, Patrick caught a glimpse of something white. He stumbled downhill towards it and saw the figure of the doctor sprawled clumsily on the ground. He gave a cry.

The figure scarcely moved, but Patrick heard the doctor's voice.

"Patrick, is that you?" he called, without looking up from nursing his foot. "I won't be coming out next week. I think I've broken my ankle."

Then he caught sight of the young man coming sheepishly through the trees. It was the first time Patrick had ever heard a note of alarm in the doctor's voice as he exclaimed, "Good Lord, man! Whatever's happened to you?"

Sporting Injuries

It's past ten o'clock on a Saturday morning when the phone rings and Bignell is on the line.

"What are you doing today?" he asks Steve.

"Nothing."

"Feel like doing anything?"

"Nuh."

"Why not?"

He has to think of the reason. "It's too hot. And I couldn't be bothered, anyway."

"What about coming out on the boat for a spot of water-skiing? No wonder you're always tired. You don't play enough sport."

Steve isn't keen. Actually, he's still recovering from the night before, and he's only just got up. He isn't thinking of anything except having a smoke to clear his head.

"Aw, come on," says Bignell, applying a bit of persuasion. "We'll make it a quiet day. Just an hour or so out on the water. It'll do you good." From the sound of it, he needs someone to steer the boat for him.

"I only just got up," Steve protests, and he raises all the other objections he can think of. He asks Bignell about the sunglasses he left in the boat the last time. He asks whether the boat's in the water, or on the trailer; whether the tow-bar on the Land-Rover's been fixed. He asks whether Bignell has got the fuel yet. There's always a lot of pissing around, going out on the boat with Bignell.

The latter reassures him. "Listen, I'm just about ready, mate. We can make an early start and beat the rush to the boat-ramp. I'll see you down there."

So Steve agrees. "Righto, I'll see you there at eleven," he says.

"Make it twelve, can you?" asks Bignell, "And bring a couple of drinks with you, and a packet of biscuits or something."

Well, Steve's got a bit of time in hand, and anyway, Bignell's not exactly the punctual type. So he pisses around a bit, himself. Smokes a cigarette, then draws the curtains and has a snooze for another half hour. Then he makes himself a cup of coffee, shoves some clothes into the washing-machine, empties the ashtrays and the cockroach traps.

He puts a record on the record-player, but it sounds shit-house, as if there's a bit of fluff on the needle. He looks at the pick-up and it's all fluff. Someone's been playing the records that got the beer spilt on them. Stupid bastard, wrecked the thing. You can ruin all your records, playing them with a needle like that.

It's still not twelve o'clock by the time Steve's had a slice of toast, so he figures he'll try and get a new stylus before the shops close. He gets into the car and runs down to Chin H.Meen's at Boroko. Of course, the shops are just what you'd expect at that hour, absolutely chock-a-block. It's as hot as hell, and he has to fight his way through crowds of Nationals, all milling around waiting for something to happen. Boroko's murder on a Saturday morning.

He manages to buy a new stylus – two actually, because he's not sure which model he needs, and he can't face going through all this again. He should have brought the old one with him. There's a whole cabinet full of different models, and they all look like the kind he needs.

He picks up a couple of things in Carpenter's Supermarket while he's about it, and tries at the newsagent for the Australian papers. They aren't in yet. That's a bugger, because Steve always feels like having a bit of a read at the weekend. So just on the off-chance, he drives past the Book Exchange, and finds it's still open. He goes in and picks up a few second-hand paper-backs, Harold Robbins, Hammond Innes, that kind of rubbish. It's hard to remember which titles he's got already.

He's feeling more wide-awake at last, so when he gets home he hangs out the washing and puts another lot in the machine. He starts on one of the books and has a bite of lunch as well. The first stylus he chose was the right one. What a miracle. The records sound a hundred per cent better.

He listens to a couple of sides and by now he actually does feel like going out on Bignell's boat. He starts to get ready; keys, money and so on, but he couldn't be bothered with the drinks. His bathers and sun-lotion are somewhere in the back of his car, he hopes. It's almost two o'clock by now, so there's no time to hang out the second lot of washing.

Just to be sure, he gives Bignell's number a ring, but there's no answer; he must be down at the boat already. So Steve heads down to the Yacht Club, and drives up and down looking among the parked cars for Bignell's Land-Rover. But he can't see it, and the boat is still on its trailer in the parking area.

The security boys know Bignell, so Steve calls out to them and asks them if they've seen him.

"No got, masta," they shout back.

For five minutes, Steve waits around in the sun. He doesn't want to go up to the Yacht Club bar. It's bound to be full of blokes he knows, and he'll never get out again before midnight. He decides to check back at his own place on the off-chance that Bignell has put in an appearance there. It only takes three minutes to whiz back up the hill, but there's no sign of him. For lack of any better idea, he heads out towards Bignell's, hoping he'll meet him on the way. There's a chance of missing him on the one-way system at Le Hunte Road, but there's no sense in spending the whole afternoon outside the Yacht Club, hoping he'll turn up. Bignell's a real pain. The bastard always keeps you waiting no matter how late you are.

There's not much traffic through Boroko now. Just Nationals, hanging around waiting for the bus; or just hanging around, full stop. There's a sheila in black sitting on her own and if Steve wasn't going waterskiing, he'd almost be interested. She's pretty presentable, and looks the type to be available this time of day. You never know your luck.

111

Steve gets to Gordons where Bignell lives, and he's just turning into Henao Drive when he thinks he sees Bignell's Land-Rover disappearing down the end of the street, with a luggage trunk or something on the pack rack. So he does a U-turn and reaches the big roundabout at the brewery, just in time to see that it is Bignell. There's a girl in the passenger seat, and by the look of her Afro hair, it's Etoro.

Steve tries to catch up to them, but he hasn't got much hope. Bignell drives like a maniac, real fast even in that wreck of a Land-Rover; and he's got too much of a start. By the time Steve reaches Gordons market, there's no sign of them. He guesses that Bignell and Etoro have had a reconciliation. They were living together until a couple of months ago. Etoro's good-looking all right, but she's the jealous type, a Kairuku. They had a terrible fight when they busted up. She tried to stab Bignell in the eye with a fork at the Mandarin Restaurant, or so they say.

So Steve gives up the waterskiing for a bad job, and since it's after three now, he reckons the Australian papers must have arrived. The paper shop is pretty much on the way home, so he calls in and gets himself a Courier-Mail and a Weekend Australian, in spite of the price. Over four kina for two newspapers, it's bloody cruel.

Steve is about to climb back into his car when he sights the girl in black again, the one from the Four-Mile bus stop. She doesn't look bad at all, just a bit overdressed. Her black dress has got a sort of silver thread around the hem, and there's a slit up each side. It's like an evening dress, a party dress or whatever you call them.

The girl is leaning against the chemist's window and looking his way, but her intentions aren't clear. Still, there's no boyfriend or big brother lurking nearby, so Steve figures he'll give it a try. Something to do, anyway. He saunters up and she challenges him straight away.

"What you looking at me for?" she demands, sort of aggressive like.

"Nothing. What's the problem?"

"Why you coming after me?"

"I'm not coming after you. I'm going to check my mailbox," he lies, gesturing towards the post office.

But she's no fool. "That's a bullshit. Where's your key then?" she asks. "I see you when you drive past, looking at me. You wanna look up my pants or something?"

"I wouldn't mind," he says.

She gives him a contemptuous snort, but that doesn't put him off. It's the way some of them are. Anyway, this one seems to have second thoughts.

"What you got at your place? You got a beer?"

"Yeah."

"What kind? You got SP?"

"Yeah."

"You sure? I don't want that San Mig rubbish. Always give you a bloody hangover."

"I've got SP," he assures her. "Come and have a drink."

"Maybe."

He heads back to the car – so much for the mailbox – and hopes she'll follow. She does. She goes straight to the passenger's side and gets in, and Steve reverses out and drives off. He casts a glance her way. Her body language is what they call ambivalent. She's friendly in a tough sort of way, but she sits with her legs crossed away from him. Still, she got in, that's the main thing.

She looks around the car with disdain. Steve's car is always a terrible mess. The floor and seats are littered with rubbish: magazines, dirty clothes, screwed-up plastic bags, empty bottles, anything you can think of.

"What sort of car you call *this*?" she sniffs, not expecting a reply.

As they drive along her mood improves. She tells him that she was out with her girlfriends the night before and they left her in the lurch somewhere, took off without her. She doesn't say where. That's why she's in a bad mood, and how come she's prowling around Boroko in a party frock in the middle of the afternoon. She doesn't want to go home for fear of meeting them. If she met those girls now, she'd kill them for sure.

Actually, this girl's not bad looking at all. A very good figure, better skin than most and quite a pretty face when she's not scowling. Her eyes are abnormally bright and alert, but with a dangerous look in them from time to time. She doesn't smell of alcohol, but she acts like she's been drinking. Maybe she's a bit drunk from last night still, or maybe just putting it on. You can never tell.

Back at the flat, she opens the fridge and helps herself to a stubby. She insists on a glass. Steve gets one down and fills it for her, and she drinks it right away. She gets a bit more relaxed after that, and she stops making a fuss any more when he tries putting his hand on her shoulder and that sort of thing. She's definitely the volatile type, all the same.

He tells her he likes her dress, the slits especially.

"That's because you wanna see my legs."

"That's right. You've got good legs," he tells her.

"That's what all the boys say at the squash club. They say 'Debbie, you got nice legs,' and they try and touch them and I tell them 'Don't touch. That's for my husband only. They belong to him'." She can manage a grin for this.

"You're not really married, are you?" asks Steve.

"You bloody stupid or something?" says Debbie, "I just say that to keep the boys away."

It only takes another stubby for a bit of smooching and hanky-panky to develop on the couch, with Debbie starting to take some of the initiative. She's got full, fleshy lips and her breath is sweet. That's one thing in favour of chewing betel-nut. She's certainly keen, and that party frock doesn't present much of a problem. Of her own accord she gets up and takes a shower.

The venue changes to the bedroom and it's well after dark when the performance is over. She's not a bad number, this Debbie, and pretty wild in bed. Bit of a nympho, even.

But after they get up, it doesn't take long for her to start being difficult. You know, moody, just wanting to give Steve a hard time. Goodness knows why.

She announces that she's hungry, so he offers to cook her something. But no, she doesn't want him to do that. She'd sooner grumble. She doesn't want him to cook rice, nor fry a steak. She

114

doesn't want bread, she doesn't like cheese. She wants fresh fish, but Steve hasn't got any fresh fish. She decides she's not hungry after all, but rifles through the fridge, anyway. She finds four hard-boiled eggs and eats the lot, shells and all. And she keeps drinking.

She wants music but she doesn't like Steve's records. They're all rubbish music. She wants string band music, so Steve manages to find that LP called Lau Vasi, the one with the picture on the cover of a Mekeo girl with big boobs. It's the only string band music he possesses, but it's one of the records he spilt the beer on. He won't let her play it with his new stylus.

She paces up and down, pulling faces, though she says she doesn't want to go home. All he wants to do is read the sport in the Courier Mail. He might feel like eating later, but for now all he wants is for Debbie to give him some peace. Originally, he was going to let her stay the night, but he starts to have second thoughts. Still, if she wants to go, he'll take her; and if she wants to stay, she can. Just whatever she wants. The trouble is, she doesn't know what she wants. She only knows what she doesn't want, and that's anything that Steve suggests.

"It's too boring here," she complains.

"Well read something!" he tells her, and points around the room, where there are paperbacks and old magazines laying wherever you care to look.

"I only read big printing," she says.

Steve thinks to himself that it's a pity he's not seventy years old and half blind, because then he'd have some of those special large-print books laying around. But the fact is that he's 26, with perfect eyesight. So he gets her some magazines, and she looks at the pictures for a while until she turns sullen again and slings them on the floor.

There's nothing she wants to do except drink. Well, even drinking she probably doesn't want; it's the being drunk that she wants. Her eyes have lost that alert look. She swears and mutters to herself, God knows what she's saying. Steve tries to ignore her, but she wants him to pay attention to her, entertain her or something. No wonder her girlfriends decided to leave her. Steve too, decides he'd like to be rid of her.

"Look," he says, "You're not happy here. I think I'd better take you home."

This really sets her off.

"I don't want to go home, I told you already. What! You want me to kill someone, you bloody bastard?" she yells. "I'll kill you next," and she looks around to snatch up any weapon lying handy, of which fortunately, there are none.

Steve is really fed up with her now. What a hassle, just for a root! This is the way it ends up half the time, with this sort of girl. So bloody unpredictable. A bloke would be better off like Bignell, having a proper girlfriend and letting her move in with him. At least he'd know where he stood, then.

Steve manages to sit Debbie down in a chair, in spite of a bit of resistance. After a while she settles down again, and then wanders off to the bathroom. There's silence for a while, and then he hears the sound of breaking glass. He dashes in and sees that she's smashed a beer bottle in the shower recess. The silly bitch is definitely out of control now. It's not just the drink, it's some innate fury. But it's a mystery what's set her off. Was it the sex? Too much? Not enough? The hard boiled eggs? Who knows, maybe she's allergic to egg-shells!

"Debbie, don't do that," he shouts.

"What you bring me here for, anyway?" she demands.

"Well, I'm going to take you home," he says. "You're not happy here."

She tries a bit of screaming and carry-on again, but Steve means business this time. He's had enough of her. She still refuses to go home, but she agrees to go to her brother's place instead, at Kaugere. She tells Steve she'll show him the way.

Steve isn't even sure where Kaugere is, but he knows the place by reputation. It's got a bad name, teeming with rascals from all accounts. The Kipsco gang hangs out there, according to all the graffiti you see. It's the sort of place where you have a good chance of having your windscreen smashed, or your jawbone. Not a healthy destination at ten o'clock at night. He hopes he'll be able to drop the girl off somewhere on the main road, and let her walk from there.

Debbie insists on taking a couple of stubbies with her, one in each hand and she gets into the car, mumbling to herself. At first, she's too drunk to give proper directions. Then they turn into Scratchley Road, where she comes to her senses sufficiently to announce that they've come too far. Steve does a U-turn and goes back slowly, pointing out the landmarks to her as they go. There's the primary school, there's the first trade store, there's the other one.

"Turn here," she says and they follow a gravel drive through the long grass until it comes to an end at the gate of a bottle yard. Bad luck: wrong way. They turn back and try again at the next street. Lining the road are run-down fibro houses with wrecked cars in front. There's a group of young blokes at the front of one of them, who all look up to watch the car pass. In the rear-vision mirror, it looks as though some of them start to follow the car down the street.

Debbie gets her bearings at an intersection.

"Go that way", she tells him.

He turns left.

"Fuck you, that way, that way," she yells. She meant him to turn right.

The road is narrow and Steve can't find anywhere to turn. He tries to do a three point turn, but his car's got a lousy turning circle. It takes him about eight goes, forward and backwards in tiny arcs, for fear of backing into some unseen ditch. He finally succeeds in turning, and by this time, there are groups of youths ahead of them, standing across the road in the light of the headlights.

They close in as he drives slowly through.

"What you want?" yells one, while the others glare and add comments he doesn't catch. They bang the top of the car, and Steve really starts to get worried.

"Keep going, keep going," mutters Debbie.

They reach the end of the road where the old admin. houses have given way entirely to squatters' huts of scrap timber and rusty iron. There's a solitary street light on a pole, and beneath it, a group of figures standing round, more young blokes. Steve approaches them at a slow speed.

117

They exchange words with Debbie and she swears at them.

"What you doing with this lady?" they demand of Steve as he swings the car round in readiness for a getaway, then comes to a stop. More of them are coming up the road to see what's happening, and the first lot stand in front of the car to prevent it leaving.

"Just bringing her home," he says. "Do you know her?"

"We know Debbie." they say. "What you been doing with her?"

Debbie is arguing violently with them, but Steve can't understand what she's saying except for an occasional English word. Bloody this, fucking that.

"Where's her brother's house?" asks Steve, trying to act cool and unconcerned.

"What brother?" answers one.

"You get out of here," say others.

There are about a dozen of them now. They close in around the car and open the driver's door. Steve leans across to Debbie's side to try to open her door, but she pushes him away.

She brandishes a beer bottle out of the passenger's side window. She's opened it with her teeth on the way. One of the youths grabs it from her and she screams abuse at him. She opens her door, but makes no move to leave. More onlookers materialise from the shadows.

Steve is out of his side by now, and the youths stand back to let him through. He walks around the front of the car to get to Debbie's open door. He's taller than any of the youths, he notes, and they only outnumber him about twenty to one. But Debbie is the centre of attention, screaming and shouting and holding the crowd at bay. None of them is game to approach her.

An older fellow in shorts and a singlet appears.

"Get her out," he orders, but they all keep their distance.

Steve approaches her, but she kicks out at him. He evades her leg and takes hold of her under the left shoulder and tries to ease her out of the seat.

"Come on Debbie, settle down now."

"Get your fucking hands...," she says.

He momentarily loosens his grip as she reaches between the seats and fumbles in the junk on the floor of the car. There's all

118

manner of rubbish there and Steve assumes she's looking for the second stubby of beer. But her groping hands alight on an old chisel, left there from goodness knows when.

Now Debbie gets out of the car and stands beside the open door, drunkenly wielding the chisel. Blunt as hell, it's still an evil weapon. The others back off, leaving Steve to tackle her alone. She lunges at him. Shouts of alarm from the crowd. He manages to grab her wrist and grapples with her, while a few of the youths close in on the two of them. Steve doesn't know whose side they are taking, his or the girl's. It's all shouts and confusion, and just as he wrests the chisel free, he feels a sharp, burning pain in his upper arm. He pulls away from the girl with a yelp, and some of the young blokes grab her from behind. The chisel falls to the ground.

"Take her away," orders the fellow in the singlet. "Always make a bloody trouble, that Debbie."

They take her, still swearing and struggling, into one of the houses, but Steve doesn't pay much attention to her, because his shirt sleeve is showing blood and he can feel the wetness dripping down his arm. He worries that a tendon's been severed, or something.

The crowd closes in for a look and Steve gingerly pulls up his sleeve to reveal on his arm, not a gash, but two semi-circles, black in that light and formed by a series of puncture marks. Blood seeps into each little dotted line, like swamp water in a footprint, and drips down his shirt. The whole bicep looks swollen and discoloured in that sickly light.

"You better get out of here," they tell him again.

"You better go to the hospital" says one. "That Debbie always bite like a bloody crocodile."

Steve doesn't need telling. He gets into the car and they close the doors for him. Someone passes the chisel in through the open window. They are laughing, but there is still menace in the air. They stand aside for him to drive between them. He takes off slowly, with only his right hand on the steering-wheel, and they pound the roof with open palms.

"You keep away next time!" they yell.

Steve finds his way out to the main road and drives to Port Moresby General Hospital. Being Saturday night, it's peak-hour at Casualty. The waiting room is dazzlingly bright under the fluorescent lights, and the place is almost full. Some of them look badly hurt, but most are hangers-on. There's an absolute pool of blood on the vinyl floor at the far end, and red-brown footsteps lead from it between the benches. An orderly appears with a metal bucket and mop. The place smells of Dettol and echoes with wails and sobs and argument.

A fellow at the desk takes Steve's particulars and has a quick look at his arm. Nothing serious; a penetrating wound, it won't even need stitches, just a dressing and a tetanus injection. Steve takes a seat on the benches. The Nationals all stare at him, the sole European. He's something of a celebrity. He studies the patient card he's been given: the injury is entered as 'Human Bite'.

As he sits there waiting, avoiding the glances of the curious, another European comes through the door. He holds his torso stiffly and his shirt is torn and soaked with blood over his chest. It's Bignell. He glances about him to see where to go, or perhaps he's noticed Steve's car outside, for he catches sight of him and comes straight over. His face brightens.

"Fair dinkum, I should have known you'd be here! What's happened to you, then?" he asks.

Steve isn't keen to divulge that. He stares at Bignell's bloodied shirt, which looks quite spectacular.

"What about you?" he says. "Injure yourself waterskiing did you?"

"Are you trying to be funny?" answers Bignell. "You wouldn't call this a sporting injury. It was bloody Etoro. She got in one of her moods and went for me again. Bit me on the tit. Look at this," he says, pulling back the torn shirt "Shit, it hurts."

Sporting injury or not, there's no doubt about the score. Nationals – 2: Expats – nil.

Snakeman

Hua is terribly superstitious – I don't know why. She's had a good education; she went to year ten at Gordons High and then to Secretarial College. But she believes anything she hears about sorcery and spirits and puri-puri and so on. You'd expect her to be beyond such things. After all, she's had a lot to do with Europeans. I suppose when they grow up with that nonsense, they can never quite give it up. Hua's best friend, Ann Marie, is your typical village girl, and she's even worse.

I remember the very first time I met the two of them. It was at a party at Korobosea and they were out on the back porch together, discussing the ghosts at Port Moresby General Hospital. I overheard what they were saying and couldn't resist joining in. They were a bit drunk, and the rubbish they were talking was unbelievable.

According to them, the corpses have a great time when the morgue closes down for the night. After the nurses and attendants have gone home, the dead bodies get up and walk round and do whatever dead bodies like to do. Apparently they enjoy answering the telephone, because you can get to speak to them if you ring a certain secret number. One of Ann Marie's friends had a relation who had just died and was laid out in the morgue. So the friend phoned the certain number and yes, you've guessed. They had a nice long chat.

"Oh yeah," I asked, "what did they talk about?"

"The spirits, I suppose," said Hua.

"None of your business," said Ann Marie.

Anyway, I kept them talking about it and got to hear about the times people had encountered ghosts at the hospital. From all accounts, it was an everyday occurrence. Both the girls had friends who had gone visiting patients there and taken a wrong turning, gone down the wrong corridor or whatever. They each had the same experience, meeting some mysterious character with white hair who talked in a strange singsong voice and told them things about themselves that nobody else could know. Then the friends noticed the mystery person's eyes – green, penetrating, like a cat's eyes. They got the feeling they were being X-rayed by the eyes, and suddenly realised that the fellow was a spirit. Then they ran away in fright. Everyone knows you've got to run for it, when you meet a ghost.

That was the start of my relationship with Hua, and at the time I found this sort of talk amusing. You'd be surprised how many of the Papuans believe it, even the Christians. In fact, especially the Christians. Hua and Ann Marie are both Catholics, and I think that when they hear that stuff about the Holy Spirit and the resurrection and so on, it all just gets mixed up in their heads.

It didn't bother me at first, but once I started living with Hua, it began to get on my nerves. She was always listening to any silly gossip from the village. As soon as anybody fell ill there, someone or other would get the blame. Death, sickness, accident – whatever it was, somebody was sure to be accused of sorcery. And you could also be sure that someone else had had a prophetic dream about it. They're always having prophetic dreams, but you only get to hear about them after the event.

Also, though Hua tried to keep it a secret from me, I'm sure she used to spend money consulting a puri-puri man when she was trying to get pregnant. That's why she used to visit Pari village, where the best puri-puri men come from. She told me she was visiting family there, but I checked with her parents. It's funny they knew nothing of any relations in Pari.

Anyway, once we had the baby, I started to get more concerned about all this superstition. I didn't want the child growing up believing that stuff. So I thought I'd try to persuade Hua it was all nonsense.

The opportunity came when a rumour started circulating in Port Moresby about a snakeman. I'd never heard of such a thing before, but someone told me it was a throwback to a character from their folklore or legends. A snakeman has the head of a human and the body of a snake. This particular specimen had recently been human, and was turned into a snake as punishment for burning a Bible. He had been sighted at Gordons Market. Ann Marie knew all about him.

Of course, I ridiculed the girls for it. I asked them why the man had burned the Bible in the first place – whether he felt cold or something, and had run out of firewood. But the girls took the rumour seriously. They swallowed the story completely. They weren't the only ones, either; there was a lot of talk about it around town. Not that I can speak the language, but I've picked up a little bit of it, and I used to hear mention all over the place about "tau gaigai". That's how they say it in Motu.

One day, I heard two checkout girls in Steamships supermarket talking about him. I couldn't understand exactly what they were saying, but I knew they were discussing him. I said to them, "Do you really believe that?"

"I don't know," said one of them. "What do you think?"

"I think it's complete rubbish," I answered.

"I think so, too." said the girl, and the other one agreed.

It's always like that. They won't argue about it with expats. But they let themselves be carried with the current of every rumour. They hear it, and their reason tells them it can't be true. Then they realise that other people believe it, and they start to wonder if it might just be possible after all. And by degrees, they go from thinking that it just might be true, to believing that it must be true. Even the intelligent ones.

Well, this snakeman business really did sweep the town. People were talking about it all over the place, and there was even a small item in the newspaper about it. Crowds would assemble at Gordons Market hoping for a glimpse of the fellow and then there would be news that he'd made an appearance somewhere else and off they'd rush. Something like mass hysteria.

There was quite a big crowd at the hospital one day. People had heard that the snakeman was there, seeking treatment to change him back into human form. There was a big mob at Outpatients, hanging about waiting. Apparently Ann Marie came around to the house to get Hua, and the two of them joined the other suckers, standing out in the sun for a couple of hours. Hua denied it later, but a friend of mine had seen them both and told me.

"What does he look like, this snakeman?" I asked the two of them, for of course they knew plenty of people who had seen him.

"Just like we said. He's got the head of a human and the body of a snake."

"How big is the head?" I enquired, trying to make fun of them.

"Medium size."

"And his arms and legs?"

"He hasn't got any."

"How does he feed himself? Does he drink milk out of a saucer or something?"

"His mother feeds him," said Ann Marie who always had the answers. Hua used to keep quiet because she knew I'd give her a hard time over it later, when we were on our own.

"How do you know that?"

"People told me."

"How do they know?"

"They've seen him."

No-one could have seen him, I told them, because no such snakeman exists. Ann Marie was inclined to argue, but Hua told her not to bother. The two of them glanced at each other and shrugged their shoulders, as if I was the one who was being irrational. Hua knew they would never persuade me; but then I hadn't persuaded them either.

"Okay," I challenged them, "find me one person who has actually seen the snakeman, and I'll give you fifty kina". And I left it at that.

From the way they'd been talking, it should have been easy for them to relieve me of fifty kina. On their information, there were hundreds of people all over town who had seen the snakeman. They only had to present me with a single witness to win the money, but the girls didn't exactly jump at the chance. In fact they kept very quiet about it. I used to remind Ann Marie about it every time I saw her, which was often because she was always around our place.

"There's plenty of people who've seen him," she protested. "Lots of people from the village did."

I remembered that remark the next weekend when I took Hua to the village to see her people. They like to see the baby, but I always find visiting a bit of a chore. I have to sit around in Hua's father's house and be nice to everybody – you know, all her relations. They're not a bad lot, but half of them can't speak English and it's an effort to make conversation. I never know who a lot of them are. I've got no hope of remembering all the names.

This time, for something to do, I challenged Hua again.

"Find me one person, just one, who has actually seen the snakeman," I said. "You could do a lot with fifty kina."

"Okay," said Hua. "I'll find Rabei. She saw him at Four-Mile."

I drank a mug of tea while I waited for them to fetch Rabei. There was a lot of animation as she came in. Some of the relations were interested now.

Rabei can't speak English well, so Hua's elder brother acted as interpreter. I asked her straight out whether she had actually seen the snakeman. There was a lot of talk in Motu, with all of them joining in. Hua's brother answered.

"She says she didn't see him, herself. It was her brother-in-law who saw him."

The brother-in-law only lived a couple of houses away, and we all trooped down there, but of course he was out fishing. Neighbours and passers-by were asking what it was all about and you could hear them saying, condescendingly; "Oh, Hua's husband doesn't believe in the snakeman. He wants to meet someone who saw him." They all volunteered some helpful suggestion – so and so's daughter was a nurse at the hospital and saw him twice, or such and such had seen him on a bus.

Wherever we went, we were referred somewhere else. We followed up the leads and really did the rounds. We tried five houses altogether and at every one we struck a snag. Either the person we needed wasn't there, or he admitted he hadn't actually seen the snakeman himself. In the latter case, we were given the name of another informant. That person, they promised, could definitely verify the snakeman's existence. Hua's little brother, whom I like best of all, knows where everyone in the village lives, and he excitedly led the way. But it was turning out exactly as I had thought. We were chasing the rumour round in a circle.

Hua was undismayed by all this traipsing around. She didn't see that the repeated failure to find a single witness cast doubt on the snakeman's existence. On the contrary, she seemed to think his existence confirmed by everyone else's belief in him. I must admit that there were a few of them who shared my point of view, or claimed to. They weren't very vocal, and they might have been trying to curry favour with me. More likely, they just enjoyed having something to argue about, though there's never any shortage of that in the village.

Earlier, Hua's elder brother had gone off on his own. Now he caught up with us again, announcing positively that Vicki Gari had seen the snakeman. She lived at the far end of the village and was at home now. She was waiting to speak to me.

We set off, a party of a dozen or more, and crossed the centre of the village, where the store and a few of the houses adjoin a flat, gravel area dotted with palm trees. Most of the village houses are built on stilts over the sea, with wooden walkways leading out to them. Vicki Gari's house was at the very far end of the village. There, a steep hill falls directly to a narrow shingle beach dotted with huge rocks.

The rough track, too narrow for a car, is hemmed in on the left by the barren hillside, all rocks and coarse grass. To our right, a view of the sea alternated with the last of the village houses. Every now and then the path was obstructed by an upturned canoe, dragged as far as possible out of the water.

"Vicki Gari's an educated girl," Hua told me on the way. "She worked for the Forestry Department before she got married. She knows what she's talking about."

At Vicki Gari's house, she and her family were waiting on the front verandah, a smallish place at the top of the steps, and piled with fishing nets and crates of empty bottles. We climbed the steps and they invited us in. Much excitement. There wasn't enough room for everybody to fit inside, and most of the observers stayed out on the verandah. I left my thongs at the door and entered barefoot. There was a window opening onto the verandah, its metal shutter hinged at the top, and propped open with a stick. The spectators outside crowded at it, and leaned through into the house itself, as if clamouring for service at a shop counter. The shifting waters beneath the house made rippling patterns of light on the unlined timber walls.

"This is Vicki," said Hua's brother, introducing us.

"Did they tell you why I came?" I asked her.

"Yes".

"It's about the snakeman."

"I know."

"They say you saw him."

"Yes."

"Is that true?"

"Yes."

There was a murmur of approval. People turned to each other with knowing expressions. Hua whispered, "I told you so."

"What did he look like?" I asked.

"He had the head of a man and the body of a snake."

"And you saw it yourself?"

"I did."

I must say I was taken aback at this. Though it was quite impossible, I hardly wanted to call her an outright liar. "You say you actually, physically saw it yourself?"

"I did."

"With your own eyes?"

She hesitated. "No."

"Then, with whose eyes?" I asked, puzzled.

"With my uncle's"

"What do you mean?"

"My uncle's eyes saw the snakeman. He told me. You ask him. He could tell you himself, but he's at the garden now."

There was slight consternation, but not much. Hua made a face as if to say "So what?" To her, it made no difference that Vicki had not really seen the snakeman at all. Somebody had, and that was good enough for her. She thought I was just being difficult. On the other hand, I felt I'd made the point with some of them. I'd done it to my own satisfaction, anyway: the rumour was a never-ending circle.

By then, it was about four o'clock; time to reclaim the baby from Hua's parents and return to town. I didn't say anything unkind to Vicki Gari. She was just a simple village girl. I said goodbye to her and her people, and made to leave. The verandah was congested with onlookers, some debating the issue, others hoping in vain for something more exciting to happen. I climbed down the steep wooden steps, and with Hua and her elder brother, made my way back along the path towards the village proper. It was then that I had my accident.

I mentioned Hua's youngest brother before. At the time, he was about seven years old, a really cute little bloke and very lively, much more responsive than most of the village kids. He used to like me to chase him. I often did, pretending to be cross and threatening to give him a spanking if I caught him. Unlike me, he never tired of the game, and squealing with pleasure, he would elude me pretty easily. This time he dashed past me, goading me to give chase and scrambling off the track and up the hillside. He dodged between two large rocks, skirting the clumps of sword grass, with me in pursuit. I made a lunge to grab him, lost my footing and stumbled. As I fell, my face brushed against the dry grass, and I felt something sharp enter my right eye.

The little boy and the others laughed as I got up and dusted myself down. It didn't really hurt, but I felt a sensation as if a liquid was running out of my eye. I thought it must be bleeding, and I expected Hua would notice. When she didn't say anything, I joined her back on the path and got her to have a look at it.

"You must have had a speck in it," she said, as I held the eye open for inspection, "but there's nothing there now. I can't see anything."

It seemed a small incident at the time, and I didn't want to make a big fuss about it. But my vision in that eye was fuzzy and within three hours, it was hurting a lot. I was awake half the night, putting eye-drops in it.

The next day I went to the doctor and saw a new fellow who had just arrived from Australia.

"Did you know you've got a cataract?" he asked me.

"That's news to me," I said. "I didn't have one last week. Anyway, I thought only old people got them."

"Well, you've definitely got one now," he told me.

As for the pain, he said it was just a bit of minor irritation; I had probably scratched the lens. He gave me some cream and told me to keep the eye covered. So for a couple of days I went round with a dressing on the eye, looking like a pirate. When I went back to the doctor, he removed the dressing, but I couldn't see a thing out of the eye. Just a hazy light, that's all. I don't mind admitting I was worried then.

He called in the other doctor, and the two of them got out some thick books on ophthalmology and worked out what must have happened. When I fell, a sharp thorn or a thistle must have penetrated the eye, and come straight out again. A real freak accident. The iris had actually been pierced. Some juices in the eye had formed an opaque blob — what they called a traumatic cataract. Traumatic all right! I thought I was going to lose the sight of it.

The doctors told me it needed attention right away. We never even discussed getting it done in Moresby: I didn't fancy risking my eyesight at Port Moresby General Hospital. The doctors made a lot of phone-calls to Brisbane and fixed up a specialist and a hospital booking. Hua and I flew down later that week. We couldn't really afford it, but Hua wanted to come with me, and we decided we may as well make the most of things. At least the baby's fare was free.

The surgeon in Brisbane told me there was a three-cornered tear in the lens, and there might be all sorts of complications. I won't go into details, but the operation went very well. It was a complete success. I did feel bad for a couple of days, and it took a few weeks for the sight to return completely to normal. But once the eye had been attended to, Hua and I and the baby had quite a nice time. We made bit of a holiday of it, and flew back to Moresby on the second Sunday.

Hua's family were hoping for presents, of course, and I half-expected a few of them might be at the airport to meet us. But it seemed like half the village was there, two truckloads of them, anyway. When they saw me come out of customs, a great buzz of talk went up. I don't know quite what they expected – dark glasses, a cane and a guide dog, perhaps. A rumour had been going round the village that I'd seen the snakeman, and been struck blind. I'd bet anything it was Ann Marie that started the rumour.

Expatriate Rates

"Don't we know each other pretty well by now, Vagi?"

No response.

"And haven't I always done my best to see they treat you right?"

She looked away.

"I mean, you know very well what the situation is. We've been over it often enough, surely. And you know what Head Office is like. It just isn't up to me."

Ian paused between every sentence, and ended each one on an upward inflection, inviting agreement, hoping for some nod of acknowledgment or acquiescence. But she just kept staring at the bottom drawer of the filing cabinet with that infuriating, sullen, Motu look. He was only repeating what he had told her numerous times already, but her moody silence impelled him to keep talking.

"It's true, what I'm saying, isn't it?"

She turned her head to stare at the bookcase now, and made that tutting noise with which Europeans encourage dogs, but which the Motu use to express disdain or contempt. Vagi knew it annoyed him, and when she felt she had provoked him sufficiently, she finally spoke.

"It's not fair."

Ian had been hoping she would say something new, but this was the same complaint she had been voicing all week long. There was some truth in it too, Ian conceded that. The firm paid her 120 kina a week, and here it was, about to engage an expatriate for 290 kina. He knew it would put Vagi's nose out of joint, but what could he do about it? It was out of his hands.

"You're the best-paid National secretary in the country," he told her. "When you hear of another National earning more than you, just let me know. I'll send a memo to Brisbane and get them to give you another raise. I mean, I always stick up for you."

"Why should she get twice as much as me, for doing the same work?"

Ian frowned. He had explained it umpteen times. Papua New Guinea needed expatriates; without them, the place would fall apart. So they had to be paid enough to attract them, to make it worth their while. That meant a salary on Australian levels plus something extra. It was a matter of paying the going rate – the expatriate rate.

On the other hand, the country couldn't afford to pay the Nationals the same. It was an economic impossibility; the country would be bankrupt. Besides, the Nationals weren't as competent as their expat counterparts. It wasn't their fault perhaps, but it was a fact, all the same. Theoretically, they were doing the same job, but in reality there probably wasn't even one in ten who was as capable as an expatriate.

The trouble was that Vagi was the one in ten, and they both knew it. Her shorthand and typing were as good as you'd get anywhere in Brisbane. She rarely made mistakes, not bad ones. It hadn't taken her long to pick up all the technical vocabulary, and she could spell the geological terms now better than Ian could. On top of all this, she was fast. He boasted to people that he had the best National secretary in the country. He really believed it.

Vagi knew Ian was proud of her. When he had a client in from Minerals and Energy, or from one of the oil companies, he used to call her in and dictate a short minute of the meeting. She'd take it down in shorthand, and bring copies back to them within minutes, word perfect. For Papua New Guinea, that's pretty impressive.

Vagi's only weakness was in the administration of the office, and sometimes in those little details that can make all the difference. She avoided responsibility even for things like re-ordering stationery, let alone maintaining the accounts or helping with the survey returns. And she didn't look the part, either. Her clothes were sometimes grubby, and she slouched round in that Motu way, round shoulders, sagging boobs and dragging her feet in the dirt.

She actually lived in a village well down the coast, and came in to work every day in the back of a truck, forty kilometres over an unsealed road. No wonder she often used to look a bit scruffy, or turn up hours late, saying the truck had run out of petrol or broken down.

Ian would let her get away with it. He tended to get a bit too personal with his staff. It was one of his failings, especially in his present situation. He was the only expat there, running the Port Moresby office on his own, and receiving very little thanks for it. Head office in Australia was hopelessly short-sighted, even threatening to pull out of PNG entirely. Except for a constant flow of unnecessary memos, they left Ian pretty well to his own devices, and then complained at the results. He felt more loyalty to his National staff than to the directors in Brisbane.

Certainly, he had become too close to Vagi. She had learned how to take skillful advantage of him, and by degrees she almost always managed to get her own way. At first he had objected when she turned up for work barefoot, but she merely shrugged, told him that she didn't type with her toes, and promised to keep a decent pair of shoes in the office for when a client called. He also had to tolerate her chewing betel-nut sometimes in the afternoon. He couldn't prevent her. She knew how much he depended on her, and exactly what she could get away with. And the betel-nut didn't seem to affect her work overmuch.

But the office definitely needed another senior secretary. The other girl, Idau and the two juniors were not up to much; Vagi did virtually all the typing single-handed, and it put Ian in a real spot occasionally, when she took a day off because her kids were sick, or when she had trouble with her husband. He was simply too dependent on her, and the directors at head office, stingy as they were, had approved his taking on an extra steno. Of course, he would never get another National as good as Vagi. So it had to be an expatriate, and for that they had to pay expat rates.

"But it's just not fair, Ian," Vagi said with a scowl, and made that tutting noise again.

It touched a raw nerve, and he suddenly flared up.

"It may not be fair, but it's the way things are," he said sharply. "There's no point talking about it, if that's all you've got to say."

She got up and slouched out of his office, and after a few minutes, he heard the glass door slam. He checked with Idau at the front desk, who said that Vagi had taken her bag with her. That meant she had gone for the day. It was exactly the sort of thing that made it essential to get another secretary. Ian hoped she would cool down over the weekend.

He couldn't entirely blame her for getting a bit temperamental about it, but it was out of his control. Even the public service had dual rates of pay for Nationals and expats. And anyway, if she was happy to work for 120 kina one week, why should it bother her what someone else would earn the next? She wouldn't be paid any less.

On the Monday, Vagi didn't turn up for work at all, which was rather a worry. But the new expat secretary did. Her name was Evelyn Fuller and she was there at the door before starting time at eight o'clock, waiting with Idau and the juniors for Ian to let them in. Her husband was an economist of some kind, and she herself had a university degree. For the extra expense, Ian was hoping she would be able to take over much of the administration of the office. While not the liveliest of the applicants, Evelyn had good references and seemed quietly intelligent and self-assured. Furthermore, she already had her work permit arranged, which was a great advantage.

Ian let her get started on a couple of tapes he had dictated over the weekend. He told Idau to show her around and let her look over the files, to give her an idea on how they set out some of the technical stuff. She seemed to take her time, but that was only to be expected. For a long while she couldn't get the dictaphone machine to work properly, and Idau and he weren't much help. It even crossed his mind that Vagi had done something on the Friday to sabotage it. Anyway, Evelyn sorted it out in due course, although she had a few difficulties with the typewriter

134

too. From reception, the sound of the keystrokes came intermittently in irregular bursts. She wasn't familiar with electric Remingtons, she said.

Ian didn't expect too much from Evelyn on her first day, especially when there was no-one there to show her the ropes, but by the afternoon he was anxious to get a couple of letters out. He noticed that the rubbish bin was gradually filling with spoiled letterhead. Finally, a couple of letters made their appearance to be signed, but quite frankly, they were of a pretty poor standard. They looked untidy, and every one of them contained at least a couple of silly mistakes. The letters were no better than Idau could have managed in the same time. Vagi would have whipped through them in about ten minutes, without any mistakes, either.

Evelyn noticed his dissatisfaction, and was a bit crestfallen, but then, it was no use pretending. Ian told her the letters were not up to scratch. He pointed out the defects. For example, although they were dated, there were no file numbers on any of them. That's something absolutely basic, surely? Anybody knows that a letter needs a reference. And if Evelyn had bothered to use her eyes, she would have seen that on their files, every single document bore a reference number. They would never find anything in the office without it.

"Oh," she said, genuinely surprised, "You didn't mention that I should do that."

"Well, I didn't tell you to date them either," he said.

Then he explained slowly that a six digit number had to go on everything connected with the file.

"And what are the letters?" she asked. "IM/va. Shall I put that on too?"

"IM," he said," are my initials: Ian Moone, and the other letters are the secretary's initials: Vagi Adava."

"So should I put IM/ef?"

"Of course," he said, coldly.

It's a peculiar thing about taking on staff, but it always seems a matter of pure chance what you end up with. Vagi herself was a classic example; nobody could have guessed how good she would turn out to be. Even when you get the applicants to do some copy typing or give them a general knowledge quiz, you still don't know quite what you've landed until they've been there a day or two. That was how it was with Evelyn. By the end of the first day, Ian had serious doubts about her.

The following day, he was relieved to find Vagi at work, and in a very helpful mood, too. She had been away because of some trouble in the village, and not through any displeasure with him. Evelyn was made to relinquish the Remington so that Vagi could catch up with the work left over from the day before. Evelyn took over Idau's typewriter, and Ian gave her some very simple correspondence which she could take her time over. Even with this, she seemed flustered and unsure of herself.

Ian noticed at once how well Vagi and Evelyn got on with each other. This was pleasantly unexpected, for he had feared the reverse, that Vagi would sulk and be difficult. However the reason was soon apparent: Evelyn constituted no rival for Vagi. On the contrary, she deferred to her and relied on her constantly for help and advice and reassurance. In Vagi's manner there was no trace of resentment. The disparity in salary, it seemed, didn't bother her, provided her pre-eminence in the office was unchallenged. Indeed, her position was enhanced for now she had an expatriate subordinate, meekly grateful and greatly dependent upon her.

By the end of the week, Evelyn was dependent upon Vagi not only for help with her work, but for protection from Ian. Vagi acted as a conduit between them, for the expatriate woman minimised her contact with him, while he made no effort to conceal his dissatisfaction with her. Of course, he should have dismissed her without any more delay, but he was reluctant to do so. It would reflect badly on his judgement in appointing her, and already there was a memo from Brisbane enquiring after her productivity. Also, to tell the truth, it gave him satisfaction to see Evelyn's patent inferiority to Vagi.

Ian suspected that Vagi was re-typing some of Evelyn's work, so he gave instructions that the latter was to do her work first in draft. This increased his grim pleasure at Evelyn's incompetence, but created more work all round. Unless he checked her letters meticulously, the mistakes he overlooked on the draft were repeated in the final copy. Even obvious, elementary mistakes of grammar would turn up in the woman's work. It was as if Evelyn was typing in a foreign language, as if English was not her mother tongue.

To take a typical example: "A thorough examination of the soil sample...," became "The thorough examination of a soil sample..."

"I'm sorry," she apologised, when he remonstrated with her.

"That's what it sounded like on the tape."

"Whatever it sounded like," he told her, "it couldn't be what you've typed. That's a definite article, isn't it? That's an indefinite article. You can't swap them round like that. It doesn't make sense. It's not English."

"I'm sorry," she said, "I didn't study English at university."

"What did you study?"

"Psychology."

Psychology degree or not, Ian reflected, the woman didn't have an ounce of common sense. It made him furious to think of what the firm was paying her, while Vagi still did most of the work. Paradoxically, Vagi had entirely lost her sense of grievance.

He called Vagi in and asked her what she thought of Evelyn.

"She's very nice. She's got two little boys, you know, just like me. She was telling me all about them."

"I mean her work."

"Well, she's a bit slow. I have to help her quite a lot. And she's scared of you."

"But she's a bloody idiot, isn't she?" he asked.

"Ian, you're very unkind. I think you make her nervous."

By the second week, Vagi was doing almost all the typing, and Evelyn was just helping Idau and the juniors with everything else. The expat woman did have a car and occasionally she made deliveries out at Waigani, which saved Ian a bit of time. That was about her only use. Getting her to type anything was more trouble than it was worth.

Evelyn worked a second full week before Ian gave her notice. Even that took her by surprise: she lacked the wits to see it coming. She was quite upset and fled the office for ten minutes to phone her husband from the post office. Vagi guessed the news immediately and went in to speak to Ian. Of course, unlike Evelyn, she had known it was inevitable.

"I thought you would," she said.

"Well I had to. She's absolutely hopeless."

But Vagi was still strangely protective of her, and suggested she might improve if she had another chance.

"Doesn't it bother you any more," Ian asked, "that she gets paid twice as much as you, for doing less than Idau?"

"Well, I feel sorry for her. It's not her fault you have to pay her more. That's just the way it is. It's a funny thing, but if you only had to pay her local wages, she'd still have a job. Now she's got nothing."

After a while Evelyn returned to the office to collect her things. Ian was paying her a full week's money in lieu of notice, and thought he was treating her very generously. Nevertheless, she plucked up enough nerve to complain that he hadn't paid her strict mileage for the times she had used her car. He had given her only enough to cover the petrol.

"My husband says you've treated me shabbily," she announced.

Ian held his tongue. It was the first time Evelyn had displayed any gumption, and he was taken by surprise. Anyway, he didn't want to antagonise Vagi by creating a scene, and for the moment, he even felt a little sympathy for the woman himself. It was a relief once she had gone.

Within minutes, the place returned to normal. Vagi sauntered into Ian's office and settled herself into the easy chair. She couldn't help spilling a few beans about Evelyn. How she used to take the spoiled paper home in her handbag, so Ian wouldn't see it in the rubbish bin. Things like that. She wasn't malicious about it, just factual. She must have grown tired of covering up for Evelyn, and re-typing half the woman's work.

"So now we're back the way we were," she commented wryly.

"Not quite," Ian said. "Get your pad and pencil and take down this note to Head Office."

He dictated as follows:

"RE: Yr Memo 861

In reply, wish to report that the new expat secretary is very satisfactory. Previous National typist is now surplus to requirements and her employment terminated. Next wage returns will reflect present situation accordingly."

For a little while Vagi looked slightly puzzled, then a grin spread tentatively across her face.

"Does it really mean what I think it does?" she asked.

"That's right. They can pay you what you you're worth, the bastards. For official purposes, you're now the expat secretary."

Vagi was not the demonstrative type, but Ian could see she was overjoyed. It was a hell of a lot more money. She took her pad out to reception, and Ian heard the brief, musical rattle of the typewriter. Then she brought the finished memo back for him to sign.

"Thanks very much, Ian," she said. "I'll try to be a real expat secretary from now on. Even in the details."

Without saying more, she pointed with a pencil to the reference at the top of the page: IM/ef.

Bighead

Even when he was only small boy Lohia is a bighead. He always tell us other boys: "Do this, do that," and if we don't want to do it, or do it too slow then he tell us off. Going fishing, playing games, he always know it better than anyone else and can do it the best. He is the one that boss all the other kids. "You just do what I tell you." That's what he's saying all his life.

Well, the kids all listen to him in those days, and even later when they grow up and go to high school and the Tech. The boys all listen to him because even though he's a bighead, he's very clever and knows a lot. People always listen to him, not just the children but the grown-ups also, and the expats.

Always Lohia got his own plan what he wants to do. But he understand that sometimes you got to wait. He can tell when is the time you got to do what the adults want, when is the time you can please yourself. So the teachers say, "Get in line like Lohia. Finish your work quietly like Lohia." But plenty of times he's not in line, and plenty of times he doesn't work quietly, but those are the times that don't matter and the teachers never notice.

So the teachers at school think that he always behave himself, and he never get the blame even for the bad things he's done. That's because he know how to make them like him. He look at them nice, he always smile. When they want to tell him things he always stop what he's doing and he look at them, even if he's thinking about some other things. That way they think he's listening to them and paying attention, and that he's going to do what they tell him to, but maybe he is and maybe he isn't.

Yes, even when they catch him that he's done something wrong, he doesn't run away. If they start telling him off, he never just look down or look away or shuffle his feet or fiddle

141

with a stick like the other boys. Instead he look straight into their eyes and say yes and no when they want him to. That's very hard to do.

Lohia can do that even to the expats. They are the ones that get angry if you shrug or look away. If you know how to look in their eyes, then they always like you. That's the expat teachers. For the National teachers, Lohia does what he want to. No need to say yes and no or look at them. They're just like us.

Another thing that help him is that Lohia look good. Skin is nice, no white spots or grilli. Not too tall but pretty strong. Hair is long, Afro style. Teeth are very good and white, no holes from too much lolly water. The expats always talk about Lohia's teeth: "Oh what a lovely smile, Lohia." You can always see his teeth because he talk a lot, but for the expats he smile special to make them like him.

Lohia's first expat friend was in primary school. The teacher's name was Mrs Fox. She tell him he's clever and can grow up to do anything he want. And he believe her. Maybe that was the time first of all when he start to be a bighead.

When all the books and pencils get handed out, Lohia always get the best ones. When there's not enough for every kid and two children got to share a book or something, it's never Lohia. At the end of the year when they give out the lollies, Mrs Fox give a special prize to Lohia; Best All-round. Even that he's not top of the grade, they still give him a prize. It's not fair because some of the kids never won a prize in their life. But we never blame the expats. It's Lohia make them do it.

The expats who make friends with him this way were Mrs Fox, Mrs Ramsay, then later at the high school was Mrs Stevens. With all of them he get up to his tricks. If he lost his book then he go and ask them for the new one. When that happen to the other boys, it's just too bad. But with Lohia he can always explain it; somebody stole it, his baby brother throw it off the canoe and nobody can get it back, there was a fire. All these sort of reasons, and every time they give him the new book.

Sometimes, Mrs Stevens used to bring her magazine to school, National Geographic magazine with the coloured pictures. They were good to look at and Lohia, he ask to borrow them. Right away Lohia can see she doesn't want to lend the magazine, but he think up a reason that he want to show his uncle the pictures of stone-fish, and he promise to bring the magazine back the next day. So he succeed to persuade her, and she give him the magazine in a plastic bag. And for sure, next day Lohia bring that magazine back in the same bag, and no speck of dust or sand on it.

Next time he ask to borrow a magazine, he can keep it for two days, next time for one week and so on. Every time Lohia look after the things very nice, never crease the pages or anything like that. Mrs Stevens think that she's teaching Lohia the things in the book, and teaching him to look after the books nicely. But Lohia know all that already. Actually he is the one teaching her. Lohia teaching her to trust him.

One Sunday Lohia decide to go and visit Mrs Stevens in her house. His excuse is to return some magazine to her. He already found out where she lived. So he got a lift first to the house of a wantok at Boroko and then he walk around to the house of Mrs Stevens. When he knock at the door, she's very surprised to see him. She let him come in and give him cool drink and biscuits. She introduce him to Mr Stevens, and when Lohia smile his best way, Mr Stevens think he's a very nice boy and can visit any time he want.

She ask him, "How did you come here?"

He tell her, "I walk here."

"What, all the way?"

"Yes, from the village. It took me one hour because I didn't know your house and I have to walk the wrong way."

"Why did you come, Lohia?" she ask him.

"Because I want to return the National Geographic Magazine. And to look at some other one, because I can't always borrow it your best magazine. I'm worried maybe something happen to it in the village."

He tell us all about this later. He tell us she's very pleased he come to read those magazine and he stay there all afternoon. Then she ask him, " What time do you have to go home? Aren't your parents worried about you?"

"They're not worried. They don't care."

143

Mrs Stevens want Mr Stevens to drive Lohia back home, but he doesn't want. He plan to go back to his wantok and he don't want her to know that he never walk all that way. Also, he want money. He tell her not to drive him home, but if she give him twenty toea he can take a PMV.

That was the first time he got money from Mrs Stevens. He got forty toea because he has to change to the other PMV in town. After that she used to give him fare money every time to come and visit her. From his father he also got the money sometimes to take the PMV. So that make double and Lohia think that he's very clever.

When he know they really trust him then he start to steal their things. First it was small money. They always keep the coins in the drawer, and he take only the copper ones, one and two toea. Then he think to himself why to take only the small money. He want the silver coins, the twenty toea and ten toea. He used to boast to the boys about it.

"I can get anything I want," he tell them.

But the boys tell him off. "Just twenty toeas, that's nothing," they say. "So what?"

"You better shut up," he tell them. "I can get anything I want. But not everything all the first time. I'm not stupid like you. I'm not greedy that I get caught just like that. I know how to wait my time."

And the next week he come back to the village with a ten kina note. He show it round and the boys ask how he got it, but Lohia never answer. He take them down to the store and buy lolly water and Twisties. Some money he give to the older boys to buy beer, and when they bring it to him down by the beach, he decide who can get a share. He has to give beer to the boys that bought it for him, and there isn't so much left. One stubby he keep it all for himself, but he give the other bottles to the boys and tell them which ones he let to drink it.

Next day at school, everybody expect that Lohia will be in trouble. Some of the boys are hoping he will get a big trouble, but no, nothing happen. Lohia walk around at school, skiting. "Why all you babies worried? I know how to do these things, I tell you that already."

And the next weekend too, nobody expect Lohia to go to Mrs Stevens' place, because for sure Mr Stevens will catch him for it. Of course, Mrs Stevens she know that money gone missing. They got plenty of money, the expats, but they know always how much they got, how much gone missing. They count their money and they write it all down in a book.

Lohia is clever, though. "I just go there same as always," he tell us. "If I don't go, that's when they know that I take the money. This way they know I don't do anything wrong. Only the guilty ones never go back again. Anyway, I want to get more money this time too." He laugh when he tell the boys this.

On Monday, the boys are waiting for him and this time he got a ten kina again. It's the same thing like before, we drink beer again, but nobody make fun at him because they want to share the beer. Also, just like he tell us, he never get caught. Must be the houseboy got the blame.

Third week again, Lohia go to Mrs Stevens' house to read National Geographic, same as before. Only this time Mr Stevens see him looking in a handbag for more money to steal. That was lucky it was Mr Stevens. His job is in the Coffee Marketing in town and he doesn't know all the tricks and excuse of the kids at Badihagwa High.

Lohia tell us everything about it later. "I admit it right away," he boast to us, "I don't want to give any excuse that they know is a bullshit. I'm too clever for that. Quickly I know I got to persuade Mr Stevens before Mrs Stevens come back in. I look straight at Mr Stevens and I try to make the tears to come to my eyes."

Lohia tell him that he need money for food. Because his little brothers and sisters haven't got anything to eat, and his father spend the wages all on beer. He tell that he only take the money once before and this was the second time. He tell them that lots of times he walk all the way back to the village so he can buy food with the PMV money.

He must look Mr Stevens in the eyes too good that time, because Mr Stevens believe him completely, even though Mrs Stevens not so sure. After that Mr Stevens himself sometimes give him money when Lohia can think up the reason why he

145

need money badly. Mrs Stevens doesn't know about that money. It's a secret only between Lohia and Mr Stevens. And us boys too, because Lohia tell us everything.

After this time Mrs Stevens always keep her eye on what Lohia doing in their house. But Mr Stevens, he's Lohia's good friend. He think that if he give Lohia money now and then, Lohia never steal again.

"That's okay," says Lohia. "So long I can get money, doesn't matter if it's from Mrs Stevens or Mr Stevens." Always he spend the money on beer.

At the end of the year Mr and Mrs Stevens got to go finish and give him all the things they don't need. Knives and spoons, plates, glasses, tablecloth that he used for a bedsheet, two pillows, food that they didn't eat it all. Plenty more things, Mr and Mrs Stevens brought it all down to the village one day.

Lots, Lohia give it to his family, but all his friends also want some present for themselves. So Lohia share all the stuff himself, he can act like the big man. Some of them get something good, some what they get is no good, and some they get nothing at all. When some of the boys ask for a share, Lohia tell them, "You piss off. Daure can get a bedsheet and Simon can get glass jars. But Augustine and Vai, they get nothing. I got all this things myself and I share them out to the boys that deserve it."

Vai go to take some glass bottle from the cardboard box. Lohia snatch it off him and they start to fight a bit, you know. They're shouting and swearing even though they still only pretty young then. Lohia grab the bottle from Vai and throw it down on the cement by the tap. He smash it into pieces and tell Vai: "You bloody get nothing. I smash these things up before I give it to you. It's all my things and I can do what I like."

That was a long time ago but everybody remember it still. They remember Vai and Lohia and the bottle. Especially Vai remember it.

After Mrs Stevens gone finish we all think that maybe Lohia won't be a bighead any more. We think he can't get money so easy now and he's going to stop acting that he's so clever.

But of course, there's plenty more expats and he make friends with them just like before. He do it next with Mrs

Ramsay. She's a nice lady, and interested in the Motu customs and legends. So Lohia, he used to tell her stories that he heard from the old people and Mrs Ramsay, she used to write it all down. She never let him come to her house but still he got things from her.

Next was Mr Gough, and Lohia was about 15 now and he drinking beer any time he can get it. Before, he used to drink beer just to show off and be like the older boys, but now he got used to the drink and he like that feeling it give him. Every time he go to Mr Gough's, Lohia used to pinch cans from the fridge and throw it over the fence into the long grass. On his way out he can pick them up and bring it all back to the village.

Mr Gough got a cupboard and it's full of different kind of drink, some is blue, some is red, some got no colour like water but with bits of gold floating in it. Every different kind of drink Lohia never saw before, some even smell like chocolate or coffee or made of fruit. All of it is stronger than beer. So sometimes Lohia used to take his schoolbag with an empty cordial bottle and he can pour a little bit from whisky and a little bit from vodka and from this bottle and that bottle. He want to try every kind. He used to bring the mixture back to the village and we boys used to go down to the beach or the cemetery and get sparked. Everyone sit in a circle and pass round the bottle and Lohia tell who is drinking more than his share.

Of course, after a while the bottles in that cupboard start to look a bit empty, but Lohia doesn't care because he think Mr Gough never notice. Mr Gough got too many bottles in that cupboard. Then one day Lohia notice the vodka bottle got a little pencil mark on the label. But that mark isn't the same place as the level of the vodka. So Lohia look at all the bottles and now they all got a little mark on the label.

Lohia start to think that something funny about all those bottles. He look at them very carefully when he get the chance and he turn the vodka bottle upside down. Now the pencil mark is the same level as the drink. That's funny. So he try all the bottles upside down and they all like that. It was a good trick, but Lohia is too clever: he find it out. After that he pour some water into every bottle and make it level to the pencil mark and Mr Gough never catch him.

Lohia pinch plenty of other stuff from Mr Gough, and to start with Mr Gough never notice because he's not married and got no wife to look after his money and things. Mr Gough was a very nice man and interested in looking at birds. He used to take Lohia into the bush with him to look for birds and take snaps, and at that time Lohia got very interested in birds, too. Just the same as Mr Gough.

But somehow Mr Gough start to worry about losing all his things. Shirts, money, food, drink, knives, hammer, cassettes, girl magazines, sunglass, hat, even Mr Gough's small binocular for looking at the birds. Lohia take the binocular and tell Mr Gough that it must be left behind in the bush. It got busted later back in the village.

So one day Mr Gough make a trap and leave a ten kina note where he know Lohia can find it. But Lohia's very clever with the thing like this, and he guess that maybe he better be careful. Still, he need money about that time, and even though he know it's a trap, Lohia can't resist to take the money, and at first he put it in his pocket.

After a while, Lohia can tell that Mr Gough going to ask him about that ten kina, so he hide it in a cupboard. Lohia got the plan to take the money later if he get the chance.

When Mr Gough ask him about that money Lohia can tell him truly that he hasn't got it.

"Mr Gough, I never take that money," says Lohia and he empty everything from his pockets and from his school bag, which that day, it's not got anything stolen inside it.

"What did you do with it, then? It was there before, and you and I are the only ones here."

Mr Gough can't believe him and start looking everywhere in the house, but he can't find that money.

Now Lohia starting to cry, and Mr Gough doesn't want to forgive him. He tell him it's no good to cry if you're a thief. But Lohia say he's not crying because he's a thief. He's crying because Mr Gough accuse him falsely when he never steal anything. Maybe the wind blew that money. This is a bullshit

148

excuse because it's not Laurabada season then and no wind blowing at all, but little by little with Lohia crying, Mr Gough think that maybe he's wrong and Lohia never steal that money after all.

Anyway, that's the way Lohia tell us the story. Maybe it happen just that way he says, or maybe he's bullshitting. He's a very good liar. But however way it happen, Mr Gough never let him into the house again, and never take him looking for birds any more. Also, Mr Gough must have told the other expats in the school because none of them is so friendly with Lohia like before.

That doesn't bother Lohia because he's so much bighead. He know he can find some more expats to trick. "There's plenty more," he tell us. "If you know how to treat the expats, you can always get what you want."

And it doesn't take long before he find some more. There's Mrs Pelosi and Mr Lowe and others the names Lohia didn't tell us. He always got a source of money. After Mr Gough finish with him, Lohia start to go to church. Not like Uniting Church in the village but those church out near Gordons Market and at Tokarara, Assembly of God, and Witness for Christ Mission, that kind.

All of a sudden Lohia got interested to read the Bible and say prayers and talk about Jesus this and that. He used to try it out with us boys when we drinking beer down at the beach, or just mucking around, and we make a good joke about it.

Lohia tell us those Christians are easiest of all to trick. All you got to do is pretend to take interest in all that stuff and then they believe anything you want to tell them. Only trouble is, they don't drink beer. Also, too much Bible reading, even though you can meet the girls there.

After he turn seventeen, Lohia go to Idubada Tech with the rest of the boys. He got sick of the Christians by now. But at the Tech he meet David McDonald, one of the trade teachers.

All the time before, Lohia is the favourite friend of those expats. When some of the boys ask Lohia to take them with him to the expats' houses, he always refuse. He want to keep them to himself. But David McDonald is a friend to all the boys, not just

149

Lohia. This make Lohia jealous and he try to make David McDonald to pay attention to him.

David McDonald used to help all the boys playing sport, and arrange the touch football and the swimming and that. When the cricket season come around, he organise the boys in the afternoon with the Tech's cricket gear. At first Lohia doesn't want to play, because he can't be in charge. Vai already is the one to do that.

But Lohia decide to join in and start to take over to get out the bats and pads before the practice. Of course, Vai doesn't like this and so they always argue. Some of the boys on the team are from the other villages or from town, and they always joke to see Vai and Lohia fighting all the time.

When David McDonald is there, Vai and Lohia always try to show off to him and he can see that the boys in the team, some like Vai best and some like Lohia best. At first he try to treat those two same as all the boys in the team, but after a while he start to favour Lohia. That's because Lohia is more clever to make himself liked. Our village boys, we know Lohia and we know what he's like, but the outside boys and Mr McDonald, they don't know him so well, and they like Lohia best over Vai.

Another reason is that Lohia start to play cricket very well. Before this time he was pretty good at all different sports, but he never bother much to play at cricket. But now when he try to impress Mr McDonald, he can bat really well. None of the bowlers can get him out and when it's Lohia's turn to bat, Mr McDonald pay a lot of attention and call out advice to him, more than to the other boys.

David McDonald start to tell him things like, "You've got a really good eye, Lohia," and "It's a pleasure to watch you play a stroke," and things like that. That talk go straight into Lohia's head and he start trying to boss the boys more than before and tell them what to do.

This make Vai very angry and he tell Lohia to shut up because he's the captain.

"Who says? We never made an election. You just think you're captain," Lohia tell him.

That's true that Vai never got elected but everybody except Lohia is happy with Vai. But Lohia mention to Mr McDonald that now the season's going to start, we got to elect a captain properly. Mr McDonald can see that there's too much argument between Vai and Lohia and so the team better decide who will be the captain.

When the time come to elect the captain, Vai and Lohia have to stand and turn their back so they can't see who vote which way. The village boys vote for Vai. But it's a surprise because the town boys too, they decide mostly that they want Vai best. They know those two are jealous about each other, and they think to change the captain will just make more trouble for the team. So Vai win the election twelve votes to four.

When Mr McDonald declare Vai the winner and Lohia to be the vice-captain, Lohia make his face very hard and he say that he refuse to be vice-captain. David McDonald is cross at Lohia and tell him that he's a bad sport. He tell the other boys to nominate for vice-captain and this time only one name nominated, and everybody agree on Felix. He's one of the town boys. So now everybody's happy, except for Lohia.

Even though they turn their faces during the election, Lohia soon can find out who vote against him and he talk very nasty to some of the boys: "You vote against me. I fucking pay you back for that".

Some of the boys say it wasn't them, that it was Timothy and Kore that vote for Vai. But the others just answer, "You bighead. You think you got to be in charge of everything. Now you got to do what the captain tell you."

"I only do what David McDonald tell me. That's all," he tell them back.

Some of the boys think that Lohia can't stand it that Vai is captain over him, and maybe give up playing on the team, but no. This time Lohia is crazy for cricket and practising at the nets at the Tech every night. This time he's really interested in the cricket, not like National Geographics and birdwatching and Assembly of God. He's really interested because Mr McDonald tell him he can be a champion at cricket, and he believe it himself.

151

The first two games of the season, Lohia play very well, 87 runs first game, 131 not out the second game. Next game, Vai getting jealous and doesn't put him in to bat till too late and the boys go cross at Vai. Maybe they're sick of Lohia but when they play, they like to win.

After that, Lohia play every game. We're only new team and even with Lohia we can't win every single game. But we do pretty good, all the same. Every time Lohia is getting better at his batting, and more and more big for his boots. Mr McDonald coach the team once a week official, but plenty of times he help Lohia at the nets with some of the other boys that he like.

"With proper coaching Lohia, there'd be no stopping you. You're a natural, an absolute natural," he tell him.

"You are my coach David," says Lohia.

"I'm no coach for someone as good as you. If only I could arrange for you to go down to Brisbane. That's where you'd get the coaching you need."

Before, it was always Lohia that tell the expats something and they believe him. This time it's the other way round. Lohia believe everything David tell to him. David lend him the cricket books and Lohia doesn't only look at the pictures, he read all the stories too. He get to know all about cricket because he want to be a famous cricket-player now. He practise all the time and get so serious about it, he even cut down on drinking beer.

And when the boys pinch the new ball from the equipment to take it to the village, Lohia go crazy at them. "You bloody thief," he tell them.

"So what?" they tell him back. "One little ball! Anyway, you are the biggest thief of all."

"That was before," says Lohia.

So the cricket can cure Lohia of being a thief, but it can't cure him of being a bighead. It make him worse. From the books and from David McDonald he learn all the special names of the place on the cricket ground, mid-on and slips and cover point and he show off, talking those names. The boys don't know the names properly and Vai when he place the boys for fielding, just tell them to go over there, or stand in that place, or go further yet. That's good enough for us.

When Vai tell the boys which way to stand to field the ball, Lohia argue with him and tell him his plan is hopeless. Lohia always shout out different orders and the boys don't know whether to listen to Vai or Lohia. And when they obey Vai and the ball go the other place, Lohia start shouting out, "You stupid, why don't you do what I say?"

And Vai is saying, "Don't listen to him. That bloody bighead."

Lohia says, "You shut up, we fucking lose the game thanks to you. You don't know anything about cricket."

"Shut up yourself, you fuckin' bighead." And so on like that, and all the boys joining in.

This sort of games are the ones we lose.

Always when Vai's batting you can hear Lohia whisper, "Fucking idiot, you finished soon," and stuff like that. And if Vai's score goes up 20 runs, 25 runs, 30 runs, he get more disappointed. Then when Vai get bowled out or hit a catch, Lohia really shout crazy: "Stupid idiot" — even though that's just the thing he's waiting for.

But when Lohia get the turn to bat, Vai can't say much because Lohia can do it very well. David has taught him everything. He can hit the ball every time, sometimes for four or for six, even. It's very pretty to watch, and Vai can't say anything what he's really thinking, that he hope Lohia getting clean bowled the very next ball.

Well, it's good to win, and after the game we have a few beer to celebrate. The town boys come back to the village with us, too. Sometimes Vai and Lohia start to argue with each other and the other boys join in and maybe swing a few punches. When it happen like this, some of the boys are sick of Lohia, but other ones they're really sick of Vai. He's too jealous to be the good captain. Also, Lohia is the best player and he knows more than Vai, but the boys already missed the chance to elect him.

These days when he start to drink beer, Lohia always boast how David McDonald's going to send him to Brisbane to get coaching. He tell us how he's going south at the end of the season, and David already started to get his passport for him. And that's the way he get money for drink too. He tell his family that he need money for passport or visa or pay for accommodation or registration fee or any excuse he can think up.

"When I'm down south, Vai can get fucked. David's going to fix up for me to join the club in Brisbane. Maybe I never come back, but just play cricket for Australia. Yeah, maybe I go finish and the team never win another game."

"Go finish! He think he's an expat now, the bighead."

"Eh, shame on him. Listen to him. We gotta call him taubada now or what?"

"Bloody hegeberi."

But these days Lohia try to cut down on drinking because beer is no good to be a champion cricket player. Sometimes, when he gone to practise with David, David can smell the beer on his breath and tell him he doesn't want to coach him because of the drink. One time too, Lohia got too sparked to go to practice, even though cricket is the only thing he's interested to do now.

Then it came the time, the season almost finished. We weren't in the final or anything like that. Plenty of the other teams been going much longer than us, and they got expat coaches too. But it was our last game and all of us really like to try hard and win.

Usually when we're batting, Vai and Lohia never share together because if Vai bat first, then he put Lohia down the list, and if Lohia bat first then Vai has to wait, and maybe never get the chance. But this time it's our last game and we're playing Davara, pretty good team. We got them all out 261 and now is our turn to bat. Davara got a very good bowler and when Lohia start the batting for us, he find it very hard to score runs. He's lucky himself a few times not to get bowled out.

One by one our boys go in to bat, but very unlucky. Ambrose get bowled quickly, then Felix caught, Kaua, Elisha, all the boys and still only ninety-something, with Vai next. This is the first time Lohia and Vai make partners together and everybody wonder that they're going to show off and lose the game.

First time Vai hit the ball, he call to Lohia to run and they start to run. But Davara field the ball very quick and when Vai call out to go back, Lohia only just escape to be run out. Some of the boys start thinking that Vai and Lohia hate each other so much, that they try to get each other out much better than the Davara team can do it.

But soon Vai get used to being at the crease and he start hitting the ball pretty well. And maybe Lohia see that and he also start to play well like usual. Sometimes they hit one run, or two runs. Then Lohia hit four and the Davara bowler start to get tired. They try the other bowlers, but that only make it easier for our side.

The score creep up and the two boys playing very nicely with each other. When one of them hit the ball, the other one know to take a single or go for two runs. Davara can field very well and Lohia and Vai also know when it's too close to try for a run. Even though they hate each other, still it's like they're thinking the same thing every time, or in contact by radio. They understand each other's minds.

But time is the problem because it's running out. Only 30 minutes left and they got to get 36 runs. The bowler now bouncing the ball close up to the batsman. If the bat touch the ball, it's a big danger to be caught by the fielders, because Davara captain move them in very close. But Vai somehow can turn the ball to go between them and score a run or two.

Lohia try the other way and move down to meet the ball on the full. He drive it to sail over their heads and the fielders run like hell to try to stop it before the boundary. But there's a danger to play it like that too, and twice Lohia miss the ball and almost stumped by the wicket-keeper. All the boys cheering and even the Davara supporters clapping for our two batsmen. Very thrilling game.

Bit by bit the score go up and we need twelve runs, ten runs, nine runs, until only the winning run needed. Everybody feel sure to win then, but still we feel excited and nervous. And Lohia too, he must get nervous because he slow down a little bit, and let a couple of balls to go past without to try a stroke.

So the bowler change ends for the new over, and Vai bang it hard, the very first ball. The fielder can't get his hand to it and the boys make a dash for the winning run. We all run onto the field and Vai and Lohia come back to each other and shake hands. David McDonald's excited also, and run to pat the boys on the back. The Davara team congratulate them both, even the bowlers. They are good sports, the Davara. It was our best game of all.

After the game David arrange it to have a party. He give us all Coke and Fanta and paper cups. Also party pies from Arrow Bakery and sausage rolls, that he paid for it all himself. And he make a speech that our team is too good and getting better all the time. Our very last game really give us something to celebrate. Next year, he tell us, we can win the shield for sure.

He says we all got to play together and not get jealous, because we all part of the team. He says it's very good that the last game of the season, the partnership was made by the captain of the team and the star batsman. Everybody cheer and clap.

But to celebrate good the boys don't want to drink just lolly water. Someone got a bottle of brandy and they put some in the Fanta and start to get a bit sparked and muck around. Fanta is all right for little kids, but after playing cricket, we all thirsty for something stronger.

David McDonald, he can smell the brandy but doesn't know who bring the bottle, and anyway, he doesn't want to get cross on the boys after the last match. All the sausage rolls got eaten up a long time back, so the boys want to go home to the village and make the party there. David McDonald let us go, and all of us take off for the village, the town boys too. Everyone that want to help to celebrate the end of the season.

The place to meet is at the far side of the village past where they dump the stolen cars. Nobody bother us there. It's where the village boys always meet and get sparked and can smash the empty stubbies against the rocks. There's plenty of broken bottles there already.

On the way to that place we pass the store to buy beer. Some of us got money already, some they run home and get the money and come back to the store. We all waiting for each other, talking who's going to buy what, San Mig or South Pacific, how much money we got, that kind of thing. We want to buy all at the same time so the beer is cold when we drink it.

Altogether we buy four cartons; each carton got two dozen stubbies. That's enough for a good party. Also, we have to leave money to buy smokes too. Billy Doi from the village is there to get beer himself, and all of our cartons, he let us pile it in the back of his ute and he give us a lift. We all sit in the back, laughing and yelling, calling out jokes to the people along the road. Straight away we tear open the first carton and everybody get a stubby, and drinking it as we driving along.

When we reach the drinking place, everybody else grab a stubby and start the party right away. We all having a good time, telling jokes and talking about the cricket. By now it gets to night time.

Of course, everybody want to get sparked as quick as possible and drinking pretty fast. Otherwise the beer getting too hot, or someone else drink your share. After a while, all the beer's finished and everyone pretty sparked. Some of the boys start throwing stones and using the empty stubbies as bowling balls. It's a good fun. The village peace officer come over and tell us to keep quiet and not to make any trouble, but we just tell him to get fucked because we're not making trouble at all, just having a good time. Only trouble is we run short on the drinks and nobody want to go home yet.

Some of the boys head off back to the village to look for more drink. If they want to buy beer now they have to get it black market, because the store is shut for selling drink long ago. But then some other boys come and they got Bacardi, and also red wine in a cask. The party is not just the cricket boys now. Anybody can join in if they bring the drinks.

When the new boys come, some of the cricket boys start to talk again about the game. Some of them skiting and acting smart. Of course it's Lohia does like that. He want to tell everybody again how he won the game and how much beer he drunk.

"Don't listen to him," we tell them, "it was the whole team won the match. All of us, like David McDonald says."

"Mostly, it was Lohia and Vai, together," says Felix.

"Fucking Vai," says Lohia, with all his words smudged. "He only score half the runs I got. He try to get me run out, anyway."

"Shut up," the boys tell him, "It was Vai that hit the winning run."

"That's because I let the ball go past so he can do it. He's the captain."

"That's a bullshit, Lohia," says Felix. "You just got worried maybe they bowl you out on the last ball."

Some of the other boys tell them to shut up because they don't want to hear Lohia skiting still. Plenty are sick of cricket talk. They want to talk about girls.

But Lohia keep talking like this and we ignore him, all except for Vai. He's the only one that can be bothered to argue. They say bad things to each other. They grab each other and wait for the other boys to stop them fighting.

Then someone run down and tell that Tom and Kore's got more drink. Everybody wonder how they got so much money to buy on the black market. But Tom and Kore hasn't got beer. Each one carry a big glass bottle and the boys whisper that they been up the Tech and broken in. That stuff in the bottle, they use it to make the stencil and print the papers at the school. It's stronger than beer, that's for sure.

"This can get you sparked quicktime," Kore tell us.

He take the paper cup and drink a mouthful and spit it out straight away onto the ground. "Shit," he says, "too strong ."

Vai grab the cup from him and try it himself. He doesn't drink it but only just taste it with his tongue and lips. He make a face with his jaw and call out to put some Coke in it.

Next time Vai drink a bit more and make a face again. "More Coke, more Coke", he call out.

Then Lohia push forward and shove his own paper cup to the glass bottle and pour some into it. Somebody add the Coke for him.

"You bloody weak or what?" he tell to Vai and drink plenty down.

The boys all looking at him.

"Taste good?"

Lohia doesn't want to stand up straight now. He sit down on the sand to drink.

"Fucking strong. Burn your throat," he says.

There's still some left in his cup and they take it off him and try to drink some. Some of them can drink it. Some of them just choke and spit it out again. Vai grab the cup and maybe he doesn't like it too much, but he has to drink it down to the bottom because Lohia already showed them he can do it.

All the other boys now start taking more from the bottles to put into their own cups. That stuff smells like the hospital. But if you put plenty of Coke, then it can taste pretty good, but strong. Those two bottles hold a lot, and got plenty for everyone. Only the Coke run short.

Everybody got very sparked now, and stagger round. They're all talking different things, but mostly you can't understand what they're saying.

As for Lohia, he can see that Vai also is drinking, and he call out from his place on the ground to get more. He reach out to try to get up but he can't stand and we all laugh. Plenty are sitting down and laughing from the drink. Every drink we make now got stronger because less and less Coke left over.

Lohia get the cup and drink down one big mouthful. This time he kind of choke and spew up down his shirt. The vomit come out of his mouth and nose too. All of it is liquid. No sign of party pies, it's too long ago.

Everybody laughing now and making jokes and nobody walking straight or anything. One by one they go to get more drink. They're all competing to drink the most and get fully sparked, especially Vai and Lohia.

Lohia lie on his side now and mumbling and gasping at the same time. He's fully pissed. Vai go over to him and roll him over onto his back and Lohia's laying there, and his eyes looking in different directions.

"Look at the big-head now. Wants to go south and he's a piss-weak."

Lohia can hear him and he try to talk back, but nobody can understand what he's saying.

"Fucking want to drink, that's okay," says Vai, and he reach out to one of the boys to get another cup of half Coke and half printing-water.

Vai sniff at it and even taste a bit more himself. He make the face again and pull his jaw muscles tight. Himself, he already drank plenty of that stuff, and having trouble to stand. And it's a bit hard to understand what he's saying too, but he's talking about Lohia: "Star batsman, eh? He better celebrate good. Maybe got a headache tomorrow." Something like that.

Vai take hold of Lohia's hair so his head doesn't flop to the side again. The other boys are helping Vai and hold Lohia steady. They got to be careful or they get the spew on them. Vai start pouring the drink into Lohia's mouth and Lohia can't swallow it all. Some of it just flow out his mouth again. But some can go down his throat, because he's coughing and choking as the drink go into him.

By now nobody can remember much what happened, because some of them already fell asleep and some others feel sick themselves and going off home to the village. Lohia is not the only one to spew. Plenty of boys are very sick, and Vai too.

The ones that drank only beer or not very sparked help some of the others. Just like a normal time, some swearing and want to fight. Others just fall asleep or they don't know what they're doing and their friends try to take them home.

They say that next day some of the boys are shaking and got trouble breathing. They got terrible headaches and can't see properly. The daylight hurt their eyes. Some of the families wait till morning before they go and find the boys, some of them still asleep in the sand.

By the time everyone in the village heard about the party, some of the boys already at the hospital. Somebody take the jars to the hospital so the doctors can see what they been drinking. But even when they know the drink, the doctors haven't got the right medicine.

Lohia and two others got tubes put into their bodies, because they don't wake up much at all. Other ones can stay in the hospital, but no special tubes. All of them feel bad and after a time they let them out.

All except Lohia. The tubes are no good for him and after three days Lohia never wake up at all. He got buried on the Thursday after the party.

Two of the boys, it's very sad for them. They were the two that lose their eyesight. One of them was the youngest boy, Timothy. That was a bad luck for him, because he never drink very much of that mixture. The other one gone blind was Vai. Nobody surprised there, because he drank that stuff too much.

Next season, nobody bother about playing cricket. No captain, no star batsman any more, and David McDonald, he feel very sorry for the boys. He want to take the blame that the boys hurt themselves. They say he's gone finish now.

Thursday Up The Club

First time visitors were always disappointed with the club. They expected some kind of Raffles hotel; palm trees outside, leather armchairs, barefooted stewards mixing gin and tonic, all that kind of thing.

The reality was very different. The weatherboard building itself was insubstantial, although the land must have been worth plenty even in those days. The ceilings were low, the shabby walls finished in semi-gloss like a cheap motel. A bar with a couple of bar-stools ran the length of one wall. On the opposite side were a couple of bar-stools, a coffee-table and two vinyl easy-chairs. The chairs were seldom used unless somebody passed out; mostly the members stood drinking at the bar.

The place was dated and depressing. A few plaques hung on the wall inscribed with the names of past Club Presidents or whatever. No present member had known them; the names were meaningless now. The plaques would be chucked out the next time the walls were painted. The framed picture of the royal family was so ancient that Prince Charles was wearing shorts. But no-one noticed. They would throw that out too, in due course.

There were two billiard tables, one with a tear in the cloth. The good table had one pair of legs recessed a couple of inches into the floorboards to compensate for the slope of the varnished wooden floor. The ceiling fans were never used now: the new airconditioning kept the place as cold as a butcher's shop.

The club had always been second-rate. The real elite belonged to the Papua Club, while here the members were the middle rankers, the assistant managers and jumped-up bank johnnies who thought they were somebody, the pen-pushers who because they were white had got a bit of power. Yet after

Independence, these were the very positions which were being localised first. So the membership was falling. The club was gradually going downhill. It had been for years.

It was open to locals of course, and there were a couple on the books. Their bosses paid their subscriptions, but they rarely showed up. You couldn't blame them; the atmosphere was scarcely congenial. In practice the club was still virtually 'expats only'. Of course, it was men only too. None of that nonsense like the Aviat Club with a swimming pool and family film nights. No, this was a real club; a place for white men to drink.

Every afternoon the regulars drove their cars the hundred metres or so up the hill and parked under the mango trees. You could say there were a dozen or so regulars, those who were there four or five times a week. They rarely missed two nights in succession.

Opening time was four o'clock. Malipu the barman was punctual, but he would often arrive to find the door already open; some of the regulars had their own keys. Galloway was one of them. He was there almost every night, often from opening time till closing at eight. He was unhappily married.

He was in his late thirties, well-built, but rather gone to seed from drink and easy living. He had a red, pugnacious face and gaps between his teeth. He was good talker and could be relied on for a yarn or a wry comment. When you got him going he was terrific company. But on a bad night, when he was feeling morose and sorry for himself, he could turn nasty. Those were the times when you had to be careful what you said to him.

In his younger days Galloway had been more easy-going, but his marriage, plus troubles at work had made the carefree in his character turn sour. "If you've had enough of the place, why don't you go finish?" they used to ask him. But he couldn't transfer back to Australia without loss of seniority, and he felt trapped. A vague resentment coloured his view of life now, and made him increasingly difficult.

Always hot-tempered, he had become in time ever more prone to take offence, even when he was sober. And the drinking didn't help. It took him a long while to forget a grudge. It was sometimes hard work to have him as a friend. Not everyone at the club liked him.

The regulars such as Galloway drank there most nights, but Thursday was the big occasion of the week. The accountants and lawyers who also belonged to the Papua Club used to make it their night to slum it. Their presence bestowed a bit of class on the club, although it was only a matter of time before they would relinquish their memberships and stick exclusively to the Pap Club.

The Thursday-nighters would arrive en masse, and tended to form a clique at the far end of the bar. Some of them might as well have stayed at the Pap Club for all the mixing they did. The club regulars thought them snobs and resented the way they kept to themselves. Galloway got on well enough with most of them as individuals, but he disliked them collectively out of principle.

There were several of the Thursday-nighters to whom he took a real dislike. Henderson was one, and the English accountant, Lucas Barlow from Burns Philp, was another. Galloway's dislikes were arbitrary; neither man had given real reason for animosity. They were a bit of a pain in the neck, true, but no worse than plenty of others. Besides, they were only there once a week.

Newly arrived in Papua New Guinea, Barlow first attended the club as a guest of one of the Thursday-nighters. The fellow who signed him in made the mistake of missing Pete and a few others when he introduced him around. You couldn't blame the Englishman himself for that; it was the fault of his host. But the omission was never rectified. It was a bad mistake with a touchy bloke like Galloway.

The Englishman was short, tubby and balding, with a mild squint in one eye. He had a cocksure manner and spoke loudly in one of those horrible, whining English accents. He had lived for years in Africa and firmly pronounced PNG backward, compared with Zambia. This brought out unexpected local loyalty in Galloway, who generally derided everything Papua New Guinean.

"He reckons they're more advanced in Zambia." commented Galloway to his mates. "They'd have to be. They got rid of that dill and sent him over here."

165

Of course, Barlow was subject to some friendly rubbishing from the Thursday-nighters themselves, and he took it very well. If only he'd been introduced to Galloway, the two of them might have hit it off. As it was, with each missed opportunity Galloway's hostility increased, and his comments about the Englishman became more and more sarcastic.

The Englishman's proposal for membership was posted and remained on the notice board for a month. Galloway would sling off: "I don't mind having a few coons as members, but we're scraping the barrel if we're taking in Poms." This, despite two other English members. "They're all right" declared Galloway of them. "They don't count as Poms. They're no worse than Kiwis."

By the time Barlow's membership was confirmed, he was well aware of Galloway's attitude towards him. If he had cared about it, he could have defused the situation by introducing himself. Or someone else could have introduced them to each other. In the event, neither of these things happened.

Then the incident of the newspaper took place. It provided Galloway with a genuine, though trivial grievance.

With security the way it was, most people carried huge bundles of keys, and for convenience they used to place them on the bar when they first arrived. It was also the practice for members to put down a pile of cash, from which the barman would draw as drinks were ordered. By six o'clock the bar would be littered with piles of coins, packets of smokes, bundles of keys.

Unusually for him, Galloway had lashed out and bought himself an airmail Australian newspaper to look up the share prices and the footy scores. He had left it on the bar with his keys and cash, but had moved away, further down the bar.

Barlow was with the Thursday-nighters and noticed the unattended newspaper. Clearly the paper was the private property of a fellow member. But he reached over, helped himself to it and began to read it. He didn't open it up, just stood there studying the first page.

"Hey Pete," said one of the stirrers, "that your paper His Lordship's reading?" drawing Galloway's attention to Barlow.

"What's this then? A fucking lending library now?" replied Galloway from the far end of the bar. "Where does he think he is? Be helping himself to the money next."

From where Barlow was standing, Galloway's tone of voice was audible, but not the words themselves. The Englishman coolly replaced the paper on the bar and turned away to rejoin a conversation. He was just in time to avoid having the newspaper snatched from his hands. Pointedly, Galloway grabbed it, pretended to dust it down and slapped it back down on the bar.

This was accompanied by loud comments: "There's some ignorant pricks in the club these days," and suchlike.

The Englishman heard the last remark, but pretended it was directed elsewhere. He neither answered back, nor offered an apology. Nor did Galloway have the matter out with him, then and there. Instead, he treated it as open season on Barlow, and thereafter never missed an opportunity for a malicious remark about him.

He ridiculed Barlow's accent and grimaced theatrically at the sound of it. "Just listen to him! Bastard can hardly speak English. If they're so smart, how come the Africans didn't give him elocution lessons?"

He mocked the Englishman's squint: "Did you hear about the cross-eyed school-teacher? – he couldn't control his pupils!" Roars of laughter.

This childish riddle gave rise to increasingly oblique remarks about teachers, schools, lessons and so forth, whenever Barlow appeared in the club. The comments made sense only to Galloway's cronies who were in on the joke.

Barlow's first name, Lucas, was corrupted to Mucous and gave rise to references to noses, nasal discharge, heavy colds et cetera. Finally, even the production of a handkerchief by Galloway would produce gales of laughter among his mates. They were like a gang of nasty schoolboys, and Barlow knew he was the butt of the joke.

One evening Neville Martin, the ineffectual Club President tackled Galloway about it: "Watch yourself, Pete. A few of the blokes are getting a bit pissed off with you slinging off at them."

It was entirely the wrong way to approach Galloway; it was bound to make him really flare up. Not that there was a right way to do it.

"I'll say what I like Neville. I've spent more money in this club than those bastards will ever earn. So if your Pommy mate doesn't like it, he can stuff it up his arse."

It was now only a matter of time before a confrontation took place. Though his appearance was against him, Barlow didn't lack guts. He was too much the smart-arse to be a coward, and was reported as having made a few choice comments to the Thursday-nighters about Galloway. In a fight, the Englishman would be no match for Pete, but clearly he was biding his time to settle scores. It only remained for the occasion to arise.

It was provided by that fertile source of friction and unpleasantness – sport. There was a Test cricket series underway between Australia and England. Australia held The Ashes, but the English were fielding their best side in years. There was endless discussion about opening bowlers and batting order and such things. It made a change from the usual topics of money and drink, but it was a bore. Galloway took little interest in it. In his opinion, cricket was a game for sissies.

One Thursday night the club was buzzing with cricket talk. The English had won the first Test decisively. Various reasons were advanced for the result, all connected with the state of the wicket, and none with the merits of the teams. In spite of himself, Galloway was drawn into the discussion. He had been drinking since four. His mood was ungenerous and the Thursday-nighters were getting on his nerves.

The Pommy's grating voice and high-pitched laughter could be heard over the hubbub. He was gloating over the English performance and predicting certain victory for the visitors in the whole series.

"What would that prick know?" commented Pete to his mates.

"You can say that again."

"He's up himself all right".

The comments were audible along the full length of the bar. They were for the benefit of the Thursday-nighters, some of whom answered back. Galloway said little but it was implicit that he was issuing a challenge to the Englishman. National honour was at stake. This time Barlow did not turn a deaf ear.

"Do you want a bet on it?" asked the Englishman. It was the first time he had ever spoken directly to Galloway.

"Please yourself," said Galloway with studied rudeness. "Easiest twenty bucks I'll ever make." He didn't condescend to look up from his glass.

"Get out the betting book," ordered Neville Martin as he pushed his way along the bar to supervise. Malipu had already produced it from the drawer under the cash-register. He was a good deal more alert than Neville and was flipping through it to find the current page.

Neville was always anxious to take charge in his capacity as President of the club. This was especially undesirable where betting was concerned because his interference often managed to confuse the issue. On the pretext of clarification, he used to take it upon himself to hedge around a simple bet with a lot of un-necessary stipulations. Once or twice there had been arguments about the terms of a bet recorded by Neville.

The last few entries were not in Neville's handwriting and were admirably concise;

> "JL bets Martini five kina that Martini's girlfriend
> is up the duff." (Won)

> "Hendo will shout everyone in the club a drink if
> there's no such country as Abassinia." (No result
> recorded)

> "Gerald Northey Esq. wagers Mr Brian Barnes five
> kina that not one drop of alcoholic liquor shall pass
> his lips before 5 pm on Thursday next." (Lost).

There was a further notation on the last one: "As Usual."

169

But Neville was first on the spot with a pen, and had taken charge of the book from the barman. Pedantry and self-importance drove him in equal measure.

"Twenty kina is it? Now what's the date today? How shall we put it? 'In the present Test series between England,' No – hang on, it's not England at all, is it? It's the MCC. Now how do you spell..."

Galloway cut him short. He wanted no ambiguity. "None of that crap for Chrissake, Neville. Just write this: 'Galloway bets Barlow twenty kina that Australia will win the Ashes'."

Neville Martin was still fussing with the date.

"You heard me. Never mind that crap. Just fucking write what I said."

Galloway was easily irritated after eleven or twelve beers, and Neville didn't want to aggravate him further. He did as he was told.

In the succeeding weeks interest in the outcome grew. It was so very much a personal feud that there was more drama in the bet than in the cricket. The protagonists ignored each other of course, but their camp followers exchanged derisive remarks. The club split into two camps, and opinion divided untidily on two separate questions.

The first was whether the English team could actually beat Australia. It would be a close thing whatever happened. There had been a couple of draws and a win each. One opinion was that with luck the visitors might actually pull it off. Some of Galloway's mates wondered what would happen then.

The second question was whether one preferred Galloway or the Englishman to win. The consensus was that Galloway had become so prickly of late that it would be good to see him cut down to size. Barlow was hardly popular, but it wasn't his fault he was a Pommy, and on the whole he had behaved pretty well in spite of provocation. At least Barlow would be a good loser; the same could not be said of Galloway.

The result all hung on the final match. Galloway himself spent the weekend glued to the radio commentary. Australia was playing for a draw, and as the afternoon wore on it became clear they would succeed. So it proved to be, and to Galloway's relief

Australia retained the Ashes. To him, the money and the game had always been irrelevant. Even the slightly dubious tactics of the Australian team didn't matter; that was cricket. After all, the Poms invented the game. The important thing had been to rub Barlow's nose in the dirt, and Galloway, having won the bet, forgot that he had ever been at risk.

On the nights after the final match, the regulars congratulated Galloway on his win. Barlow would not be along until Thursday, and they looked forward to his appearance then to settle the debt. Actually, it crossed a few minds that Barlow might try and save face by sending Galloway a cheque. No-one could have blamed him. It wasn't Galloway's style to be magnanimous in victory. Indeed, Galloway had already stated his policy: "I'll take the prick's money, but I'm not shaking his hand."

By Wednesday there was no cheque and it was clear that Barlow would turn up to pay in person. Ironically, the English-man was proving to be the winner in the whole affair: he was showing himself to be a decent bloke. Opinion now crystallised firmly in Barlow's favour. Everyone likes a good loser.

About six on the Thursday night, Barlow and his cronies arrived and parked themselves at their end of the bar. Of course, there was little gallantry from Pete's mates. But the cries of "Got your wallet tonight?" and that sort of thing were relatively inoffensive.

In Galloway's mind, the Englishman's obligation was clear. He should have come straight over and settled up. It was not for the winner to go begging – it was for the loser to pay up, and without any pissing around either. Had the Englishman done so, Galloway for all his bravado might perhaps have done the right thing by putting the money on the bar and shouting the Pommy a drink.

But the longer the delay, the more Galloway seethed. Comments about the bet came thick and fast, yet Barlow pretended not to understand. He and his mates ordered drinks and ignored the remarks. Galloway could see now that Barlow was trying to act smart with him, trying to make him grovel for his twenty kina.

171

Then the whisper went around that there was going to be trouble, that the Pommy was going to welsh on his bet. Galloway heard the rumour too, but he didn't believe it. Even a weasel like Barlow wouldn't do that; a bet was a bet in anyone's language. Galloway said nothing, but from the way he stared into his glass you could see his temper building up.

Galloway looked up from his glass and stared with narrowed eyes at the liqueur bottles along the wall behind the bar. That was a bad sign. Those who knew him best waited for a move. The sense of expectation was communicated along the bar and conversation petered out into an unnatural hush. By the time Galloway was ready to speak, the silence was complete. He still didn't turn to face the Englishman. His words came out almost softly, but the effect was electric.

"Have you got my twenty kina, Barlow?"

The Englishman looked towards Galloway, and the drinkers who had been leaning on the bar stepped back slightly. Barlow peered insolently along the full length of the bar to Galloway's scowling profile.

"What do you mean?"

Galloway's eyes blinked and he cocked his head quizzically to one side. He still stared directly ahead. Even those who hadn't seen him like this before knew that sparks were about to fly. They loved it. The merest whisper ceased.

"What do I mean?" His tone was venomous. "I mean you owe me twenty fucking kina."

"Not that I know of," said Barlow, smugly. "I don't owe you anything." The man was a smart-arse, and he obviously had something up his sleeve, but just then his whining voice possessed a certain dignity. You had to admire his nerve.

Slowly, Galloway spoke as if he were thinking out loud. "Doesn't owe me anything, eh?" he began with a mock-puzzled expression, his gaze still fixed on the row of bottles behind the bar, which fortunately were well out of reach. "From what I remember, we had a bet."

"That's right," interrupted the podgy Englishman, "And you lost."

Galloway ignored the interruption and continued at his own steady pace. "We had a bet. And I won the bet. And you owe me twenty kina." At this point he turned dramatically to face Barlow.

Barlow was shaking his head. "The bet was that Australia would win the Ashes and they didn't win the Ashes."

"So where's the Ashes now? Fucking England are they?"

The Englishman stood his ground, while Malipu, showing considerable initiative, was hurriedly removing empty glasses from the bar.

"The Ashes are in Australia because she won them two years ago. Australia didn't win the Ashes this year. She kept what she already had. The result was a draw. Nobody won anything. That's what a draw means."

Galloway was looking at the wall again. "Australia's got the Ashes, but she never won them. That's what you're saying?"

"Not this series. You can't win what you've already got."

There were mutterings from the onlookers:

"He's got a point, you know."

"Doesn't sound right."

"Typical Pom."

There was no agreement; in that charged atmosphere nobody could think it out clearly. Even the Englishman's mates, with whom he'd discussed it earlier, were undecided – on the morality, if not the logic. Someone had taken out the betting book, and fellows were craning their heads to see how the bet was recorded. It was Galloway himself who thought it through and expressed the issue most neatly.

"So if Australia held the Ashes, she could only keep them or lose them. Is that right? According to you, I could never win that bet, only lose it."

That surely was the Englishman's argument, but when it was put like that, it hardly seemed a fair bet.

"That's your lookout, Galloway. You wrote the bet yourself, dictated it anyway. You should have thought of that before."

Now there were murmurs of disapproval, and "Steady on you blokes," from Neville Martin. The Englishman's eyes darted towards his mates, seeking support. His nerve seemed to weaken slightly. No wonder, for the storm now broke.

"YOU..." Galloway spat out the word with venom as he reached the Englishman in four purposeful steps. There was a pause between each word. "You... Pommy... cunt!" His voice was slow and deliberate. Nobody intervened. Sympathy was with Galloway now. At last the Pom had really done something to justify Pete's hatred for him.

He stood a foot away from Barlow, glaring down with loathing. He was too out of condition to be much of a fighter but he was bigger and heavier than the Englishman.

"I'll give you three hits start and still lay you out, you cunt."

For the second time, and before anyone else realised it, the Englishman took Galloway exactly at his word. With a sudden, violent movement he brought his knee into Galloway's groin. The effect was instantaneous. Some of the blokes claim they heard the thud as Galloway's balls copped it; others reckon it was his gasp for air.

Whichever it was, Galloway uttered a kind of gurgle and doubled over. But as he did so, his right hand shot out in a kind of reflex action, smashing against the Englishman's nose. He hadn't even had time to form a fist, but the blow with the heel of his hand was delivered with surprising force.

Barlow fell backwards and hit his head on the edge of the billiard table. He was unconscious by the time he hit the floor. There was blood everywhere.

Someone rushed a bar-stool to Galloway and eased him onto it. His face was quite grey and had the goggle-eyed, gasping look of a goldfish. They thought he was going to throw up until someone gave him a sip of rum and he came good. Meanwhile, Malipu got a dishcloth to the Englishman's nose as they carried him off.

For the next week rumours circulated that Barlow's nose was broken, that the two men were going to sue each other, and so on. None of it was true.

The following Thursday, to his credit, Barlow fronted the club again. Nothing was said about cricket matches or gambling debts, for tempers had cooled. The two men ignored each other, but no insulting remarks were uttered on either side. Some person unknown had written 'Draw' beside the entry in the betting book.

In the end Galloway even conceded privately that Barlow had been right. That was the feeling in the club, too. As time passed, it became the general opinion that both men had come out of the incident honourably. It was said that Pete's blow to the English nose had been no lucky chance, but prompt retaliation to an attack below the belt. They meant no criticism. You couldn't expect a bloke to wait for another two like that.

His Honour's Associate

It's always a pleasure to accommodate His Honour here at the Lodge. By His Honour, I mean Mr Justice Hadley, he being the only judge who stays with us these days. Until the hotel-motel was built, all the judges used to stay here – they had no choice. Now Judge Hadley is the only one, and we see him rarely. The National Court visits only six times a year, and the judges take turns in coming. Our little town is one of the quieter, more pleasant parts of the country and I understand there's competition among them to come on circuit here. They all want to avoid the highlands, and I can't say I blame them.

The National Court sittings are good for business. Even the judges who stay at the motel frequently come to the Lodge for dinner. Everyone admits that our catering is light-years ahead of the food at the motel. We pride ourselves on our cuisine here. Even His Honour is highly complimentary about the food, though he criticises the menu. Alphonse insists on writing it partly in French, and some of the descriptions are a bit on the flowery side. The judge accuses us of being pretentious, but I have to keep Alphonse happy. He's a marvellous chef, but terribly temperamental, and I can't risk offending him. The Lodge would be uneconomic without him. It's touch and go as it is.

My own contribution to the catering section is the decor in the dining-room. The Lodge building is 1950's weatherboard, but it has a certain charm, and I have tried to exploit the period ambience. I had the place done up in Melanesian/Colonial style and originally we sported an extensive collection of stone axes, shields, fishing spears and so on. Unfortunately, I had to modify it after a seminar of Provincial Education Ministers got rather out of hand six months ago. I'm not saying they actually pulled the weaponry off the walls, but it might have come to that if the riot squad had arrived any later. Since then, the decor has run more to Tapa cloth and basketware.

At the far end of the dining-room is the bar, and this is where His Honour likes to spend his evening after a hard day sentencing our local criminals to terms of imprisonment. The judge is in his fifties, getting portly, with a pink, almost child-like face and blue, staring eyes. His manner is distinguished, a bit pompous in fact, and he chooses his words with great care. He's an excellent raconteur with a colourful turn of phrase. Though I laugh at his jokes, I'm always careful to show him proper respect. I wouldn't be game to cross the man.

His Honour has a reputation as a brilliant jurist. Of course, I'm not qualified to express an opinion myself, but I have it on good authority. The senior partner at Gadens told me, and he ought to know. They're the best law firm in the country. I use them every time I go bankrupt.

We always have quite an entourage in town during the court sittings. There's the judge, a state prosecutor and the defence counsel from the Public Solicitor's Office. They travel the whole circuit together, doing the final week in our town, which has the best golf course. The judge is also accompanied by his associate, which makes four altogether.

The associates are a peculiar breed. They're meant to be a kind of personal secretary to the judges. Before Independence they were always expats, mainly retired army officers whose brains had been shot out during the war. These days, they're no better – Nationals who never had any brains to get shot out. I really wonder where they get some of them. Straight out of the village, I suppose.

Gideon, Judge Hadley's associate, is in a different class altogether. A complete exception, in fact. He has a pleasant, intelligent face, and he's extremely quiet and reserved. At first glance, his manner towards the judge seems almost shy. I used to think he was intimidated by the judge's powerful intellect.

But Gideon possesses quite an intellect himself, although he has a diffident manner and goes to great lengths to avoid conversation entirely. I remember the first chat I ever had with him. In the course of it I asked him whether he had ever been to

Australia, and when he said he hadn't, I made some remark or other about Brisbane. He must have thought I was being condescending.

"How does it compare with Washington DC?" he asked, no doubt guessing that I was in no position to say. He then told me he'd visited America twice, both times with the university debating team.

"You were lucky," I said. " Did the government pay?""

"The US State Department paid the first time," he answered, "and the CIA the second."

When I took to studying Gideon more carefully, I realised that he wasn't in awe of the judge at all. In fact it was more the opposite; he treated him politely, but almost off-hand. Certainly, I never saw Gideon trying to ingratiate himself with the judge as did the rest of us, the lawyers especially. I always noticed how careful they were not to get more pissed than the judge. As for Gideon, for a long time I thought he was a teetotaller.

At breakfast and lunch, Gideon and the judge would share a table. For dinner, the prosecutor and defence counsel often joined them and sometimes, by invitation, one of the planters or local bigwigs. Gideon would take little part in the conversation and at an unobtrusive moment, would often sneak away altogether.

The judge thrived on an audience, and if the lawyers left early and there were no other expats around, he would call me over as a last resort, and indulge in some humorous banter.

"Wiggins, I've noticed this place is deteriorating."

"In what way, Judge?"

"You're getting a lower class of patron here since the motel opened. Last circuit, I had a fraud trial to hear, and the two accused used to have dinner here every night. Bloody inconvenient. I should have revoked their bail."

"I'm sorry about that, Judge. It's the excellence of the cuisine that attracts them."

"But their manners, Wiggins! The time before, there was a National fellow at that very table there. Blew his nose into the ashtray. First one nostril, then the other. Disgusting. Chap was thorough though, I'll give him that."

179

What could I say?

The judge continued: "Pretty poor clientele altogether now. The standard's dropped. You'd better do something about it, Wiggins. I might decide to stay at the motel next circuit if things don't improve. Eh, Gideon?"

"Yes, Judge," said Gideon.

"Well, we still have a lot of distinguished patrons," I ventured. "His Grace the Archbishop stayed three days with us last month."

"That cretin!"

"And Dr. Spurr dines here frequently."

"Never heard of him."

"He's our new medical practitioner, Your Honour. That makes four doctors in the province now."

Mention of Dr. Spurr provided the judge with an opening to his favourite topic; medical complaints in general, and his own health in particular. As I mentioned, the judge is witty and amusing most of the time, but he can be something of a bore on medical matters. I've heard about all his troubles from diabetes to dengue fever, and the account of his prostate trouble was positively grisly. None of these health problems seems to affect his appetite, though. Or his thirst.

On every occasion he's stayed at the Lodge, it seemed to be the case that His Honour was suffering from some more or less serious medical condition. Once long ago, he reported to me with a mournful expression that he had been bleeding overnight from the back-passage. He almost abandoned the circuit, thinking it was cancer of the bowel. Later, he confided it was only his haemorrhoids – one of the grapes had burst. Personally, I would have kept quiet about it.

One evening the judge was in good form. He had invited the two lawyers down from the motel to join himself and Gideon for dinner. The defence counsel was Mrs McNab, a widowed, middle-aged Australian lady. The discussion was on some abstruse legal point or other, and I could hear the judge's voice ringing out.

"Sodomy, it may have been. But consensual, without a doubt."

"But, Judge...," came a female voice.

"My dear McNab, what's your opinion of consensual sodomy? You must have turned your mind to it many times over the years."

"As a matter of fact, Judge...,"

His Honour caught sight of me, and interrupted her.

"I say, there's Wiggins. What about some rum! You must have rum here, Wiggins. What sort do you keep?"

"Well, we've got Bacardi."

"Bacardi, Bacardi! Call that rum? Do you know what I call it?"

"No, Judge."

"I call it cat's piss, Wiggins. That's what I call it."

"Well we've got Bundaberg, Judge, if you prefer dark rum."

"That's no better, Wiggins. As a matter of fact I suspected you'd have nothing decent here. I thought to myself, 'That Wiggins is not a bad chap, but you can't rely on him for rum.' No, I knew I wouldn't find decent rum here, so I came prepared, didn't I Gideon?"

"Yes, Judge."

"Be a good fellow then, and go up to my room and fetch that bottle I brought. I'll teach Wiggins a thing or two yet about rum."

"Yes, Judge," said Gideon and disappeared with the judge's room-key, to return shortly with the bottle of rum. At the judge's insistence we all partook of it, Mrs McNab included; and it wasn't bad, either.

In due course the four of them ate dinner, sharing a couple of bottles of wine and finishing up with port and liqueurs. About nine o'clock, the judge unexpectedly quietened down and declared that his ulcer was bothering him. Murmurs of sympathy. After another five minutes, he abruptly announced that he was going to bed, and the party broke up. The lawyers departed and Gideon was left to settle the chits.

"Another pleasant evening, Gideon?" I asked him. "The judge is certainly good company."

"He is, Mr Wiggins," agreed Gideon.

I was surprised to see you drinking tonight," I remarked. "I've never seen you drink before. I always thought you were a total abstainer."

"No, I'm just a little more abstemious than some of your guests, Mr Wiggins."

"His Honour, for example?"

"You could say that."

It must have been the rum and a single glass of wine, for Gideon was more forthcoming than usual. It was mid-week and the dining-room was fairly empty, and I pressed him to sit down and have a drink and a few words with me. I'm very interested in the administration of justice, especially where it touches on the idiosyncrasies of members of the judiciary. Before long, we were sitting at one of the vacant tables, and Gideon was talking.

My opening comment was how much I admired the judge. Gideon looked thoughtful and then began to speak. Once he got going, the words flowed beautifully. His command of English was extraordinary. ("You speak it like a native," I told him.) Articulate, fluent, grammatical: he was judge material himself.

"Well," said Gideon, "unlike some of the judges' associates, I'm quite interested in the law. So I applied to be Judge Hadley's associate while I was still at university. He had all the intellectual qualities I most admire, and he seemed a very nice man.

"I was excited, thrilled even, when His Honour agreed to have me, and we got on very well together. Just occasionally he was aloof or prickly, especially when his health was poor.

"The very first time we went away on circuit, I was quite apprehensive. You might think that making travel bookings, arranging the government car and so on would be a simple thing for a university graduate. Of course, it is really. But it was my very first time, and I wanted everything to go well.

"When we arrived in Wewak, all the arrangements were in order. The hotel was expecting us; the car turned up; none of the judge's trunks was lost, the ones with the law books that we have to carry around with us. I was so relieved and pleased with myself that on that first night when the judge and I had dinner together, I drank more than I should have. The judge encouraged me.

182

"First we had some aperitifs, things I had never heard of even when I went to America. Then at dinner he insisted on ordering a bottle of white wine with one course, and red with another and so on. You know how he is. I lost count of what we drank.

"By the time we'd finished dinner, I was rather under the weather. That's very rare for me. I was feeling exhilarated I suppose, because over dinner the judge had begun to confide in me. He divulged a most closely-guarded secret: his health was extremely precarious. If the Chief Justice or the National Executive Council knew exactly how ill he really was, they would insist on his retirement, so he begged me to treat what he was saying with the utmost discretion.

"He told me a lot about his illnesses and used terms you would only find in a medical dictionary. It all sounded dreadful. He explained that while we were on circuit it would be an important part of my duties to ensure that he took the correct medication at the proper times. To miss even one dose might have serious consequences. The extra responsibility worried me, but I was determined not to let the judge down.

"When dinner was over he invited me up to his room for a nightcap, and the two of us helped each other upstairs. When we got to his room, the judge somehow slumped to the floor and I was afraid for a moment that he was having one of the attacks he'd described. Luckily, it was only a momentary thing and he was really quite all right. But it was comfortable on the floor, so we stayed there, chatting together. The judge produced a bottle of port and we shared it from the same glass until there was hardly any left.

"At one point, the judge got to his feet, went into the bathroom, and came back with handfuls of bottles and plastic phials. This was his medicine, and he arranged it all on the bed, explaining its purpose and dosage to me, one by one. It was very hard to remember it all, but he was emphatic about one thing.

"The most important thing of all, he explained, was to make sure he took his pink pills. They had to be taken twice a day without fail, at six in the morning and six in the evening. They were something to do with his heart. He explained it all to me, how the valves have to be co-ordinated with the flow of blood,

183

and so on. The only part I really followed was when he warned what would happen if he forgot to take the pills. He lowered his voice to tell me: unconsciousness; coma; even death. The thought was horrifying.

"When I finally managed to make my way to my own room, my head was reeling. All I could think about was those pink pills. I was worried that I might oversleep and fail to wake the judge. When I felt myself dozing off, I tried to force myself to stay awake. Every thirty minutes, I checked my watch by the light of the bedlamp. I knew that the judge's health, even his life, depended on me and on the pink pills.

"The next thing I remember was that it was light outside. I looked at my watch and saw it was almost seven o'clock. I rushed up to the judge's room and knocked at the door. There was no answer. I knocked again: still nothing. I knocked over and over, each time more loudly, but there was no sound from within. I was sure I was too late and that the judge was dead. Dead because he had trusted me! It was too awful.

"I completely panicked, I admit it. I pounded the door with my fists, until I heard the judge's voice call out faintly, 'Who is it?'

"Mr Wiggins, I could have cried with joy, I was so relieved. There was still time for the pink pills to save his life.

" 'It's me, Gideon,' I shouted back. 'Quickly, Judge. It's after six o'clock. Take your pink pills.'

"I could hear him shuffling about in the room, but even then I didn't know what I should do. Should I continue to shout, or force the door? Perhaps at that very moment, he was swallowing his life-preserving medicine. On the other hand, perhaps he was lying prone, grasping helplessly for the pills while I stood inches away outside his door. I kept pounding the door, and calling to him 'Judge, please. Your pills. Quickly.'

"Suddenly the door burst open and the judge stood there in a dressing-gown.

" 'What the devil do you want?' he shouted at me.

"All I could answer was, 'Your pills, your pink pills.'

" 'Pink pills, be damned! How dare you. At this hour of the morning.'

"He was furious. He called me an insolent kanaka. I think he even used the term rock-ape. I find that especially offensive. Anyway, he said a lot of insulting things and slammed the door in my face. At breakfast later, all he said to me was: 'Don't you ever do that again. Do you understand? Never.' He didn't offer me a word of thanks.

"I felt so ashamed and humiliated that I could hardly bear to look at him. But when I did, the judge didn't look to me like a man who had narrowly cheated death by taking a pink pill in the nick of time. On the contrary, he just looked hung-over.

"After that, Mr Wiggins," concluded Gideon, "I have been more, shall we say, circumspect about everything His Honour says."

He got up to leave, and politely thanked me for the drink.

"Don't mention it," I told him, "I'll add it to His Honour's bill."

At The Wide Bend

At the Fifteen-Mile point on the Sogeri Road there is a wide, sweeping curve to the right, just before the driveway entrance to the Adventist vocational school. Before and after this bend there are much sharper curves on the winding bitumen road. This one is so open and the visibility so good, that a driver can be tempted to take it a little too fast. It was on this curve at around four o'clock in the afternoon, that Jacob Nangoi, aged nine, was struck from behind by a Mazda 929 and killed instantly.

At the time, the boy was accompanied by his uncle and an elder brother. The fourteen-year-old brother was leading, followed by the uncle, a villager of around fifty. Poor little Jacob, with a five kilo bag of rice slung across his back, was last in line. The three of them were returning home from a trade store four kilometres down the road. They were walking to the left of the road, with traffic outbound from Port Moresby, of which there was very little, approaching them from behind. It was a Sunday afternoon, and the traffic was mostly oncoming – people returning to town after a day up the range. Through the grass on the left of the road, there was a well trodden path. Whether the group was keeping to the path or was walking on the road proper became a matter of dispute.

The driver of the Mazda was Rodney Miller, an accountant with the Banking Corporation. He was a tanned, fit, handsome Australian in his mid-thirties. Miller's wife, Sandra was his ideal counterpart; attractive, lively, intelligent, and like her husband, a pennant standard squash player. Their two children, a girl of five and a boy of seven, sat in the back of the car with their mother seated between them.

Occupying the front passenger seat was a visitor from Australia, Dennis Underwood. He and Rodney had been at school together, but had not seen each other in years. It was only by chance that Rodney had overheard Dennis's name mentioned at the bank, and learned that he was to visit Moresby on business. Rodney had tracked down his telephone number, and given him a ring in Sydney; Underwood was taken completely by surprise. Both had looked forward to renewing the friendship. At school, they had been close friends.

Dennis arrived on the lunchtime flight from Sydney, and was met by Rodney and his family. He was booked to stay at the Travelodge, but the Millers drove him to their home first. Rodney was doing well for himself. He wanted to show Dennis their house, the view, the pool; and the winter-pale Underwood was duly impressed. The Millers' domestics were usually given the weekends off, but this Sunday Rodney had kept them on call at the house. He wanted to exhibit them to the visitor, and order them around a bit in his presence.

Rodney and Dennis chatted away about old times, and traded news with each other of their school contemporaries. Dennis had already eaten on the plane, so Sandra made sandwiches for her own family. The men had a few drinks – or rather Dennis Underwood did – for Rodney had only one, a Scotch and water, while Sandra didn't ever drink alcohol.

Dennis had been intrigued by the little he had seen of Port Moresby. The barefoot crowd at the airport, milling around in noisy confusion beneath the banks of ceiling fans. The market at Six-Mile, where he had wanted to stop and look. ("Don't be mad," Rodney had told him. "There are much better markets than that.") Glimpses of ramshackle squatters' huts, and of luxurious expat houses, their graffitied walls spattered with betel-nut spit and topped with razor wire.

Dennis's schedule for his three days in Port Moresby was very full. The rest of the afternoon was his one chance for sightseeing, and he hinted hopefully to the Millers that a short guided tour would be much appreciated. It was almost three, rather late in the day, but they were happy to oblige. After a brief discussion they decided to take him on the standard out-of-town excursion; up the range to Sogeri. There was still time enough and it was an afternoon out for the children too.

They were quickly under way. Sandra, in the back between the children gave Dennis a running commentary. To him of course, Port Moresby was exotic and unfamiliar, and he was gratifyingly curious about everything he saw. It encouraged the Millers to show off. They answered his questions with an assurance not really justified by the state of their knowledge.

"Chimbus for sure," declared Rodney, in answer to some enquiry by the visitor about the occupants of a passing truck. "No, that's not the same as Southern Highlands – another province entirely, miles away, I couldn't tell you how far. No, our house girl wouldn't speak their language; she's got her own. Place-talk we call it."

Once out of town, the country was more open, and Dennis was a little disappointed at its resemblance to the ragged bush of northern Australia. The look of the country was different up on the plateau, the Millers assured him.

As they passed the racecourse, Dennis noticed the sign to Bomana War Cemetery. Rodney had not intended to stop; there had been a few incidents there recently, and it was not altogether safe. Besides, the mosquitoes were ferocious. But Dennis was undeterred. He insisted on their turning down the side-road for a quick look, and was much struck by the sight of the white headstones set in the well-watered gardens. He and Rodney walked around for ten minutes, while Sandra and the children waited in the car with the windows up. Dennis signed the visitors' book and wrote: "Very moving. Lest We Forget" in the Remarks column, before rejoining the others in the car.

The road to Sogeri follows the course of the Laloki River on the left, with the impressive escarpment of Hombrum's Bluff beyond, and hills closing in from the right as well. The detour had set them back a few minutes, and Rodney was keen to get to Rouna Falls – they were something really spectacular. He hoped there would be a decent flow of water. In another few kilometres, the road would begin to climb steeply to the Sogeri Plateau. Sandra, from the middle of the back seat was leaning forward to chat with Dennis and answer his many questions. And then it happened.

As the car entered the wide bend, Rodney glimpsed a small party of Nationals walking along the left side of the road, heading in the same direction as themselves. It all happened so quickly that it was hard to be sure of anything. He remembered they had their backs to them. How many there were he couldn't say, but the last one was a little kid only slightly older than his own boy. He was carrying something on his back. Rodney couldn't say for certain, but they seemed to be walking on the gravel shoulder of the road, perhaps even on the bitumen itself.

The next thing... Well, the boy was suddenly right in front of the car, and there was nothing Rodney could do. There was a ghastly thud, then another, and the windscreen exploded into frosted ice. The children screamed and the men in the front flinched as they were showered with rice and particles of broken glass. Rodney couldn't see to steer, and in his blindness lost all control of the car. It swerved across the road and into the grass on the other side. The five of them were thrown forward against their seat-belts as the car hit a ditch and ploughed through the long grass. It cut a swathe forty metres long and came to a halt. Rodney closed his eyes. He was sure something terrible had happened.

The men were in a state of shock, and the children were crying in fear and confusion. Only Sandra was at all composed. She comforted the children and checked that they and the men in the front were unhurt. Dennis Underwood, his body trembling, was the first out of the car, opening the door with difficulty against the wall of grass. Rodney, still half-stunned, struggled out of his own side. His hands too were shaking, as he helped his wife and children out and hugged them each in turn.

As always happens on a deserted road, people materialised from nowhere. There were shouts and cries, and people came running from the direction of the vocational school. First came the students, then local people, for there was a Koiari village in the bush somewhere behind the school. Passing cars were stopping, too.

Afterwards, Rodney could give no clear account of the sequence of events, or the intervals between them. By the time he had followed the corridor of flattened grass back to the road, a group had gathered on the opposite side around the boy. He made to cross over to them, but was held back by bystanders on his side of the road. The body had been thrown some distance, and the cry had gone up that the boy was dead. Rodney had known it all along.

A passing car had already left for the store to phone for the police and ambulance. Other motorists urged Rodney and his family into their own cars to drive them away. It was better to leave and go straight to the police. This wasn't the highlands, but it was risky to wait around. Nobody could tell what might happen. So Rodney organised his family into a car where there was room, and asked Underwood to go with them. He, himself insisted on staying.

There were perhaps forty or fifty people there now, but in two groups. Around the car collected a mixture of students and motorists – Nationals from various provinces – and a few expatriates too. They stood as outsiders, powerless and pitying. Few ventured near the second group gathered around the body on the other side of the road. They were local people, Koiaris. The group parted as a woman desperately pushed among them and let out a heart-rending wail. The others restrained her as she threw herself on the body in a frenzy of grief. It was harrowing. Rodney was crying himself.

Some of the villagers started to carry the body away, while others made for the car. The bystanders stood aside to let the Koiaris through and they laid into the Mazda. They took no interest in the presence of the driver, but visited their rage on the car alone. They kicked it and smashed all the windows and lights. They found sticks and beat at the bodywork. They made dents all over, the front and bonnet included, and by the time their fury was spent it was impossible to tell which damage had been done in the accident, and which by the crowd.

After some time an ambulance arrived, and the police later still, in a convoy of three vehicles. They stood around importantly for a time, while some of their number went down to the village. By then, the area around the Mazda was completely trampled underfoot, and it was difficult even to tell the course the car had taken through the grass. It was much the same on the other side of the road. It was anybody's guess now where the point of impact had been, and where the body had been thrown. No proper enquiry was made by the police, and no measurements were taken.

Rodney returned with the police to Boroko Police Station, and phoned Sandra from there to tell her he was all right. They had him sign a brief statement, and released him about midnight. By the time he reached home, Dennis had long departed for the Travelodge. Rodney only saw him once more before he returned to Australia.

Back at the house, Dennis had offered to stay with Sandra for as long as she wished, but once she knew her husband was safely at Boroko she had shown much presence of mind. She assured Underwood she could cope on her own, but insisted on their discussing the accident before he left for the hotel. Painful though it was, she was determined they go over it while it was still fresh in their minds. Her strength of character was impressive.

"I'm just not sure of anything," Underwood told her. "I know we had a few drinks before we left."

"You had a few, Dennis. Rodney only had one."

"I thought he had the same as me."

"No, he only had the one. You had three, remember? And anyway, you had a few beers on the plane, didn't you?"

"A couple."

"You might not have noticed, but I did. I always watch when Rodney's going to drive with me and the kids. I'm very strict about it. It was only the one, I'm certain of that. It wouldn't have affected him at all."

Then they tried to reconstruct the circumstances of the accident.

"To tell you the truth," admitted Dennis, "It's all just a blur. It happened so fast, and I was turning round to talk to you."

"Well, I was facing forward," said Sandra. "I was looking straight between the front seats. I saw it all. The people were on the road, right in our path. Rodney had no chance. I mean it's an awful thing, I'm a mother myself. I grieve for them, but it wasn't Rodney's fault. These things happen. They shouldn't have been walking on the road like that."

"I just remember driving in the grass."

"You mean on the other side of the road?"

"No, before that. When the windscreen broke, I looked to my left out of the side window, and I remember seeing the long grass brushing past."

"But that was after we'd hit the boy."

"Was it?"

"Of course, Dennis. It was after the windscreen broke, you said so yourself. Once we hit the boy, the car went into a skid. It went in to the left first and through the grass a bit. Then we swerved across the road and into the ditch on the opposite side."

"I just can't remember any of it clearly."

Dennis left the country on the Thursday morning without having made a statement to the police. Sandra made one a week or so later. She described exactly what had happened. She was clear and definite about the details, even their speed, which she put at around 55 kph. She was a driver herself, and good at estimating speed; that was how she could tell. She would have noticed if they had been going any faster. And she mentioned Dennis Underwood too, how he could confirm most of what she said. They could arrange to get a statement from him in Sydney, if the police wanted them to.

Rodney needed a lawyer. He knew several through the bank, but they were commercial lawyers and didn't deal with cases like this. It gave Rodney an excuse not to engage them. Somehow, he would have felt uncomfortable consulting people he knew. Like a man with an embarrassing illness who avoids the family doctor, he went to a lawyer he'd only heard of. Gaffney had a reputation for this sort of thing.

Rodney was hoping to be reassured, but Gaffney was guarded about his prospects and said he could do little until a charge was laid. There were two possibilities. One was a charge of negligent driving, which would mean a stiff fine at worst. The other was under the Criminal Code, a charge of dangerous driving. That carried a jail sentence – up to five years, with hard labour too. Gaffney suggested they negotiate with the police, and offer to plead guilty to the lesser charge. Their approaches came to nothing and Rodney had to endure the wait until the charge was laid. It was a full month before the police served the papers on him: he stood charged with dangerous driving causing death.

Gaffney explained the procedure. First, there would be a committal proceeding before a magistrate. This would decide whether there was sufficient evidence to commit Rodney for trial before the National Court. It was most unusual to mount a full defence at the committal stage. If the prosecution case was at all strong, it was best for the defence not to show its hand. However, Rodney's case was different. Gaffney recommended they go all out at the committal.

His reasoning was simple; the accused driver was an expatriate, the dead boy a National. The magistrates were mainly Nationals, while the judges were mainly expatriates. And the judges were only human. Expediency and appearances could sometimes play a part in a case like this. A National magistrate might let Rodney off, but an expatriate judge would find it much harder. It would hardly look impartial, a white man acquitting another white over the death of a black, and a little boy at that. Indeed, if Rodney were committed for trial, his chances would be poor.

"What you need," the lawyer summed up, "is a black magistrate with the brains to listen to the evidence, and the guts to act on it." It was a tall order.

Another two months passed before the committal was listed for hearing. The week before, Gaffney went out to view the scene. He met the Millers out there, and the three of them paced out the distances and inspected the view from different angles. In the intervening months, the appearance of the place had changed greatly. The dense, shoulder-high grass had withered and been burned off. The roadside now was covered with a rough black stubble through which new green shoots were on the point of emerging. It made it easy to see every contour of the verge, and to trace the meandering course of the footpath beside the road.

The path snaked through the burnt grass, mostly well clear of the road, but coming at its closest point to within a metre or so of the gravel shoulder. If the boy had ever been on the path, it must have been here that he left it and started to walk along the road itself. On Rodney's estimate, the point of impact had been just beyond this spot, with the dead boy positioned on the gravel. Sandra put the boy even further into the road: well onto the bitumen. They were agreed that it was the extreme left of the front of the car which had struck him. Among the extensive damage to the car, there were dents consistent with this.

The Millers and Gaffney walked up and down the road in the hot sun, trying to reconstruct the other details. It was difficult to say exactly where the car had ended up. There was no trace of the swathe it had cut through the grass; there was no longer any grass. There were no wheel ruts, clues of any kind. The Millers did their best to estimate.

They walked back in the direction of Port Moresby so that Gaffney could see the view of the road as the car came into the bend. He took notes and drew a sketch-plan in an exercise book. Crossing their path, a dirt driveway led to a gate in a wire fence some distance off the road. Visible beyond was a small run-down house, the closest building to the accident scene.

"What's that place?" asked Gaffney. He had never noticed it before, though he had driven up to Sogeri on this road many times, himself.

"It's a house. It belongs to an old bloke," said Rodney.

"What old bloke?"

"They call him old Mick, or Mad Mick."

"Did he see anything?"

"No," said Sandra firmly.

"How do you know? Have you spoken to him?"

"We've asked about him. They say he's long-long."

"A National?"

"An expat," answered Rodney. "He's an old bloke who was in the army here at the end of the war. I don't think he saw any action. He worked with the War Graves Commission, going round digging up bodies, sorting out the Australians from the Japs. They say it was the work that turned him a bit funny. He never even goes in to Moresby. He just sticks to himself. They all know him out this way."

The lawyer thought they should try speaking to the fellow, just in case he had seen anything. As they walked towards the gate, a couple of dogs – big ones – came rushing out from behind the house. Their savage barking stopped the three of them well short of the gate, and Sandra insisted they were wasting their time. She had made enquiries already. Old Mick was virtually a recluse, and indeed, though the dogs barked continuously, there was no sign of life from the house. Besides, Gaffney reflected, if they could find a witness at all it was a black one they needed, not a long-long white.

The committal hearing took place in the Port Moresby District Court. The magistrate was Mrs Damena. Gaffney said

195

they could have done worse. She would at least listen, and she might have the courage to do the right thing, despite the presence of the dead boy's relatives.

The windowless courtroom was lit by flickering fluorescent tubes. The PNG flag in the corner rustled gently from the blast of air from a too-powerful airconditioner, and Rodney shivered from nervousness and the cold. The procedure was painfully slow. Every question and answer was taken down by a National girl on an ancient manual typewriter. The case proceeded at the speed of her typing, and came to a complete halt at the end of each page, while the girl bravely did her best to reload the typewriter with six fresh pages and five sheets of carbon paper.

Gaffney was greatly encouraged by the start of the prosecution case. Apart from the doctor who certified death, the first witnesses were virtually irrelevant. The police were hopeless. They had made little enough enquiry into the accident, and their account even of that was completely garbled. After lunch, the dead boy's elder brother gave evidence. He had been first in line, with his back to the traffic. He heard the bang and ran away. That was as much as could say, and it took the entire afternoon to get it out of him. He was scared stiff.

The prosecution's case depended on the uncle. He was a dignified fellow, not really old, but he spoke with the deliberation and self-assurance of an elderly man. He gave evidence through an interpreter. That can often become a fiasco with the interpreter arguing with the witness and interpolating his own comments, and everyone generally at cross purposes. For once, it went smoothly, and the uncle gave his evidence well.

He said that all three of them had been walking along the path. They were in the grass, well off the road. The car came round the corner too fast. He heard it approaching. It left the road and hit Jacob in the grass.

Gaffney cross-examined him. Did he admit he was walking with his back to the traffic? Yes. And did he agree that it would have been much safer to have faced the on-coming traffic? Yes. Why then, were they walking on the left? The uncle waited until the typist had recorded the question, then gave his answer. Because there was no path on the other side of the road.

It was a better answer than Gaffney had expected. He tried to recover the lost ground. "Ah," he said, "But you weren't walking on the path!"

"Yes, we were," stated the uncle.

"You yourself were, perhaps. But where was Jacob walking when he was hit?"

"On the path, same as me."

Everything turned on the truth of that answer. Was the uncle speaking from knowledge or conjecture?

"Jacob was walking behind you, wasn't he?" asked Gaffney.

"Yes."

"Just before the accident, did you look back at him?"

"We left together from the store. I saw him then."

"But just before the accident, immediately before the accident, did you look back at him?"

"I did not."

"Then at the time of the accident, how do you know where Jacob was walking?"

"I know."

The lawyer looked meaningfully at the Magistrate. Mrs Damena did not lack intelligence. She surely understood that this was not direct evidence of the boy's position at the moment of the accident. It was inference only. And it would be contradicted by evidence from the Millers. Mrs Damena appeared to make a note.

"How can you assert that?"

"What?"

"You didn't see it. How can you say that?"

"I can say it."

"But you didn't see it."

No answer.

"You don't know where he was walking, do you?"

"I know."

"How do you know?"

"He followed me."

Gaffney left it at that. He hoped he had made his point.

It was now the turn of the defence. There was no obligation to call evidence, and it was an unusual course for a defendant at a committal. But it was the plan they had adopted. Both the Millers gave evidence, Rodney first, then Sandra.

Somehow, it did not go as well as they had hoped. Rodney seemed unsure of himself, and became rattled when he was cross-examined. Sandra was the opposite. She was precise, articulate and sure of herself, but too much so. The boy had simply stepped into their path, she said. She had an answer for everything, and under cross-examination she became more dogmatic. There was something unsatisfactory about her evidence, something unconvincing. Neither was as impressive as the uncle had been.

Mrs Damena invited submissions. The prosecution said nothing, but Gaffney had his submission prepared. Dangerous driving, he argued, required a very high degree of blame, and the position of the boy on the road was all important. No tribunal could be sure on these depositions that the car had left the bitumen. Far from it. On the other hand, it was open for the court to make a finding of careless driving. In Papua New Guinea there is always the chance of encountering careless pedestrians on the road. His client perhaps had failed to guard against that possibility. He asked Mrs Damena to dismiss the charge under the Criminal Code.

But Mrs Damena would not take the bait. She didn't have to decide whether Miller was guilty of dangerous driving causing death, but merely whether there was enough evidence to send him for trial. The position of the boy was crucial, and there was a conflict. On one side there was eyewitness evidence and on the other there was inference. But it was not for her to choose between the two. That choice could be made elsewhere. Accordingly, Rodney Miller was committed for trial at the National Court.

Gaffney took the result worse than his client. The Millers still hoped for luck at the National Court, but privately the lawyer was gloomy. His strategy had failed. He half blamed himself and wondered whether he had handled it wrongly. A life had been lost and an expat judge would feel obliged to convict. Things looked very bad for Miller.

The next day, Gaffney drove out to the scene alone. He wondered whether he had overlooked something, some clue that was the key to it all. He walked along the path which snaked through the short grass like the untidy parting on a head of hair. There were so few landmarks, and the place looked different even from the time he had inspected it with the Millers. He tried to locate again the places they had pointed out. The point of impact. The skid. The car's course across the road, and where it came to rest. He found where the path came closest to the road and stood there, lost in thought.

Suddenly, he became aware of somebody's presence. He looked up and saw an elderly expat man, arms folded and standing only six or seven metres away. Two big dogs sniffed around at a distance. So this was Old Mick. Mad Mick.

The fellow had a leathery, intelligent face. He wore loose faded shorts and boots without socks. He had a trade-store shirt. His hands were blotched where years of sun had migrated the melanin into brown patches. They were an old man's hands, but his arms were strong. The fellow looked tough still, and far from mad.

The lawyer nodded to him, and Mick spoke.

"That's where it happened, just where you're standing."

"What?"

"The little kid, where he was killed. That's what you're looking for, isn't it?"

"Yes," agreed the lawyer.

"Thought so. I seen you the day you came with the driver and his missus. They've come a couple of times. They all come, the police, the road people, some-one from the insurance."

"What have you told them?"

"Nothing. You're the first bloke I've spoken to. And I wouldn't be talking to you either, except that I come out to find my dogs."

Gaffney looked down. His feet stood on the path, a full metre from the gravel shoulder of the road.

"You say this is where the accident happened?"

"Right there, mate. Right where you're standing."

"Here on the path?"

"Right there," said Mick, with irritation and emphasis. "The car took the corner wide and come into the grass along here." He indicated its course with a sweeping slash of his spotted arm.

"He's not the first to come into the grass. A lot of them do. The bend's sharper than it looks."

"Where were you when it happened?"

"Me? I was down at my place. I come out a few minutes later when I heard the commotion. I just watched from my gate there for a minute, then I went back. I didn't want to get mixed up in it. There was enough of them there already."

"So you didn't see it happen?"

"Course not. I told you I was in the house. I heard it. Then I come out."

"So how do you know where it happened?"

"I could see."

"But how?"

"The rice, mate. The little kid was carrying a sack of rice. Didn't they tell you that? The car hit him right where you're standing and the rice burst out all over there," and he made another sweeping gesture with his hand in a direction down and away from the road.

"But the car was moving at speed. Surely the force would throw the rice well clear of the boy's position?"

"Don't you believe it. It was the corner of the bumper bar that got him, wasn't it?"

"Was it?" answered Gaffney without thinking.

"Don't you know anything about it? Listen, mate," Mick continued, pointing towards the road this time, "this other way, there was no rice, nothing. It all started here in the grass. This is where that little kid copped it."

Gaffney took a deep breath. "Did you tell the police this?"

"I never spoke to them."

"Did you tell anyone about it?"

"No-one, mate."

"Why not?"

"No-one ever asked me," he answered, shrugging. Then he corrected himself with an afterthought. "Except for the bloke's missus. She asked me, but I was forgetting her."

Entertaining Mary

Jamie had picked up a pamuk, and now he wished he hadn't.

It wasn't even as if he'd really been on the prowl; he'd only gone out for milk, when he noticed her at the corner of Chinsu-rah Street, near the shops. She just about flagged him down, so he stopped to give her the once over and she wouldn't take no for an answer. It was Saturday afternoon and there were plenty of people around. Jamie didn't want to attract attention to himself by blocking the road, so he leaned over and released the door lock.

She was a big girl and you wouldn't have thought she could move that quick. But in she jumped, pleased as a puppy. She was a Highlander with a face like a boxer, and tattoos into the bargain. They were horizontal lines, three on each side of her face, and when she grinned they looked like a cat's whiskers.

Worst of all, she was on the nose. She smelt pretty badly from a distance, and when she got in, it just about knocked you down. At first, Jamie thought of driving round the block and kicking her out. But she didn't understand English, or pretended not to, and twice when he stopped and leaned across to open her door she refused to budge. He should never have let her get in.

She prattled away in Pidgin, as fast and staccato as a machine-gun. It was impossible to make head or tail of it. Jamie only knew a few words of Pidgin. He could understand it a bit, but not at this speed.

Naturally, her name was Mary, and she was in no doubt as to what she was in the car for. They were hardly on their way before she reached across and grabbed at his groin, kneading it roughly like bread till she felt him stiffen. With a cheerful leer, she giggled and chattered, something about master do this and do that, obscene probably. In a way, Jamie was half in the mood, and the girl seemed so determined that he thought the best thing was to take her home, make it short and sweet and then get rid of her.

He lived right at the top of Goro-be Street. He had a terrific view, but the access rather lacked privacy. Tracks led off the road to a series of squatter settlements extending through the hills all the way into the back of Murray Barracks. Goro-be Street was always alive with Nationals carting firewood, beer, fishing nets, vegetables; trudging up to their makeshift homes in the folds of the hills. And the kids! Scores of them, and cheeky buggers too. The expats who lived in the street were used to it, but few other Europeans were game to drive up. They had no reason to, anyway. It's a dead-end road.

Beneath the canopy of huge raintrees, Jamie's car snaked slowly up the hill. As usual, there were easily thirty or forty pedestrians ahead. Most walked in the middle of the road, not giving a thought that a car might approach from behind. Others, emerging from the tracks on the high side of the road, took a keen interest as the car neared them. Jamie was far from eager to be seen in present company, but Mary was proud as Punch. She rested her beefy arm on the open window, eyeing down the pedestrians and occasionally yelling out some remark or other.

She was showing off. She was in the master's car, going to the master's house: and soon to be screwed there by him. This was probably the gist of her random shouts to passers-by. Jamie winced and counted the corners till they got home. He had no success in shutting her up.

That useless garden-boy, Samson, was under strict orders to keep the gates closed at all times, but of course they were wide open again. For once it was for the good; Jamie didn't have to get out and fiddle with the lock, while curious onlookers scrutinised his companion. He drove straight in and marched Mary into the house.

As soon as she was inside, she started making herself at home, poking into cupboards and peeping into all the rooms. She walked through the lounge and opened the glass doors onto the verandah. Jamie peevishly ordered her back in case the neighbours in the house below were looking. Or their domestics.

He caught another whiff of her B.O. It was really bad. A decent shower was what she needed first of all. The girl was quite short, but solid as a rock: she must have weighed more than he did. He grabbed her to steer her into the bathroom, but she took the gesture as love-play and went into a clinch, rubbing herself against the front of him.

"Not yet Mary, for Chrissake. Wash-wash."

He disentangled himself and shoved the bathroom door open. He grabbed a towel and tossed it to her. She answered with a fusillade of Pidgin and wrapped the towel around her middle. All Jamie could make of her talk was, "Sexy man too much." He couldn't get her near the water and he gave up trying. He was more intent on getting the performance over with, and whizzing her off as soon as he could, with a ten kina note.

She had found her way into the bedroom and was busy untying her laplap underneath the wrapped towel. Her pants dropped to the ground and Jamie could scarcely bear to look at them, such was their condition. She undid the towel and laid it on the bed.

The smell was dreadful and Jamie thought of his sheets. Fully clothed, Mary looked solid. Now, with her abdomen bare, she verged on the obese. That huge protruding belly merged with two massive thighs and overshadowed the small black triangle of steel wool. She pulled up her nylon top and let free two large breasts whose appearance was more presentable than expected.

Jamie was half undressed himself. It was not desire, or passion; he was merely resigned to do what was expected of him and so be rid of this malodorous but strangely cheerful girl. He worried too, that she would grab him again and further contaminate his clothes. Sheets and a towel were quite enough, and the wash-boy wouldn't be in till Tuesday.

She bent her legs and opened them wide, pulling Jamie between them. He was half attracted, half repelled, but after all that's often the way. Suddenly, he remembered and reached to the bedside table. Mary watched, irritated but curious, as Jamie fumbled for a condom.

He pulled out a line of them in their flat sealed packets and tore one off. Mary snatched the packet from him and turned it over in her hands.

"Me no like."

"It's a condom, Mary." He picked up the plain paper envelope in which they came modestly packaged, and found the instructions in Pidgin.

"Lookim you. All 'e call 'im gumi." And he tried to read the instructions out to her. He opened the instruction sheet and she squinted at the line picture. It showed a hand pulling a condom over a cylindrical object the size of a log. She shook her head sharply.

"Me no like," she repeated more aggressively and tossed the packet towards the door.

"Too bad," said Jamie tearing the next packet off the line. With his teeth, he ripped it open and unrolled the condom onto himself. Mary nodded in partial comprehension.

Then she reached out and took his penis in her hand and guided it inside her. She was content now, and wrapped her powerful mountain-climbing thighs around him. The large splayed-out feet with soles as tough as crocodile hide were interlocked at the small of his back, and she squeezed.

She rocked him back and forward and the movement was all hers. She bit at his bottom lip and babbled in Pidgin. She paused and looked directly into Jamie's eyes to deliver her most intimate confidence: "Me like European fuck. European fuck good. Native fuck no good," and she had her moment of release. Jamie groaned inwardly and gasped for fresh air.

When it was over for him too, Jamie withdrew and became aware of footsteps in the house. He gave a start, and heard Philip's voice calling to him.

He knew at once who it was, but playing for time, he yelled out, "Who is it?"

"It's me. What are you doing?" answered Philip.

They were the best of mates.

"Why didn't you blow your horn? How'd you get in?"

"The gates were open."

"That bloody Samson," Jamie shouted. "Give us a moment will you, I'm just having a shower." Then, sternly to Mary he said, "Just stay here. Don't move." At all costs he had to keep her out of the way. If Philip caught sight of her, he would never live it down.

The door at the end of the hallway was open and, checking that Phil was not looking his way, Jamie scampered across to the bathroom, unpeeling the condom as he went. He flung it into the toilet, pressed the flush and quickly got under the shower.

He was out again in a flash and could hear Phil prowling about in the kitchen and lounge. He was calling out at intervals, "Step on it mate. What are you doing? Have you got a beer?" and so on.

Jamie ran to the bedroom and grabbed his clothes from the floor. "Get your clothes on," he gestured to Mary, who was in no hurry at all. Any moment, Phil might be wandering up the hallway, poking his nose in.

As Jamie slipped on his thongs, he became aware of the smell on his own clothes. Mary's smell. He slipped back to the bathroom and splashed aftershave on his shirt and shorts. Then he sauntered down to the kitchen, with a pretence of being at ease.

Phil had helped himself to a beer. He instantly noticed Jamie's edgy manner.

"What are you up to? Come on, you're up to something."

"What are you talking about?" answered Jamie feebly.

"Fuck me, what's that stink?"

"I can't smell anything."

Philip leaned towards his friend, screwing up his nose and sniffing at him like a dog.

Jamie was trying to back away. "It must be my aftershave," he volunteered unconvincingly.

"No, something else too. Ugh, it's bloody horrible." Then he twigged. "There's a sheila in there isn't there?" he asked and Jamie's reaction left him in no doubt that he was right. "Come on, let's see her."

"Mind your own business. Piss off," muttered Jamie as Phil jostled with him, advancing towards the hallway.

"Come on. Out with her. Introduce us. Where's your manners?"

"No, no, she's very shy. Leave us alone, you bastard."

"Shy to be seen with you. I don't blame her," said Phil, who was enjoying himself greatly.

At that moment and without warning, the bedroom door opened and Mary stepped out, the towel around her, thank goodness.

The effect on Phil was dramatic. His eyebrows shot up. "Bloody hell. What's this?"

"This is Mary," said Jamie, mortified.

"Hel-lo Mary," said Phil, and Mary, unabashed, greeted him in Pidgin.

Jamie somehow managed to herd his friend back to the kitchen, the latter muttering and exclaiming all the way. He was beside himself with laughter and incredulity.

"Jesus wept. I don't believe it. James, I tell you this is your worst ever, your absolute worst." Jamie couldn't silence him. "But where did you get her? Wait till everyone hears about this!"

"Fair go, Phil."

But Phil was deaf to him. "Give us a camera, give us a camera. I need evidence, they just won't believe it."

By now Mary had joined them in the kitchen and peremptorily demanded beer. Jamie grabbed her a stubby. Phil traded Pidgin ribaldries with her: "Em 'e strong too much, eh? Number one kokoruk," and so on, while Mary grinningly agreed.

Every now and then Phil would mutter an aside; "But couldn't you give her a hose down first? She stinks. I mean, how could you do it?"

It so happened that Phil and Jamie were both facing the kitchen window. They had a view of the drive and noticed the car at the same time. It drove in through the open gates and stopped behind Phil's car. A couple of Nationals stood at the gates too, watching.

"Here's trouble" said Phil with glee. "Anyone you know?"

Mary joined them at the window and they all three peered out, but Jamie didn't recognise the car at all. He had never seen it before in his life. And for a moment, he didn't recognise the occupants either, even when they got out, locking the doors all round. Then it dawned on him. He went almost faint with panic.

"No, no. Oh shit". He moaned with such feeling and vehemence that even Phil was taken aback. "You've got to help me, Phil, you've got to. It's my cousin, my bloody cousin."

"I didn't know you had a cousin."

Jamie gestured frantically at Mary. "Just keep her out of the way. Just stay put. Whatever you do, don't let her out. I'll get rid of them," he said of the three pale figures, man, woman and child who were now making their way down the stone steps towards the house.

"What am I meant to do with her?" asked Philip.

"I don't care, I don't care." Jamie was beside himself. "Do what you like, entertain her."

Phil and the girl let themselves be pushed towards the bedroom, and as he passed the fridge, Phil deftly opened it and grabbed a couple more stubbies. Jamie was at the front door now, intercepting the visitors just as they knocked.

"Morris, Shirley, lovely to see you again. I meant to call you." And he wished he had.

His cousin Morris, overweight, blotchy face and a bit of a dill, had arrived the weekend before on a one-year stint for some church or other. Jamie had done the right thing by the family and welcomed them at the airport. He had promised to ring them at their billet. Morris was a printer by trade and had been tolerable enough until he'd got bitten by religion after he married.

The wife Shirley was ghastly, an out-and-out Bible-basher with the thin face of a ferret, straightlaced and spiteful. It was just like her to turn up unannounced to take him by surprise. She was sure to be busting to report back to her mother-in-law that afternoon, knowing that within minutes it would all be passed on to Jamie's mum.

The day Jamie had met them at the airport, the church people had turned up too, falling over each other to take the newcomers home to tea. The preacher was putting them up until their flat was ready.

"Yes," said Shirley, "We only picked up the car this morning and were just driving around, when we noticed your street by chance. Goro-be Street, such an unusual name."

"You should have given me a ring first. I'm actually a bit tied up at present."

But they stood at the front door expectantly, and Shirley pointedly reminded him, as if it was some big deal, how they had brought a small parcel for him from his parents. "Did everything in the parcel arrive safely, James?" she asked. "We never let it out of our sight."

"Yes thank you, Shirley." And he felt obliged to ask them in.

"Just for a moment," said Shirley. "We'd love to see the view from your verandah. Your mother showed us the photos before we left."

Jamie reluctantly ushered them into the lounge.

"Hope we're not interrupting anything Jamie," said cousin Morris. "We're only here by chance."

Jamie would have bet quids that they had been driving in circles for hours to find the street and ambush him like this.

"Yes, we had to drive to the top," said Shirley, "because there was nowhere to turn round. On the way down we noticed your car in the drive. Belinda saw it first. She's so observant, she recognised it from the day at the airport. Those dents on the passenger's side."

Belinda was about ten or eleven and the spitting image of her mother, but skinnier and with glasses. Her character was the same: nosy, malicious and smug. No wonder Morris looked more grey and flabby every time you saw him, living with those two.

"Yes, we almost didn't stop when we met those natives at your front gate. They were really quite, well, menacing. Not at all like the lovely natives, I mean Nationals, we've met through the church."

"Jamie, you're sure we're not intruding?" asked Morris again. "You're not busy with anyone else?"

Jamie acted all innocent. He would die if they caught sight of Mary. "No I was just going out, actually. I'm on my own."

"Because there is that other car there, the blue one."

Jamie's mind went blank just for a moment. He realised he had made a silly mistake. Why had he said he was alone? He tried to make good his error.

"I don't mean all alone. The blue car belongs to a mate, but he's in the other room."

Just then, Shirley and the daughter came in from the verandah, where they had been admiring the view. With exaggerated delicacy Shirley asked whether Belinda could use the loo. Without thinking – and he could scarcely have refused – Jamie directed her up the passage to the bathroom.

Small-talk had scarcely resumed when Belinda sidled back into the room with an aggrieved air. "I don't like the black lady, Mummy. She looks like a tiger, and she growled at me." The girl looked around the room to see the effect she had made. "She frightened me."

"Whatever do you mean, darling?" asked Shirley, putting her arms around her. But Jamie was up the passage before the observant darling could add another incriminating detail.

He burst into the bathroom to find Phil standing sheepishly, while Mary emerged dripping and grinning from under the shower. "Get her out of here," Jamie screamed, in a whispered shout.

"It was hard work getting her in. She doesn't like water."

"Get her out!"

"You said to do whatever..."

"Out. Out. Out."

"Well, she did stink. I thought I'd done you a favour."

Jamie shoved the two of them, Mary dripping, into the room opposite and snapped the door shut with a forceful click.

He tried to compose himself, and returned to the lounge. Belinda was still in the maternal embrace and well aware of the mischief she was creating.

"Terribly sorry, Belinda, the bathroom's free for you now," he muttered with a forced smile, as if it hardly warranted explanation to have found a tattooed pamuk leering at the dunny door.

"I say, is everything quite all right?" asked Morris, looking a bit grim now. "I mean, what's going on here?"

209

"Just a lady, that's all."

"I thought you said a mate," snapped Shirley.

"Yes my mate. And my mate's friend. It's really none of your business."

Shirley exchanged glances with her husband, and Jamie regretted the last remark. The knives would be out now. He should have just humoured them. It was starting to turn nasty.

Playing for time, Jamie ignored the parents and addressed himself to Belinda. "Come on, dear. I'll show you the way."

"I don't feel like going now, Mummy," said Belinda, but Jamie was firmly ushering her in the manner of a thoughtful host. "This way, Belinda," he smiled, and the girl allowed herself to be led reluctantly to the bathroom door.

The girl stepped over the drips and puddles on the floor and entered the toilet. She closed the door behind her and Jamie heard the flush.

He returned to the lounge where the parents had obviously been exchanging words. Shirley assumed her classic do-gooder expression and said, "Your mother did ask us to keep an eye on you, and I think she'd be rather disappointed if she could see you now."

Jamie wished he could tell her to get stuffed, but he lacked the courage. Instead he said: "Whatever do you mean?"

"Well, James," began cousin Morris, "you did say a mate and that wasn't true. And where native girls are concerned..."

"Just a minute," interrupted Jamie. "My mate has been..."

But he was himself interrupted by Belinda, sneaking back into the room and heading straight to her mother again. "Mummy I don't want to go any more. There's something nasty in the toilet." She watched to see the effect on Jamie, and it must have been everything she hoped for.

"It's a spider," he yelled, springing to his feet.

"It's not a spider," whined Belinda. "It's like a horrid jelly-fish. I pressed the flush three times, but it won't go away."

Jamie shot into the toilet and reached into the toilet bowl. With his thumb and forefinger he gingerly snared the condom by the tip and flung it into the corner of the room. It was sheer luck, but his aim was good; the jellyfish hit the wall a few inches above the floor, then subsided out of sight behind the plastic toilet brush.

Just as well, because Morris was behind him now, muttering aggressively, "What the devil's going on?" No doubt Shirley had ordered him down to make trouble.

"It's all right," answered Jamie, "I've got rid of it. Everything's under control."

"Just what's going on?"

"I've killed it, I tell you."

Morris's eyes were darting about. "How could..?"

"With my bare hands," insisted Jamie, waving them claw-like in the air.

Then a tattooed face peered round the corner. Mary was irked by her confinement and had heard the commotion. Morris was taken aback. "Oh, my goodness," he said.

Phil was on her tail whispering, "I couldn't stop her. She's out of control."

Jamie was triumphant. He pointed to Phil. "See, there's my mate."

Morris was gesturing at the bedroom door and stammering in consternation.

"Excuse me, Morris," declared Jamie in mock outrage. "They *are* engaged. This is Phil and his lovely bride-to-be".

It was hard to know whether Phil or Morris was the more aghast at this remark. At any rate, it was enough to send Morris back to the lounge to rescue his wife and offspring. As they made ready to flee, the parents whispered to each other for Jamie's benefit: "fornication," "disgusting," "his poor mother," and so on.

They were on their way out now, and Jamie followed up their retreat with sarcastic yells of, "What about a cuppa! Do come again!" To hell with the bastards, he thought.

He looked at Mary, who was also slightly taken aback by the turn of events. He offered her another beer. Pissed or sober, smelly or scented, she was a bloody sight better person than any of that three.

Phil was shaking his head with a wry grin; "Jeez, you get yourself into some strife."

But it was not over yet. Morris's car had come to a halt at the end of the driveway. There was a crowd of Nationals obstructing its exit. You could hear the hollow sound as they banged the bodywork with their open palms, and the younger kids were clambering onto the bonnet to prevent the car leaving.

"Wantok belong me," said Mary, and she headed for the door.

"You go with her," yelled Jamie, "I wouldn't trust myself with my bloody relations."

So Phil joined Mary and the crowd around Morris's car. There was a lot of shouting and carry-on. The ringleader was acting tough and aggrieved, the way they do when they want something out of you. It was the usual routine: Mary was their cousin sister – they demanded compensation.

Mary was giving them hell, telling them to clear off, and if it wasn't for the car trying to reverse through them, she and Phil could have got rid of the mob relatively easily. But Morris and family were newcomers; they didn't know how to handle the situation at all. They had wound all the windows up, and they looked pretty scared.

Phil figured he'd kill two birds with one stone. He walked around to the driver's side and tapped on the window. Morris wound it down an inch.

"There's going to be trouble here, mate. You'd better give them twenty kina," he said solemnly to Morris.

"Whatever do you mean?" came a woman's voice from within.

"They heard what you were saying. They're her relatives, you know. You've insulted them."

Morris was white with fear. "We never said a thing about your fiancee, sir. We do apologise. It's all my cousin's fault."

Phil ignored the olive branch. "You can't talk about people that way here, mate. Pay up quick." He gestured with his hand to quieten the wantoks down, but nobody could shut Mary up.

A twenty kina note was poked through the top of the window, and Phil took it and waved the car back. It reversed out onto the road. Phil handed the money to the ringleader and gestured contemptuously at Morris. He slapped the roof with his hand. "Get going," he shouted, and the car drove away.

Mary continued to lambast her relatives. They too, were now keen to leave, for Mary was laying claim to the twenty kina on her own account. Phil called her off, and pulled the security gates closed. The two of them returned to the house.

Jamie opened three stubbies and they sat together on the verandah. Mary didn't smell so bad now.

"They just won't believe all this when I tell them," said Phil.

"If I were you, I wouldn't be telling anyone," commented Jamie.

"Oh yeah, and why's that?"

"Because," answered Jamie jubilantly, "as cousin Morris and I are well aware, you are engaged to young Mary here, and have just spent a romantic half-hour alone with her in my bedroom. The reason for that, as I shall let it be known, is that you weren't game to entertain her at your own place."

Phil tried to protest, but Jamie exploited his advantage. "And furthermore, since your car is blocking the driveway, I think you'd better drive her home as soon as you've finished that beer. I've decided I should write a letter to my mum."

Jisala Mission

I

By reason of its altitude, the valley enjoys a wonderful climate, almost a perpetual springtime. The days are warm and sunny, the nights cold, but rarely frosty. The seasons vary little over the course of the year. The rains are reliable and floods and droughts infrequent. The soil is fertile, and the valley produces an abundance of crops: taro, sweet potatoes, yams, bananas, carrots, tomatoes, pumpkin. On the slopes of the surrounding mountains there is timber and game for the taking.

From the air, there is a splendid view of the Meru Valley as the aircraft banks to make its approach to Balamoi airstrip, on the southern side of the range. The green valley, dotted with native gardens, nestles in the enclosing mountains, while on the far side, the eye is drawn to the cluster of buildings which form the mission. As the aircraft turns and descends, the valley disappears from sight; and later, from the airstrip, one sees to the north only the rugged barrier range, with no hint of the Meru valley beyond.

From the Government station at Balamoi airstrip, it is as if the valley does not exist. That is part of its charm, that it is remote, secluded – a world of its own. Thus did it appear to the Reverend Stanley Cox, that day in 1976 when he first glimpsed it from the aircraft window, and sensed with a flash of certainty that this was the very place for which he had been searching.

Even then, in 1976, access over the range from the airstrip was scarcely more than a track. Originally a bridle path, it was impassable except on foot or by motorcycle. The Reverend Dodds, who was at that time the sole European at the mission, did own a motorbike, but he had long ceased to ride it. After two nasty falls he had lost his confidence and at 58, he felt it was beyond him now.

For practical purposes, the mission would have been much better located on the southern side of the range. The problems of access and communication would have been much less, and the mission could have served the much larger population on the Balamoi side. But during the sixties, the Catholics, long established on the coast, were extending their territory inland and were quietly lobbying the administration to exclude newcomers. The best therefore that the Gospel Baptists could obtain was a lease in the valley; and Dodds, who was there almost from the mission's inception, had stuck it out tenaciously for almost twelve years. During that time, and in spite of all difficulties, Dodds had grown to love the valley and its people.

On that first visit, Stanley and Margot Cox had been returning to Australia from a sabbatical study tour of Europe and the Holy Land. It was their last stop on the way home. Since childhood, Stanley had wanted to visit New Guinea. Unconsciously, he now pinned his hopes on it. The thought of his return to Melbourne left him downcast; he felt stifled and obstructed there. He had confided to his wife that if he found a favourable prospect in New Guinea, he would arrange to stay. She had agreed at once.

The Coxes were running short of both time and money when they reached Port Moresby. So the location of the mission was ideal; only twenty minutes' flying time by the twice-weekly Cessna. Meru Valley Mission at that time received few visitors despite its proximity to the capital. Nobody could have called the mission a showpiece, but it was probably the lack of vehicle access that discouraged most visitors. Few in those days relished a gruelling trek over the Meru Gap, even with the mission boys to carry their bags. Sadly, among Christians too, there were many faint of heart.

Perhaps the valley's inhabitants also served to deter visitors. It must be admitted that their appearance is unattractive to European eyes. Their heavy browbridges and deep-set eyes impart a scowling, hostile expression to their faces. Furthermore, outsiders tend to confuse the Meru with the Tauade people beyond, who are notorious killers. The Meru's ill-repute is mainly undeserved, for they are not especially violent. In fact, even compared to the coastal people they are relatively civilised, and with more initiative of course. Stanley was aware of all this. In readiness for his visit, he had read the brief entry on the Meru in his encyclopedia.

The Coxes were met at the airstrip by some well-spoken boys from the mission, who took their suitcases and led the way. After two hours of strenuous climbing, the party reached the pass and were there rewarded with another spectacular view of the valley. Stanley and Margot found the descent from the pass even harder going than the climb. Their knees trembled from the unaccustomed exertion. The terrain took them by surprise; it was tougher than they had ever imagined. They had difficulty keeping up with the boys, and paused frequently to recover their breath, and also to take in each successive view. At every turn they were vouchsafed another glimpse of the mission buildings with their sheltering trees, and of the native gardens beyond.

At last they reached the valley floor, and saw approaching in the distance a grey-haired, slightly stooping figure escorted by a horde of black children. This was the Reverend Dodds, who walked the last kilometre to greet them, apologising that he had not come to meet them at the airstrip. There was a sense of occasion about the scene. In his exhilaration, Stanley felt almost as if it were Dr Livingstone whom he was meeting in this wild and exotic place. It was not, he felt sure, mere chance which had brought him here. The Lord had called him; and it was the Lord's work which he would carry out in this remote and beautiful valley.

Together they covered the final lap to the mission, Dodds leading and Stanley, with renewed energy, close behind. Though the track was wider, its unevenness and the crowd of natives prevented the two men from walking abreast. Conversation was impossible until the whole party reached the mission compound and came to a halt in a large open space between the buildings. There, Dodds lined up the children outside the ramshackle mission school for an official welcome.

In spite of the excitement of the occasion, Stanley observed that the mission buildings were less impressive close-up than they had appeared from the air. The children were agreeably polite, but they wore the sullen look of which the encyclopedia had warned. The adults milled around in noisy disorder behind the ranks of the children. They were as excited and inquisitive as the youngsters, and beyond the curiosity in their eyes, the Reverend Stanley Cox perceived clearly their thirst for the gospel message of salvation.

Stanley and Margot could spare only three days with the ageing Dodds, who did his best to be hospitable and make them comfortable. Naturally, they uttered no word of complaint, but secretly Stanley was unimpressed with how little had been achieved by Dodds over the previous decade. The place lacked even basic amenities. At night, Dodds depended on pressure lamps for lighting. The small generator appeared to have been out of service for years. The home-made plumbing was ingenious, but unhygienic. Almost all the buildings were of bush materials, for there was scarcely a sawn plank in the whole place, and only the medical dispensary had an iron roof. Even the church itself looked like a glorified native hut. Picturesque it's true, but hardly a proper monument to the glory of God.

Carefully avoiding any hint of disapproval, Stanley asked Dodds why the church was not properly roofed.

"Our support has dwindled over the years, I'm sorry to say," explained Dodds. "Everything has to be paid for, and it all has to be carried by hand from the airstrip. We have to make do with what we can afford."

"Of course, but why is the dispensary roofed and not the church?"

"Well, you understand, the church is full on only one day of the week, while the dispensary is used every day."

Stanley was taken aback at the answer. It showed an unexpected attitude on Dodds' part. A doctor might look at things in that way, but surely not a missionary. Public health was very important of course, but it was the government's responsibility. To the mission, medical work was entirely incidental. The mission existed for one purpose: the saving of souls. That would be Stanley's firm policy if he were in Dodds' place.

Though they noticed inadequacies and lost opportunities wherever they looked on the mission, the Coxes found the valley itself enchanting. Stanley was filled with enthusiasm for the task ahead. Their last full day in the valley was a Sunday, and the hillsides resounded to the mission bell, actually an empty gas cylinder hanging from a tree and beaten with a stick by one of the boys. It seemed that the entire population turned out for the service. In many ways the Meru were more fervent Christians than people back in Australia.

The church was filled to overflowing, the congregation sitting cross-legged on the earthen floor. The elders of the church looked a picture, solemn and dignified in their white laplaps, and some even in white shirts and ties. The singing was an inspiration, and Margot, the more musical of the two of them, thrilled to the strident voices, the strange words and the rich harmonies which transformed the familiar hymns into something entirely new.

With great formality, the Reverend Stanley Cox was invited to take the pulpit. The congregation was attentive and respectful. Not all of them understood English of course, but with the aid of the Holy Spirit, even a tone of voice can convey an eloquent message. Stanley delivered a powerful sermon, and the Meru responded with all their heart. Did they accept the Lord Jesus as personal sin-bearer, confident of salvation through the unmerited favour of God through faith alone? They did. To Margot it was an unforgettable scene. She wished she had a movie camera.

The following day the Coxes left in good time for the afternoon flight. By then it had been agreed that they would return as soon as possible to join Dodds in the valley. On each side there were slight misgivings. Stanley worried whether Dodds was doctrinally sound. Dodds, for his part found Stanley humourless and inflexible, and Margot insipid. Still, she was pleasant enough and unlike her husband, she at least showed some rapport with the Meru people.

Whatever Dodds' reservations, the fact remained that he had worked alone for the past three years. He felt himself neglected and forgotten by the subscribers in Australia. He was tired and going stale, and he ran the mission on an absolute shoestring. Stanley had promised him the finance to support himself and Margot, and to develop the mission too. It was an offer Dodds could not refuse. He knew that nothing better would turn up.

Back in Australia, the Coxes set to work to acquire the pledges of financial support they needed. They did the rounds of the local churches with their colour slides and projector. Stanley's colleagues gave wholehearted support. In the past, his strong personality had sometimes given rise to discord within the church community, so now there was enthusiasm for his missionary aspirations. The Meru valley was a satisfactorily long way from Melbourne.

By the time the Coxes had returned to the Meru valley, a new house had been built for them. Though it was of bush materials, it was well constructed, with walls and floor of woven pit-pit cane and a skilfully thatched roof. The surrounding garden was already planted with a hedge of crotons, their variegated leaves a pretty blend of red, yellow and green. The colour photos came out perfectly, of Stanley and Margot standing in front of the house, Stanley holding his Bible in folded hands, and Margot beside him. Several of the more photogenic black kiddies sat admiringly at their feet. It was a shame the pictures had to be printed in black and white for the fundraising brochures.

Of course, it was inevitable that upon returning to the valley, Stanley and Margot would take some time to adjust to their new surroundings and way of life. Stanley knew he would encounter obstacles which he had failed to anticipate on his first, brief inspection months before. The first was something that he had entirely overlooked: he proved to have no aptitude for languages. Though he tried conscientiously for some weeks, he made scarcely any progress, and indeed never succeeded in learning anything of the local language, and hardly more than a few words of Hiri Motu or even Pidgin. At first this threatened to limit the effectiveness of his preaching.

Dodds was a very good linguist and spoke both dialects of the local language well. However, he gave Stanley no encouragement and little help. He was at first impatient, then almost contemptuous of Stanley's efforts. His attitude was so off-putting that very soon Stanley ceased to turn to him for assistance. It was difficult not to take offence at the way Dodds flaunted his fluency in the native tongues. Certainly, it was distasteful to hear him exchanging jests with the natives, provoking peals of irreverent laughter.

After expending so much effort on the study of the Meru language for so little reward, Stanley devoted serious prayer to the matter. He questioned too, whether Dodds' fluency really availed in bringing sinners to Christ. Perhaps what God intended for himself was to work through the native catechists and the deacons, all of whom had a smattering of English. This, Stanley began to do, relying on them to pass on his words in their own language; and it worked very well. In time, Stanley concluded that this was indeed God's plan, and that he and Margot should therefore devote themselves to building up the mission in a material sense. Improvement of the physical facilities was clearly essential to carrying out the real work of the mission.

The second problem was the greater, and the more unexpected; it was Dodds himself. Within weeks of the Coxes' arrival, the fellow became moody and unco-operative. He was resistant to change, and where local knowledge was concerned, a know-all. He was indulgent with the natives, but autocratic and argumentative with Stanley. His resentment of Stanley's presence was undisguised.

He was also very possessive about the mission. Stanley had half-expected that: Dodds had seemed the bossy type. But it created an unnecessarily difficult situation, and called for much patience and restraint on the Coxes' part. They went to great lengths to avoid ruffling the old man's feathers. At least, they did to begin with.

In time however, Dodds began to prove quite impossible. He was incapable of accepting honest criticism in the spirit in which it was offered. For every shortcoming Stanley pointed out, Dodds would offer an excuse. Instead of welcoming new ideas to develop the mission, Dodds raised objections and created difficulties. There was always a reason why something could not be done, or would not work, or could not be afforded. It was extraordinary. He objected even to the first, indispensable step upon which all future progress in the valley depended: putting through a proper road to the airstrip.

His attitude went beyond officiousness, or a wish to preserve his solitude. There seemed to be a deeper reason for it which Stanley could not fathom. There was no rational explanation. Not egoism, for Dodds appeared to gain no pleasure from the exercise of power. Indeed, the fellow was almost modest in a strange way. Stanley could only conclude that age or isolation had slightly affected his wits.

Stanley tried hard to be tolerant, but the effort taxed him. Before long he wondered whether he was really duty-bound to exercise patience. Why should his ministry be thwarted by misplaced politeness? The projects under discussion were to be funded with money which he and Margot had themselves raised. What right had Dodds to exercise a power of veto? Stanley ceased to try to reason with the man: he resolved to spend his own monies as he saw fit.

As for the regular mission funds, Dodds simply misused them. It was no wonder the place was in a state of dilapidation. Dodds allowed the Meru to take ruthless advantage. They openly stole tools, food, fertiliser, vegetables from the mission gardens, kerosene. Dodds tolerated it, though it was theft pure and simple. Whenever supplies were carried in from the airstrip they shrank by half on the way. Boxes were lost, bags dropped and spoiled, but the contents somehow made their way to the Meru's huts. Dodds' attitude was infuriating.

When Stanley confronted him on the subject, he shrugged it off as a matter of no importance. "We have enough for ourselves," he said. "It's a form of exchange, like paying rent, almost. The mission is built on their land, after all."

Statements like this were simply untrue. They both well knew that the mission was built on a Government Lease for ninety-nine years. It was completely official. The mission was not built on Meru land at all.

"They don't see it like that," said Dodds. "We use their land and they expect something in exchange. A gallon or two of kerosene hardly matters."

Such arguments resolved nothing. They merely increased friction between the two men.

Occasionally Dodds appealed privately to Margot who, though she knew her husband was right, tried to keep on cordial terms with Dodds. She felt sorry for him.

"Your husband doesn't understand," he told her. "He should have more respect for the people. I've worked with the Meru for a long time. I came to help them, not to destroy their customs. I respect their way of doing things, not because it's quaint or old, but because it's theirs. They have as much right to their own ways as anybody else. To me, spreading the gospel doesn't mean bribery or bullying – it means sharing with them the best things in my own life. I try to show them by example. That is why I live simply."

Therein lay the gist of Dodds' strength, and also of his weakness. He drew strength from the very modesty of his achievements. He took pride in the mission's simplicity. It was consistent with his conception of Christianity; humble, frugal, simple.

But this same indifference to material things was also his weakness. The mission was small, ramshackle, rundown. Even in the valley, people knew what things were like on the coast; the Western-style buildings, electricity, roads, tractors, outboard motors. Some had visited Port Moresby. They knew how poorly the mission compared. Though they liked, even loved Dodds, they were bewildered by him. It was hard for them to revere a man who lived in a hut little better than their own, and who aspired to nothing more.

Dodds understood that he remained a contradiction to them. He knew sadly that in this respect, the Meru were closer to the newcomer, Cox. They valued power, position, wealth. It was he himself who offended against Meru ways by living too simply. The people respected a 'big man', with wealth to show and bestow on his favourites. They saw Cox as the big man, and they were attracted to him. His power and wealth and personality began to dominate the mission.

Dodds reflected wistfully on his time in the valley. Years before, an incident had taken place which he had never confided to anyone: the night he showed a film on an outside screen of the

223

life of Christ. They had come from all over the valley to watch. When the film reached the scene where Jesus is beaten and humiliated by the Roman soldiers, it was greeted with shrieks of laughter. The audience was entirely on the side of the Romans. Anyone who allowed himself to be treated like that was a 'rubbish man'. Anyone who had wealth and power at his disposal and did not use it was a fool. Dodds wondered whether he perhaps had been a fool all these years.

As the months passed, he became more touchy, and relations on the mission deteriorated further. Dodds avoided the Coxes, sometimes for days at a time. Stanley did not mind. All the time he was asserting his authority more strongly within the valley. As far as he was concerned, Dodds could do as he wished, busying himself ineffectually in the school, or supervising the dispensary, or interceding in petty, local arguments which were none of his business. Such prayers as he conducted were poorly attended, while Cox's services filled the church to overflowing. The deacons and elders saw who held sway, and were drawn to Stanley.

From time to time and for no apparent reason, relations thawed. The Coxes would have Dodds over after dinner and he would weary them with stories of the Meru and the early days of the mission. It was especially tedious for Stanley, who was not interested in the past, but the future. Dodds would pronounce at length on Meru customs and ways. He had made a lot of notes and records about them, and obviously considered himself something of an anthroplogist. Some of the details were disgusting: mutilation, nose-piercing, circumcision ceremonies, the Meru's contempt for physical weakness, their revulsion for human waste. It was beyond Stanley why a man would want to study such things. And why talk about them? Stanley had no wish to know about Meru customs. He was there to change them.

He tried to close his ears to the talk, and instead to study the man himself. Addled or not, Dodds surely realised they were unwilling listeners. Yet he talked on. He could not help himself. In a way, Dodds was independent of an audience. It seemed not to matter to him whether they listened or not. And another thing; how fast the man talked. As if time was running out. Stanley

224

wondered whether Dodds was perhaps aware that his time was short, that his authority was waning, and that by degrees he was becoming dispensable, irrelevant.

Still, Dodds talked. He told them of the beginnings of the mission in the valley. For years its presence puzzled the Meru. Why had the white men come? What did they want of them? To the Meru it was incomprehensible that people as powerful and wealthy as the whites would come to live among them for no personal advantage. Dodds explained how the concept of self-lessness, much less that of the Lord's sacrifice, was alien to them. The people took advantage of the mission certainly, for they did not understand it. It took time to gain their confidence and bring them to a knowledge of Christ. By his personal example and by learning their language and their ways, Dodds had gained the confidence and friendship of the headmen, and finally their faith for Jesus. And the people had followed.

In spite of himself, Stanley could not help taking in some of the torrent of words which poured forth from the old man. And gradually, he began to piece together an answer to the riddle that Dodds' person presented. Stanley considered him a failure who had accomplished little, but charitably, he had always given the man credit for his sincerity and his good intentions. Now Stanley wondered whether he might not have misjudged the man. Dodds' words were leading him to disturbing conclusions.

One evening, he resolved to draw the old man out. He would get him talking, and he would pay careful attention.

For the first time, Stanley displayed an interest in Dodds' stories. He asked questions about the Merus' traditions, their customs and practices, and Dodds was happy to answer. He had an explanation for everything. The practice of buying and selling women, for example – otherwise known as brideprice. According to Dodds, it helped to secure relations between families. It gave each clan a stake in the permanence of the marriage, for the brideprice had to be returned if the marriage failed. It reduced the incidence of divorce, Dodds argued. Anyway, it was a very widespread, almost a universal practice in Papua New Guinea. You would never eradicate it even if you tried.

Dodds defended the feasts and sing-sings, though in fact they were an orgy of waste. No work was done for days on end, and masses of food (and probably drink too, smuggled in from the airstrip) were gorged in a single week-long debauch. To Dodds though, they were innocent festivals. To him it was simply Meru custom: they were not a yam or grain-producing culture, he explained. Traditionally, they had no means of conserving food over long periods.

So it went on. Dodds could find a reason to excuse any practice, however debased. Stanley disputed nothing. He was learning much from the old man, more than Dodds guessed. For in his eagerness to talk, the old man was revealing himself, and with every sentence he was confirming Stanley's suspicions.

Stanley asked about the sorcerers. Yes, some were a force for evil, but many were merely traditional healers. The lewd dancing? Well, it was rather shocking at first, but it was part of their culture, their courtship rituals. It was wrong to judge them by Western standards. The people had a more natural attitude to nakedness and were free of notions of false modesty. Meru burial customs? Yes, they were insanitary. The mission had put a stop to them long ago.

By the end of the night Stanley had drawn his conclusions. He knew he was right. Now it all made sense. He knew why the old man resisted change and resented Stanley's presence. Dodds' years in the valley had infected him with these heathen beliefs. Dodds had not converted the Meru at all; they had converted him.

With painful clarity, Stanley recognised his earlier mistake. He had misjudged Dodds very badly. Dodds had not simply weakened, or yielded ground. It was more sinister than that. His were not mere errors, but dangerous errors, and the fact that he could make them sound almost plausible made him more dangerous than ever. Though the people thirsted for Jesus, they were headed for damnation. It was the old man's doing. No wonder he had always been hostile to Stanley. He feared to be exposed.

Now everything was clear to him, Stanley reproached himself for his earlier blindness. He had heard rumours from the church elders of what took place elsewhere in the valley. Though the people observed the sabbath and assembled in their white Sunday clothes, Dodds had suffered vice to flourish. Beyond the mission there was evil: idleness, fornication, idolatry, sorcery (traditional healers indeed!). Dodds knew of it, and he did nothing. Nay, he connived at it.

Stanley saw his duty. He determined to do it. The bell would be rung twice daily. He, himself would lead the prayers. They would be in English. He would tolerate no faltering, no backsliding, no slackness. He would insist on the minor virtues too: punctuality, thrift, sobriety. And most of all, he would see to it that the source of contamination – Dodds, was removed. But how?

As time passed, it became an obsession. The need was urgent, but Stanley could see no way to be rid of Dodds. For practical purposes, much of the power and control of the mission was already Stanley's. But the real instruments of control remained in Dodds' hands. He was the sole signatory to the official bank accounts. He alone held the mission records, the mission lease, the land title, the deed of trust. Some means had to be found to prise them from his grasp. But Stanley had no plan; he could only pray for guidance. Meanwhile, patience and stealth were called for. More than ever he had to humour the old man.

Forbearance came to Stanley only with difficulty. He was sorely tested to bear Dodds in silence, while the scoundrel undermined their work and spread contagion through the valley. Stanley knew what Dodds was up to. The Meru are great gossips and tell-tales, and the deacons and some of the younger people came regularly to his office with news of Dodds. Stanley guessed that some of them in turn reported his own doings back to the old man. For the time being, they played the two men off against each other. Though Stanley despised intrigue, it was unavoidable. The situation required it. If Dodds saw fit to scheme and plot, then Stanley would respond in kind. The people were making their choice and by whatever means, he must capture their hearts for Christ.

He tightened his grip on the mission. The devout were rewarded from the Coxes' supplies of prayerbooks, medicine and clothing. Even more valuable, they earned Stanley's stern approval. As the numbers of his adherents grew, Stanley looked for a way of distinguishing them from the others in the valley, the drifters and those weak souls still misguided by Dodds. He and Margot ordered batches of T-shirts from Port Moresby. (They were carried in from the airstrip by trusted followers without a single loss from pilferage.) A devotional slogan was stencilled on to each one: Stanley had hit on the word JISALA: Jesus Is Saviour And Lord Almighty.

The shirts were distributed as a sign of recognition among the loyal Christians, and there was a hierarchy of colours, determined originally by the colours and sizes available from the suppliers. The students wore bright blue, new converts yellow, the baptised green, the leaders red. They were a source of pride, a symbol that the wearer was a worthy follower and in the case of the rarer colours, a designation of status. Furthermore, they could be confiscated from backsliders and thereby formed a means of discipline as well as reward. In due course the T-shirts, a uniform of faith, came to predominate within the valley.

The numbers of the faithful grew too large to accommodate in the church, which in any case Stanley now had no wish to share with Dodds. Daily, they worshipped in their hundreds at morning prayers, dressed in their Jisala shirts and assembled in ranks on the sports field. The massed colours were spectacular. Every morning was a veritable pageant.

But Stanley was all the time tormented by Dodds' presence. He could still see no method to wrest full control from him and expel him altogether. Just as he was drawing on his last reserves of patience, the Lord's plan was revealed. All of a sudden Dodds' health deteriorated.

The man's health had not been the best for several years. His shortness of breath was quite pronounced and he had occasionally been laid up with arthritis. Then, one day while inspecting a rubbish pit, he suffered what he called a 'bad turn'. At the time Stanley was busy with the red-shirts, the brigade leaders, and the boys ran to Margot for help. She organised for the old man to be taken back to his house.

She radioed the symptoms to Port Moresby, but the diagnosis was obvious in any case. The chest pain and faint pulse indicated that Dodds had suffered a mild heart attack. The fellow himself had acquired considerable medical knowledge from his work at the dispensary over the years, and he knew better than the Coxes what ailed him; he was plainly worried. And now too, he was disadvantaged by his own unwisdom and lack of foresight. Short of chartering a helicopter, which was out of the question, there was no way to reach the airstrip and fly to Port Moresby for treatment, except by trekking first on foot over the Meru Gap.

After ten days of bed-rest, Dodds took things very easily for several weeks and dosed himself with the medication which had been sent in for him. When he felt sufficiently recovered, he announced that he would travel to Port Moresby. Despite Margot's pleas, he insisted on walking the whole way to the airstrip himself. He positively refused to be carried or helped over the range. He left the day before the flight was due, and stayed overnight at Balamoi station. The effort took a lot out of him.

Dodds' illness provided the opportunity which Stanley had prayed for. It was unthinkable, he said, to allow Dodds to travel to Port Moresby alone. So, walking to the airstrip early on the morning of the flight, Stanley joined Dodds in the Cessna. Once at Port Moresby, he accompanied Dodds to the hospital and helped get him admitted. He showed great tact and kindness towards the old man, but was firm in insisting in view of his health, that certain formalities be attended to concerning the mission.

While Dodds underwent tests and observation, Stanley made appointments with the lawyers, the accountant and the bank, and explained the situation to them. They were very understanding. They visited Dodds at the hospital, bringing with them the necessary documents – authorities, transfers and so on – just formalities, it was explained. At his bedside, the professional men declared themselves confident that Dodds would soon be fully recovered, but in the meantime... They gave him the papers to sign, and Dodds complied.

The Meru people, if nothing else, are shrewd and observant. When Stanley returned to the valley alone, they drew their own conclusions. Here was the outcome of the trial of strength which they had witnessed over the previous two years. Even their ancient social values of which Dodds was so well-informed, played their part. In Meru society there is no general feeling of respect for old age on its own account. Indeed the process of ageing is an object of ridicule to them, and knowing this from Dodds' own lips, Stanley exploited it. To the elders, he referred to Dodds as 'the poor old man' and 'the sick man', and confided to them that Dodds was seriously ill and unlikely to recover.

With Dodds gone from the valley, the Meru transferred their allegiance entirely to Stanley. Those few who had not been wearers of T-shirts were absorbed into the new regime, and issued with the lowest colour in the hierarchy. A charge was now introduced for the T-shirts, but no-one wished to be excluded. Somehow they managed to find the price, either in cash or by undertaking unpaid labour for the mission. The people prospered. They became more devout, more disciplined, and they shared in the contentment that comes from righteousness, and from the increased material wealth that the Coxes were bringing to the valley.

Stanley reflected on his contest with Dodds. He thought of it in terms of a parable: two forest vines competing for the light. The one was sturdy and upright and fruitful; the other old and exhausted, and poisonous into the bargain. The struggle was unequal. It had been inevitable that the stronger would overcome the weaker. The analogy was apt, for Dodds' resistance was ending in the same way as that of a forest vine. Just as in the forest, it was ending not in a violent death-spasm or a sudden climax, but in a gradual, but complete strangulation.

In fact, within a month Dodds did return to the mission, but he did so almost as a visitor – no longer as someone who belonged, and he stayed for only three weeks. The fact that he had recovered sufficiently to walk over the pass again and into the valley was ignored. Morally, he was a spent force, a supernumerary. He came only to attend to his personal effects, and there were few enough of them. He treasured most his notes and the artifacts he had collected. Margot found it sad in a way: even Dodds' plans to return to Australia were vague. He had it in mind to write a book, he told her.

The Meru knew Dodds was soon to leave them for the last time. A steady procession of visitors came to pay him court and say goodbye. Mainly they were the older people, those who had once been leaders, but who now like Dodds were aged and feeble. He received his old friends quietly, and then one day he simply took his leave. This time he allowed himself to be carried to the airstrip. Some villagers had made a kind of litter for him. There was no valedictory service, no sing-sing, no speeches. It was the way Dodds himself wanted it done, and it could not have suited Stanley better.

II

Great changes had been taking place at the mission well before Dodds' final departure, and now they continued in earnest. The first and most crucial step was to upgrade the track over the pass into a trafficable road. The blasting was paid for in full, but much of the earthmoving was done from the Balamoi end by a Department of Works bulldozer, informally placed at their disposal by a sympathetic works superintendent. His generosity had to be recompensed from mission funds, but it still represented an enormous saving. The concrete pipes for the culverts were also acquired at much reduced cost; the same superintendant found them to be surplus to requirements and made them available to Stanley. These irregularities caused Stanley no embarrassment. The government itself should have built the road. It was benefitting from the mission's exertions.

Of course, most of the work was done by hand by teams of villagers or the brigades of children willingly conscripted from the mission school. Here, a young man who was only lately converted from the influence of Dodds, proved of great assistance. This was Rahe, around nineteen years old, and better looking than most in the valley, for his mother was from the coast. He was a natural leader, intelligent and of strong character. Once he understood where his duty lay, Rahe proved to be one of the mission's most valuable workers in spite of his youth.

In fact, he proved to be the most capable of all in organising the work teams on site, and keeping them working to best effect through the day. Stanley had tried a few of the church elders as superintendents, but they were useless. He was anxious to complete the road by Christmas, and when work fell behind, it was upon Rahe that he relied most. The young man was even excused attendance at morning parade and prayers, so that time was not lost on the road project. He was empowered to lead the workers in a short prayer and a hymn at the start of every shift. Their labours were blessed with success. By mid-December, the job was as good as done. In recognition of his efforts, Stanley bestowed upon Rahe the most prized of rewards, a red Jisala T-shirt.

The arrival over the pass of their very first vehicle, a second-hand Land-Rover, was marked with festivity and thanksgiving. The valley's isolation was breached, and the event heralded a flow of supplies and improvements for the mission. Building materials, spare parts, medical supplies, schoolbooks, clothing; and a few richly deserved luxuries in the form of imported foods for the Coxes. Within months, improvements and extensions to the mission buildings completely eclipsed what had been there in Dodds' day.

All these things however, cost money. Finance became the most pressing problem. Despite every possible economy, the construction of the road had consumed more of his funds than Stanley had bargained for. Furthermore, upon Dodds' departure, the true state of the mission's finances came to light. There had been no regular income from Australian supporters for years. Even worse, Stanley discovered that the senile Dodds had been drawing on the capital as well as the income from the mission's only major endowment. There were no financial reserves what-ever, and only the Coxes' own funds to keep the mission going. Paradoxically, Stanley was almost glad of this. The mission would truly be his own creation now, his very own. Under his sole stewardship, he was determined the mission would flourish as never before.

As a break with the past and as a symbol that the mission, like the people themselves, were truly reborn, the mission's name was changed. Hitherto, the mission had been known by a mere geographical tag, the Meru Valley Mission, or by its initials, MVM. Henceforth, it would have a name which was truly Christian. The choice was obvious: Jisala Mission. It was an improvement which required no expense, and it expunged the final reminder that Stanley owed anything to his predecessor's efforts.

Stanley always remembered his first view of the valley from the air. This was the same view which his overseas visitors would behold; visitors whom he now planned to attract as a source of funds for their work. Part of the hillside behind the mission was cleared and rocks arranged and painted to spell out the word Jisala. Rahe proved himself yet again on this project. The white painted letters were a spectacular landmark to every incoming flight, and an inspiration from any vantage point for miles around.

All the Coxes' energy and ambition were channeled into the expansion of the mission. Over the years they achieved great things. Naturally, a new and bigger church had been the highest priority. After that came the library and annexe, the girls' dormitory, the new dispensary, workshops, paving and fencing. Stanley prevailed upon officialdom in Port Moresby to recognise the mission as an accredited Education Agency. This provided a flow of government grants for the operation of the school.

But finance remained the overriding problem. As the mission expanded, so did the costs of running it, for there were now salaries to pay, the school boarders to support, the road to maintain, fuel, airfares, clothing, insurance – the list was neverending. From financial necessity the Coxes became adept at cutting corners and minimising expense generally.

The salaries were for the helpers whom Stanley had recruited from Australia. In due course these comprised two teachers and a trained mothercraft nurse, together with two other lay helpers. Stanley insisted that each subscribe to a doctrinal statement which he had taken many days to compose. None but sincere, practising Christians were wanted at Jisala Mission, and only once did a newcomer prove to be a troublemaker. Stanley quickly arranged for Immigration to cancel his visa.

A government road of sorts now connected Balamoi with the coast, and when the road was open, freight could be brought in at a fraction of the cost of flying it in. A comfortable guesthouse was erected to accommodate the stream of overseas visitors. As Stanley had hoped, the visitors often proved to be a source of substantial donations. Prayer parades always impressed them, and a mass baptism of converts was sometimes scheduled to coincide with the visit of a particularly promising benefactor.

The visitors, who now averaged a small party every fortnight, were an important part of the mission's life and financial support. To transport them more comfortably to and from the airstrip, the mission purchased a brand-new minivan. Rahe, who was now twenty-three, was appointed the official driver and guide. He was ideal for the position because of his intelligence and looks, as well as his reliability. The visitors always took to him at once.

Some came from America now. Stanley had developed contacts with churches in Tennessee and Missouri, and the mission's fame grew by word of mouth and by fund-raising letters which together with the book-keeping, were Margot's main responsibility. The presence of the visitors gave Stanley scope once more for real preaching: an educated white congregation, though small, provided more satisfaction than his now infrequent sermons to an audience of attentive but uncomprehending Meru.

It was through an American Christian foundation that the mission acquired a new diesel generator. It was a magnificent machine and was installed by four young American volunteers who stayed for three weeks, doing much other work besides. The generator transformed life on the mission: for the first time they did not have to stint themselves, since the donors had also promised to meet the fuel bills for two years. Now there was unlimited lighting, constant hot water for the Cox's house and the guesthouse and there were plans to put it into the dispensary, too. There was power for a microwave oven, extra freezers, an airconditioner (rarely needed at that altitude), and a video and television set (devotional and educational programmes only).

The mission thrived, the Lord's work prospered. Hundreds bore witness daily to Christ. Stanley was admired, respected and fulfilled. The school attracted scholars from outside the valley and the Meru people, more devout, more disciplined, and happier for it, assembled for prayer morning and night. All took God's bounty for granted. Perhaps they had become complacent. Perhaps that was the reason for what happened next, for at first even Stanley had difficulty divining the Lord's intentions in the tragedy which followed.

An elderly couple from Tennessee was due on a two-day visit, and as usual Rahe drove in the minivan to collect them at the airstrip. Two girls from the school went for the ride, making five in all on the way back. As a driver, Rahe was entirely trustworthy. Stanley never for one moment blamed him for what happened. Indeed, it was established later that a stone must have flown up just prior to the accident and broken the brakeline of the van.

On the return journey, they reached the top of the pass without mishap. The van then began the descent towards the first of the series of sharp hairpin bends. It was just at the point where the JISALA letters first become visible through the trees. The rock surface of the road there was extremely rough, hardly better than the bed of a watercourse. On the left rises a solid wall of rock where the road is cut into the side of the hill. On the right, the hillside falls steeply away to the valley floor below. For a kilometre or two it is impossible to drive much faster than walking pace.

With the downhill grade, the van's speed increased. Rahe applied the brakes, but there was no response. The minivan gathered speed and jolted violently over the rugged rock surface of the narrow road. The luggage was hurled against the cabin walls, and the girls screamed. Rahe panicked. He lacked the presence of mind to engage first gear or apply the handbrake or steer towards the embankment so the van would at least remain on the road. Their speed increased until Rahe lost all control.

The van pitched forward to the very edge of the road, where its righthand wheels dislodged the loose rocks. Part of the edge subsided under the weight and the vehicle tipped over sideways, plunging down the hillside of grass and low scrub. As it rolled, Rahe either jumped, or more likely was thrown, from the van. The others remained in it as it rolled over three times until, by the grace of God, it hit a clump of trees and came to rest.

The scene was frightful, the battered van on its side, its doors burst open and its contents scattered like washing down the hillside. A party of Meru men who had been clearing new gardens nearby actually saw it happen, and were on the scene within minutes. Even before reaching the van, they had raised the alarm and shouted the news down into the valley. The message was taken up by successive voices until it reached the mission compound. There, a group of boys burst into Stanley's office,

236

telling him that there had been a terrible accident; the minivan had gone off the cliff and everybody in it had been killed.

It took a moment for the shattering news to register fully on him. Then Stanley ran to the Land-Rover and headed for the range. As the vehicle climbed out of the valley, he caught sight of the scene of disaster far above and to his left. Through the gaps between the trees, he glimpsed it again and again, closer and from a different angle as he rounded each bend. A small crowd could be seen milling around the minivan, while others at the edge of the road peered downwards at them. Between the two groups, a traffic of figures moved among the scattered debris of clothing, boxes, papers, prayerbooks.

Beseeching the Lord, Stanley's lips moved mechanically as the Land-Rover reached the scene. His eyes searched among the crowd on the road. Surely, he saw a European among them? Yes, a white man, tall and grey-haired – and unhurt. And there was a white woman too, standing to one side, comforting some small girls. Stanley could scarcely believe his prayers had been answered so soon, but there was no doubt. He closed his eyes, and they were moist from gratitude and relief.

The crowd was easily forty or fifty strong. The white man came forward and Stanley struggled to regain his composure. "Thank God you've arrived," said the man as he and Stanley shook hands. The American woman came forward, and Stanley greeted her too. She had suffered a gash, and her forearm was wrapped tightly in a bloodstained shirt. Both Americans talked uncontrollably in a strong accent. Stanley glanced around and took in that the two girls, now surrounded by their Meru kin, were also saved. All four were bruised and shaken, but they were not badly hurt. It was a miracle.

"The driver's hurt," said the American woman, pointing to the group halfway down the hillside where Stanley could see them fussing around Rahe. At once he scrambled down the embankment and picked his way around the scrub and boulders to the boy, who lay face upward, evidently conscious. His red Jisala T-shirt was dirty and torn, and they had put a folded jacket beneath his head.

"Rahe!"

"I am sorry, Mister Cox."

"Are you all right?"

"The van is broken, Mister Cox. I couldn't stop it. It went by itself. It fell down the hill and bumped the tree."

"But what about you?"

"Me, I am not so bad as the van."

The boy was so calm that it put Stanley at ease. "Let us give thanks," he said, and they closed their eyes and said a short prayer.

"Mister Cox," said Rahe when the prayer was over. "Only thing, I can't move my legs. But it's not so bad. It doesn't pain at all. Only my hand hurt a little bit." But they had bound it with a rag already.

In excited snatches, the bystanders told Stanley what had happened, how Rahe was the only one to be thrown from the van. Halfway down, they had see him thrown out and into its path. The van had rolled over him.

Stanley climbed back to the road and rejoined the Americans. He issued instructions, and a party scoured the hillside and collected the littered cargo and piled it in the back of the Land-Rover. It was clear Rahe's injuries were severe, but all they had done was bind his mangled hand. Stanley ordered him to be carried up to the road. Several men took him by the shoulders and feet and brought him up. They arranged some cushions in the back of the Land-Rover and placed Rahe on top. Stanley drove him as gently as he could to the airstrip, from where they radioed at once for a plane to evacuate him to Port Moresby. The aircraft arrived at Balamoi within the hour.

The Americans chose not to return to Port Moresby, but gamely continued with their visit to the mission. By nightfall they were settled into the guesthouse, sorting out their salvaged belongings. The next day they joined in a special thanksgiving service at morning prayer parade. They offered thanks to the Lord for sparing the lives of all those involved in the accident. Though there were grave fears for Rahe, his calmness and courage were an inspiration to them all.

Within a couple of days, Stanley's fears for Rahe were confirmed by the news from Port Moresby. The doctors advised that his spinal cord had been severed and that his paralysis was permanent. Faith and staunchness were now more necessary than ever. It was not for them to question, but to accept. God had a plan for each and every one of them. For all the ingenuity of medical science, it was beyond man's power to restore Rahe. Only prayer could do that now.

Stanley resolved that everything humanly possible would be done for Rahe. Now was the time to repay him for his faithful service to the mission. Stanley himself made a visit to Port Moresby to confer with the doctors, but in spite of all their hopes, the news remained the same: nothing could be done.

For seven weeks, Rahe remained in the hospital in Port Moresby. The doctors wanted to keep him longer, but Rahe yearned to return. He was homesick for the valley and it was affecting his morale. He was losing heart badly in the city, the doctors said. It was better to send him home.

Stanley rejoiced at his planned return. Everything was made ready for him. During his absence, a special house had been built. It was low on the ground with an entry ramp for a wheelchair. It had bathroom and toilet, both especially spacious, and equipped with metal handrails. Hot water was connected. The paths around the mission had been graded and rolled smooth, so Rahe could wheel himself around. It was hoped to make him as independent as possible. With God's help, he could continue to lead a useful life, bearing witness to Jesus Christ in spite of all afflictions.

Stanley examined his conscience, and found himself free of all blame. Rahe had been fully instructed and licensed. The van was not much over a year old, and had been properly maintained. The rupture of the brakeline was pure chance. No human agency could have prevented it. But still he felt troubled.

A complication had come to light shortly after Rahe's evacuation to Port Moresby. It was this that made Stanley uneasy. Somehow they had forgotten to renew the minivans's registration, and at the time of the accident it had been technically unregistered and uninsured. Stanley's enquiries revealed that Rahe would nevertheless receive the best medical treatment available in the country. That was a relief. It had been his main worry.

Of course, there was a chance that the mission might be fined for allowing an unregistered vehicle on a public road. Stanley always had so much on his mind, running the entire mission operation that he had simply overlooked it. He had just forgotten; it was as simple as that. Anyway, he wondered, was the road really a public road? The mission itself had constructed it. Perhaps the minivan had not needed to be registered.

What Stanley learned with more dismay however, was that the insurance fund could claim from the owner of an uninsured vehicle any compensation which it was obliged to pay out. This meant that ultimately the insurance company might ask the mission to meet all the compensation and medical costs for Rahe. Stanley received notice from the insurer that it intended to do exactly that.

A letter in reply was sent at once. Margot wrote it for Stanley to sign. She was better at that sort of thing, the soft answer which turneth away wrath. It dealt with everything that was relevant: how the accident had happened – sheer misadventure; the condition of the vehicle – perfect; the years of dedicated service to the community by Jisala Mission; the efforts they had made and the monies expended to make provision for Rahe on his return; the prayers that had been offered; and lastly, how the vehicle had come to be driven while uninsured.

> The very Monday before, I had given instructions for the vehicle to be taken down to Balamoi Government station to be re-registered, but on arriving there, it proved to have a headlight not working on high beam. It had probably blown that very day, and of course the vehicle is never used at night due to the condition of the road.
>
> Hence the van was driven back to the mission without being registered, whilst we awaited a new bulb to be flown in from Port Moresby. For some unknown reason the spare part was not forwarded to ourselves promptly (I am sure you know what it is

like at an out-station), and so the vehicle was not presented again for registration before this tragic accident happened.

Therefore it came to pass that on the following Monday, only three or four days later, the vehicle was uninsured, the only such instance in the long history of Jisala mission (formerly known as Meru Valley Mission).

A cheque was enclosed to bring the premium up to date, and the letter concluded by requesting the insurance company to grant them cover despite the gap of a few days.

It was the company's lawyers who replied. They pointed out that the policy provided for fourteen days of grace. If the contents of the letter were correct, then the mission would be entitled to a full indemnity. The lawyers would now make enquiries from their client insurer.

The reply caused Stanley foreboding. Everything in his own letter had been entirely accurate to the best of his knowledge. The part about the headlight was completely true, except perhaps with regard to timing. Stanley wondered about the interval between the expiry of the registration and the happening of the accident. Possibly, it had been rather more than four days.

Before long, another letter arrived from the lawyers. Their client's records disclosed that the minivan had been unregistered and uninsured for eight months and eleven days. The insurers would therefore seek to recover in full against the mission.

Soon after this, Rahe was brought home. In appearance, he was a changed man. His body looked strangely old and shrunken. His face was drawn and his skin grey and lifeless. Only his eyes were bright. At the mission they had all been looking forward to his return, but his actual arrival at Balamoi airstrip was a sorry anti-climax. The Cessna taxied to a stop and Rahe was clumsily manoeuvred out of it and into his wheelchair. It took so long to settle him in and wheel him over to the Coxes and the reception party, that all spontaneity was lost. Stanley had planned to rush forward and embrace him, but in the event he

241

could not bring himself to do so. Rahe stank: he had soiled himself on the flight. They shook hands instead.

Rahe brought with him instruction books from the hospital about the nursing care he needed, together with boxes of supplies. There were catheter tubes and colostomy bags, condoms (to collect his urine at night), suppositories and sanitary pads for his bowel movements, sheepskins, inflatable cushions, and an inflatable mattress whose alternate aircells inflated and deflated to avoid pressure sores while he slept. Stanley made a mental note that they would need to keep the generator going all night now to power the compressor. There was special cream to minimise pressure sores, medicines to treat renal infection, drugs to control depression. There was more to nursing Rahe than Stanley had anticipated.

For a day or two, but no more, a spark of the former Rahe returned. In hospital at Port Moresby, all he had lived for was to return to the valley. He had pictured himself still in command of the work teams; strong, red-shirted, uninjured. Irrationally, he had somehow hoped that on his return all would be well again and his life in the valley would resume as before. After the brief pleasure of returning home and rejoining his people, disillusion followed. The awful truth dawned on him.

It was pitiful. He was as helpless as a baby. He was dependent upon others for everything – to be woken and dressed, to be fed, to be cleaned, to be sheltered, to be moved around. For a short while he was an object of curiosity; they came to see his wheelchair. But the novelty wore off. Among the Meru there is only contempt for physical weakness. They showed him little sympathy, and did nothing to spare his pride.

His toilet functions were the greatest humiliation. Rahe was doubly incontinent. Throughout the day his urine trickled into the colostomy bag strapped to his leg. The bag needed emptying, washing, sterilising. And somebody had to clean him after he had moved his bowels. He had no control at all and was unaware of his motions until with revulsion he would find himself nestled in his own filth.

The Meru feel a great abhorrence for human waste, and Rahe's physical plight revolted them. At first some of his family helped nurse him, but before long they abandoned him completely. The others would not eat with those who had handled human shit. Even the hope of sharing in his compensation was not enough inducement. So his care was left to those at the mission who were not Meru, the relatively few from the Balamoi side or from the coast.

Rahe brooded. His helplessness and unhappiness were translated into hatred of others, and of himself. He ceased to make any effort to be independent, even in the simplest things like wheeling himself around. He claimed he could not do it because of the injury to his hand. He became morose and ungrateful, and lost all hope. Even his English deteriorated.

Stanley tried to comfort Rahe and they prayed together. Stanley assured him of the Lord's continuing love for him.

"Why He do this to me, then?" demanded Rahe.

"He's testing you, Rahe. You must keep faith. The Lord is all. Don't lose faith now, or you'll lose everything."

"I lost everything already. I want to die."

"Rahe, you must trust in Jesus," pleaded Stanley, but the boy answered in his own language.

"I can't understand you, Rahe. Speak to me in English."

"Mister Dodds always help us, but you chase him away," cried the stricken boy. "He can speak our language. He understand us. He was like Meru people." The boy relapsed into his own tongue, and his tears flowed.

Meanwhile, a letter arrived from the lawyers informing Stanley that the total liability to Rahe would approach a hundred thousand kina. It was unbelievable. Margot wrote the reply for Stanley in feverish haste. He still hoped for mercy. He had not tried to mislead them over the expiry date of the insurance. His wife had made a slip. He, himself accepted full personal responsiblity for allowing the vehicle to be used on that ill-fated day. By the letter of the law he was to blame. But his years of devoted service to the people of the country, the school, the dispensary, the road, electricity, the word of the Gospels, did they count for nothing? A single mistake in all those arduous years, and a freak accident too, could he not be forgiven that? Copies were despatched in desperation in all directions: to

Members of Parliament, Judges, the Insurance Institute, Cabinet Ministers, the Melanesian Council of Churches.

When these proved to no avail, Stanley at last realised the truth: the insurance company and the lawyers intended to destroy the mission. He took over the correspondence himself. He scrutinised the names on the lawyers' letterhead, and speculated that they were Catholics. Or even Jews; lawyers were often Jews. But he could not tell from their names.

His own letters had a different tone from those Margot had drafted. He explained that the mission possessed no saleable assets. The lawyers would never get their money. The iron would have to be stripped from the roofs, the buildings demolished, the generator dismantled and sold. Their vehicles were old, secondhand, worth next to nothing. The lawyers had suggested the mission appeal to its overseas contributors, but Stanley refused to contemplate such a thing. He was determined they would learn nothing of the problem. And a hundred thousand kina! They could not raise a fraction of it. It was beyond human power. Only the Lord could provide.

Rahe too, had need of the Lord. Offers of payment were insufficient to attract helpers. Stanley resorted to compulsion, and the older children were ordered out of school in turn to perform nursing duties. They did so unwillingly and unconscientiously. They quickly used up the disposable urine bags. The reusable ones were emptied, but rarely washed. They neglected to launder his soiled clothes and blankets. The sheepskins were flung into the rubbish pit because nobody wanted to clean them.

Stanley exhorted the conscript nurses on the need for absolute cleanliness, but it made no difference. They could not understand the risk of kidney infection or pressure sores. Even those few who tried to do their best were antagonised by Rahe's ingratitude and his violent moods. It was a struggle all the time. It needed constant supervision by Stanley or one of the other expatriates.

Stanley's growing fears for the future of the mission manifested themselves in furious efforts on Rahe's behalf. Unconsciously, Stanley identified the survival of the mission with the survival of Rahe. He bullied the students and they

244

rebelled. They ran away sooner than tend Rahe and defile themselves with his body wastes. Their defiance made Stanley more ruthless and erratic in dragooning those who remained. He was completely distracted from the normal operation of the mission. He was obsessed with Rahe, and with the threat to the mission. He neared his wits' end.

The mission had never asked to be represented in any legal proceedings. Stanley did not wish to contest Rahe's claim. There was no point. The accident had happened: the victim must be compensated. But the magnitude of the claim was another matter, and Stanley realised that he could dispute the amount of the compensation. It gave him a pretext to delay the settlement of the claim until something turned up – until their prayers were answered.

He applied his mind to the correspondence. The amounts mentioned so casually by the lawyers were astronomical. Stanley examined the breakdown of them. A large proportion was to compensate Rahe for pain and suffering and for what they called his loss of enjoyment of life. But mainly the expense was to cover the cost of Rahe's medical requirements for the rest of his life. His life expectancy, they predicted from statistical tables, was a further 42 years. Yet in his present condition it was a struggle to preserve his life even from month to month!

To Stanley, the whole business seemed ludicrous. It was contrary to common sense. Compensation for the death of a grown man with dependents was only a fraction of what the insurer was ready to concede to Rahe at the mission's expense. It was a conspiracy. Thousands were to be paid over to cover the cost of medicines which it was presumed Rahe would need for decades to come. But he might die at any time before the 42 years was up. And if he did, the money would be a windfall for his family who now neglected him. Yet the lawyers were pressing to finalise the claim at once.

Now Stanley understood the saying that it was cheaper to kill than to maim. It was cheaper by a long shot. For here was Rahe, young, unmarried, childless. If he had died outright, his relatives would have received but a few thousand. The longer he survived, the more he cost, the greater his need for drugs and wheelchairs and nursing and all the rest of it. And the greater his pain and suffering.

Suddenly, everything became clear to Stanley. It was all so obvious. The solution. He had fathomed the Lord's intentions at last! For if Rahe sickened and died, then his suffering in this world would be over and he would join our Lord. He would have no need for years of futile treatment, and the mission would be spared a crushing financial burden. Only the boy's estate would have a claim. Four or five thousand kina would cover it. And that was a figure the mission could find, somehow.

Stanley's course was clear. He wrote at once to the lawyers. There must be no settlement of the claim; the mission wished to be represented. It had no funds to spend on lawyers, so Stanley would do it in person. The mission would enter a defence. The figures were speculative. The calculations were wrong. The matter had proceeded with undue haste and the mission had been prejudiced. Further time must be allowed.

Stanley's confidence returned, his sense of direction. To think he had almost succumbed to despair! He felt again the sure hand of the Lord's guidance and looked with pleasure beyond the neat mission compound to the tranquil beauty of the valley. Shortly, he would be able to turn his mind again to the future: extensions to the school, a reviewing platform for the parade ground, a sawmill, the pastors' common room.

But first there was the present to attend to. The mission had become too lax. Too much time was wasted on distractions. The school for example – there were too many absences. Children were needlessly missing classes. Their education was suffering.

And Sunday observance had become too slack. The sabbath had been profaned by work. He would put a stop to it at once. There would be no work of any kind on the day of rest. No laundry. No cleaning. No unnecessary indulgence of the infirm.

One's duty to the Lord must come first from now on.